THE HALF
THAT WORKS

Laurie Horner

dfb

FICKLING

David Fickling Books

OXFORD · NEW YORK

THE HALF THAT WORKS

Acknowledgements

Thanks to Sophie Hannah, David Fickling and Bella Pearson, for being so much nicer than they needed to be.
Soph and Doug, for getting me started.
My parents, for keeping me going.
Everyone at D'Arcy, for being nothing like the employees of Laurent Création.
And most importantly, Joe, for showing me that modern art is never rubbish.

*'I know half of my advertising works,
I just don't know which half.'*

Advertising adage, adapted from an original quote by
Lord Leverhulme

Prologue

Chapter One

In which Dave does not have greatness thrust upon him

In artistic terms, Dave was 'technically competent'. He could draw a nice straight line. He could assemble colour with the eye of a reasonably talented interior decorator. His sculpture was pleasant but unchallenging. His watercolours were magnificently average. The weekend watercolourists of Cornwall, had they seen them, would have liked them. Dave's use of perspective was conventional. He favoured the figurative over the abstract. His work lacked dramatic devices or humour. Even irony, which could have saved him, was absent. He painted landscapes. He sculpted pots.

Dave's A level art show failed to raise an eyebrow amongst a determinedly biased audience consisting of all of his friends and most of his relatives. His grandmother, who suffered from chronic conservatism, thought he could have been more inventive.

'Very nice, dear,' she said, peering at Dave's efforts bifocally.

'Thanks, Gran,' said Dave.

'Next time, I'm sure you'll be a little more adventurous.'

'I'll try, Gran,' said Dave obediently.

'Good boy. Now walk me to the cafeteria. I fancy some rock cake.'

These comments were all too typical of the reactions to Dave's A level work. At the school's public viewing, he was submerged in a lake of faint praise.

In fact, almost all the work on display at the A level show was considered trite and predictable by those who observed it. Given that the viewing public were represented by peers and parents with no formal (or informal) training in art, this was comment indeed. The students were supposed to be angst-ridden seventeen-year-olds who had been urged to express their tormented world-views within the cocoon-like safety of the studio. Their tormented world-views were apparently best expressed by painting fruit in bowls and sketching old buildings.

The external examiners, confused at first, eventually chalked this anomaly up to the staggeringly middle-class structure of the catchment area and went off to find some inner city colleges that could produce more embittered work. If they'd been around during term time, to see Mr Cliffguard teach, they might have reached a different conclusion.

Mr Cliffguard was an art teacher from the old school. Indeed, he appeared to have learned his tuition methods in the late eighteenth century. Only a man with an artistic rubicon over one hundred years old could have purged the syllabus so methodically of anything onwards from cubism. Mr Cliffguard was vaguely aware of something called 'Modern' art, but disapproved of it so much that he pretended it did not exist. His disapproval encompassed Picasso, whom he regarded as a key perpetrator of the gradual descent towards 'Modern', and a greasy little European to boot. He was prepared to teach Matisse for his use of colour, but told his students the painter had died young and that any abstract work was clearly the work of impostors. Bacon, he said, was just plain evil, and if anyone mentioned Warhol, Mondrian or Pollock, he sent them to sit in the corridor.

In sharp contrast to most of his charges, Mr Cliffguard was fond of the Pre-Raphaelites – so much so that during one unfortunate lesson he attempted to recreate one of their more famous works using a suitably red-haired student and a small rowing boat in the local canal. His class were diligently rendering this scene when a human turd floated past the subject, causing her to scream and rear backwards in her vessel. When she emerged from the canal, she bore some hundred yards of duckweed, as well as the cause of her hysteria, which had become lodged in her extensive white skirts. The poor girl was too traumatized to continue with her studies, and Mr Cliffguard miserably abandoned his plans to restage *The Raft of the Medusa* in the same location.

Early on in the course, Mr Cliffguard demanded a reproduction of Cézanne's famous *Still life*. He placed a small bowl of oranges on a romantic white table-cloth, and set down his students in front of it. Returning half an hour later to check on their progress, he was not pleased with Dave's inter-pretation of the material.

'What is this?' said Mr Cliffguard, levelling a hairy finger at Dave's spreadeagled painting.

'Oh, I thought it might be interesting to explore the colours of the oranges,' said Dave. 'I think it's the different light sources in here. They make each orange look a slightly different colour.'

'But this orange is blue,' said Mr Cliffguard. He prodded it with venom.

'Er, yes. It's the fluorescent light overhead. It gives that one a blue tinge. You see?'

'You cannot have a blue orange,' said Mr Cliffguard, his eyes stalking with outrage. 'Oranges are orange. That's the whole point of them.'

'Sorry,' said Dave. 'I just wondered if it might be more interesting to paint them as I see them.'

'It is *not* interesting,' said Mr Cliffguard. 'It is *not* interesting to change the colour of oranges. Did Cézanne paint a bowl of blues? He did not. He painted a bowl of oranges. Wonderful oranges, which, unless I am very much mistaken, were bloody well orange.'

'Sorry,' said Dave, dipping his paintbrush in assent.

'*Oranges.* Do you hear me?'

'Yes. Sorry.'

'*Oranges,*' said Mr Cliffguard, who was full of artistic distemper.

This incident epitomized the nature of Dave's learning curve throughout his A level course. Over the next two years, Mr Cliffguard taught him the importance of exactitude in art, the vitality of representing the world as it is, rather than as it was meant to be. He forced the use of complex forms upon Dave, so the poetry of simple forms was impossible to see. He demanded the use of conventional media, even considering collage to be too risqué. For Dave's one attempt in this field, Mr Cliffguard allotted an F and the words 'Untidy' and 'Babyish'. He bludgeoned his student into submission, recreating the young artist in his own image.

Sadly, Dave did not resist this punishment. The forthright opinions of Mr Cliffguard were the straws that broke his back. Under such an assault his artistic voice, which was already muted by a towering lack of self-confidence, quietened to the point of non-existence. He was a shy boy, not given to outspoken behaviour or rebellion. He did not argue, doubting himself when others did not and hesitating when others jumped. Stern parents and a reductionary school system had poisoned him with compliance, adding a topping of humility to his natural self-doubt. When confronted with his teacher's absolutist opinions, Dave therefore listened to the voice of authority. He swallowed his educational medicine and did as he was told. If monochrome seemed more interesting, he used the primary colours that Mr Cliffguard suggested. When abstraction beckoned, he clung to the realism that was advised. Dave bowed his head so often that he forgot what his own predilections looked like. By the time of his A level show, he was almost an artistic technician, decorating the canvas but achieving little more.

'Very good, David,' murmured Mr Cliffguard in their final lesson together.

'Thanks,' said Dave, his nose two centimetres from the painting. Mr Cliffguard had asked the class to reproduce a detail from Seurat's pointillist masterpiece *Sunday afternoon on the island of la Grande Jatte*, and Dave was carefully copying out a blanket of impressionistic spots.

'Perhaps this one should be a little darker?' said Mr Cliffguard, pointing to a portion of his student's work.

'This one?'

'No, that one.'

'This one?' said Dave, trying to locate the errant daub of paint.

'No, not that one,' said Mr Cliffguard. 'Up a bit from there.'

'Here?'

'No. Left a bit,' said Mr Cliffguard. 'A bit more left. There. That one.'

'Ah,' said Dave. He amended the offending pinprick of colour.

'Much better,' said Mr Cliffguard. 'Now, that one's a little too large . . .'

In fairness, Mr Cliffguard was not the sole cause of Dave's artistic decline. Though his ministrations marked the final crumbling of Dave's talents, there had already been significant erosion at the base.

As a young boy, Dave had been obsessed by the plaster models they made at primary school. The plaster was smooth and organic, moist and perfect. It was like the flesh of deities. Dave would spend hours turning the models over and over in his hands. His teachers thought he loved the models because they were renditions of his favourite film characters, but Dave was attracted by their aesthetic qualities, not their personality. One day, when his teachers were out on a cigarette break, Dave snuck into the supply cupboard and stole a packet of the white powder from which the plaster was made.

Dave's mother arrived home that day to find her sink thick with plaster stalagmites. Her son, similarly encrusted, was beating egg cups against the tiles of the kitchen floor.

'*For God's sake, David!*' she screeched. '*What the hell do you think you're doing?*'

'Oh. Hi, Mum,' said Dave, largely absorbed by his creative task. 'I'm just trying something with these egg cups.'

'*You little hooligan!*' she screamed. '*Look at the mess you've made!*'

'Sorry, Mum,' said Dave, staring vacantly at the wreckage around him. 'I was just trying something out. That's all.'

His mother heaved indignantly, her tempers fermenting.

'Sorry,' said Dave. 'I just thought it might be good.'

Following this exchange, Dave's mother dragged

15

him upstairs and thrashed him senseless with a copy of *Wonderful Homes*. It never occurred to her to help him liberate the contents of his egg cups, and even if she had done so, she wouldn't have realized the significance of what was inside. Dave had filled the receptacles with plaster. The idea of pure white half-eggs appealed to him. He knew the containers would create objects that were simple and beautiful. Perfect mushrooms. Silent tears. At the age of ten, Dave was interested in beauty rather than function.

Over the course of Dave's secondary school years, this artistic interest in the world, this love of colours and textures, was gradually shouted out of him. Though Mr Cliffguard completed the process, Dave's parents built the coffin into which he drove his educational nails.

When he was thirteen, Dave painted a rim of skyscrapers using dirt and glue. The buildings were veined with grime and misery.

'For heaven's sake boy, can't you paint a nice English landscape?' said his father. 'All the best artists paint nice landscapes.'

'Really?' said Dave.

'Absolutely,' said his father, flipping the pages of his business section and casting firm glances Davewards. 'Just look at Turner. Hardly painted anything else.'

'OK,' said Dave. 'I'll try.' And he walked up to the top of a nearby hill and painted a sweet little landscape that was stripped across with lines of barbed wire. He had been meaning to produce a dappled scene of greens and blues, but he couldn't help focusing on the barbed wire. As he sat on the hillside with his sketchpad, it was the most interesting thing he saw before him.

'What on earth is that?' said his father. 'It looks like barbed wire.'

'Er, yes,' said Dave. 'It is.'

'No, no, no,' said his father, rattling the business pages angrily. 'That's no good at all. I meant a proper landscape, like Turner. You don't see barbed wire running through Turner landscapes, do you?'

'Actually,' said Dave, 'I'm not sure they had barbed wire when . . .'

'Don't argue, boy,' his father interrupted. 'You know what I mean. A proper landscape. With fields and horses.'

'I'll try,' said Dave.

And gradually, as they were reiterated throughout his youth, Dave's landscapes became attuned to the political composition that his father desired.

Dave's mother was equally unadventurous in taste. When Dave came home with a clay sculpture that looked remarkably like a tongue, she wrinkled her nose in disgust.

'What's that?' she said.

'It's a tongue,' said Dave. 'They asked us to think about the way clay feels, and I thought it would taste funny. You can always taste it in the air when you're working with it.'

'It's disgusting,' said his mother. 'Why can't you make some nice pots, like a proper artist?'

Dave came back the following day with a pot. He

had slashed its sides before he sent it to the kiln, so the object bore challenging and confrontational wounds.

'No, no,' said his mother. 'A proper pot. One that I can put on the mantelpiece. I can't put that anywhere, can I? I've got the Kingsley-Smiths coming round for dinner tonight.'

'I'll try,' said Dave.

And gradually Dave's pots became just pots.

So by the time Dave started his A level, his artistic spirit was already limping and wounded. Mr Cliffguard, with his fascist tutelage, finished it off. He cut Dave's hamstrings, and his work became technically competent but nothing more.

Dave was not completely oblivious to the abuse he had suffered. He felt, on some unconscious level, that the end products of his labours were not quite right. Not quite *him*. However, he could not argue with the opinions of his betters. He was a worker, not a fighter. They were adults and he was still a child. He had to listen to their advice if he was to improve. Dave's instincts counselled diligence, and any ideas of his own, any glimmers of talent, were trapped in the prison of standardization that he had allowed others to build around him.

Needless to say, the only people who liked Dave's A level art show were his parents and Mr Cliffguard.

When he received a D grade from the external examiners, Dave reacted predictably. He blamed himself. Perhaps, he reasoned, he had followed the syllabus with insufficient precision. Perhaps he had wandered too far from the path of accepted wisdom. Perhaps he had not listened closely enough to Mr Cliffguard during his two years of tutelage. Dave internalized his failings, as his character advised, and he never questioned the system's low opinion of his talents.

'I realize it's not the grade you were hoping for,' said Mr Cliffguard, 'but you should think yourself lucky. I dread to think what you would have been awarded for the experimental rubbish you were producing two years ago.'

Dave nodded miserably.

'I really try,' he said. 'I try to do things the proper way. I just find it hard not to make changes. I have all these crazy ideas in my head.'

'You must resist your impulses,' said Mr Cliffguard. 'Art is bigger than you are. You cannot hope to improve on its perfection. After all, nobody seeks to reinterpret *The Mona Lisa*, do they?'

'I suppose not,' said Dave.

'If you want to continue with this subject, you must do as you are told,' said Mr Cliffguard. 'Art has little patience with those who do not respect its achievements.'

'I'll try,' said Dave.

'Try *harder*,' said Mr Cliffguard. 'If you follow the example of your betters, I'm sure you will improve.'

'I'll try,' said Dave, his eyes on the table in front of him.

Though Dave's poor A level result made it difficult for

him to continue as an artist, he did not give up his dream. Art was the only thing he enjoyed in life, and he could not imagine a career doing anything else. A D grade made his university applications redundant, so he was forced to look around for a reserve option that would allow him to continue working within his chosen field. An art foundation course at one of the local colleges seemed the most likely crucible for the reincarnation of his talents, but even these establishments were scornful of his mere technical competence.

Despite the cushion of his ingrained modesty, Dave's A level grade affected him adversely. He became depressed. Then, to make matters worse, he did something that no aspiring artist should ever do. He went out on a date with someone more talented than he was.

Jessica was the only student in Dave's class to receive an A grade from the confused pack of external examiners. She was the daughter of wealthy parents, who had happened on a fortune whilst still in their twenties. Her father, then a young laboratory worker at Solihull School of Engineering, had been assigned to develop ring-tones for the first generation of mobile phones, and whilst plugging his ears with cotton wool in a bid to avoid insanity, he had spotted a potential gap in a future market.

Intelligent enough to realize that this incessant shrieking would one day be commonplace, Jessica's father foresaw an eventual need to escape from the din. Handing in his notice and swabbing out his ears with alcohol, he began searching for a piece of equipment that could enable this goal. When he rang an electronics importer in Surbiton, he found not only the bandwidth blockers he was looking for, but also his future wife, who answered the phone. She altruistically assumed that he would be unwise to *buy* the little black boxes he needed, and promptly stole the details for their manufacture. She then resigned and negotiated a fifty per cent profit share with him. Once they had circumvented the patent laws and had time for it, they were married in a small registry office in Clapham. The pre-nuptial agreement concentrated mainly on the division of their new company ('Blocks Clever') in case of divorce.

By the time Jessica was walking, her parents had a contract with the government, who needed to stop mobile phones from going off within the military theatre. By the time she was eleven, their boxes were being installed in all the major airports, to remove the confusion from air traffic control, and by the time she had started her A levels, they were even beginning to examine options within the public domain. Jessica's parents could provide the one thing mobile phones had eliminated. The sound of silence. Their little black boxes were in constant and increasing demand, and their daughter lacked for nothing.

When Jessica began to show an interest in art, her mother and father researched the subject, determined that there was at least a little prestige in it, and then planned a strategy. It was agreed that her father would develop her abilities by taking her to positively-reviewed shows around the country, while her mother stayed at home and looked after their business concerns.

'You'll see it all, darling,' said Jessica's father. 'You'll see every piece of art that's worth seeing.'.

'Thank you so much, Daddy,' said Jessica, scrunching up her nose. 'Are you absolutely sure it's all right?'

'Nothing's too good for my daughter,' said her father, puffing up his chest like a pigeon. 'We'll see every decent piece of art in the land.'

Jessica threw her arms round his shoulders and planted a daughterly kiss on his cheek.

'Oh thank you, Daddy!' she gushed enthusiastically. 'Thank you! Thank you! Thank you!'

Jessica's father took her to see the great old galleries first. The Louvre and the National. Jessica however, was only fourteen, and soon became bored of the cracking paint and the need for historical or religious context. She began to push for trips to ever more modern shows. Soon they were attending Pop Art homages and Readymade retrospectives. Her father was confused.

'This is a load of crap,' he said, confronted with Manzoni's immortal tinned excrement.

'That's right, Daddy,' said Jessica. 'Good, isn't it?'

'Very good, cupcake,' agreed her father, wondering why this was the case.

On another occasion they came upon Duchamp's legendary urinal.

'This is a urinal,' said Jessica's father.

'Yes, Daddy,' said Jessica. 'Isn't it beautiful?'

'Beautiful, cupcake,' her father agreed, wondering if he was looking at the right thing.

He soon gave up. He was clearly not capable of understanding his daughter's passions, but she was his angel and he didn't want to interfere. He supplied her with a huge monthly allowance to further her artistic endeavours, and went back to his seat on the matrimonial board. Jessica's allowance was of sufficient size to allow visits to London, and even the occasional flight to New York. Her enormous confidence and striking good looks made her noticeable at the private views she attended, and she was soon installed on the circuit as an artistic genius-to-be. Her place at the London Lightschool, Britain's premier artistic institution, never seemed in doubt.

Jessica's A grade was more of a credit to Mr Cliffguard than he realized. Because she had become used to more adventurous examples, Jessica made his small-minded and horribly restrictive syllabus the subject of her work. She used cuttings from the school photo to print her classmate's faces onto the heads of her nudes, peering out at the viewer like lice. She pursued extreme abstraction in her landscapes, which were of the school grounds (Mr Cliffguard and her fellow students were again present, reduced to pathetic stick figures supporting the buildings from beneath). Her sculpture consisted of a poorly constructed artist's stool, on which she sat, making conventional sketches of trees. The examiners would normally have been taken aback by this level of sarcasm, but given their considerable dislike for the show in general, they were inclined to be lenient and reward any originality they saw. Jessica's place at the Lightschool was sealed when it transpired that one of the external examiners happened to sit on the school's selection board and also knew her father. It was apparent that she wouldn't even need an art foundation qualification. She could go straight there in September.

Mr Cliffguard, who loathed Jessica's work, was appalled by her imminent stardom.

'I don't pretend to understand how this has happened,' he said to Jessica, 'but I will do everything in my power to overturn the decision.'

Jessica smiled at him.

'Well, you must do whatever you think best,' she said.

'You show none of the humility that is so important to an artist. Your work mocks the respected conventions of the discipline.'

Jessica nodded. 'My work is quite modern,' she said. 'I thought it might not be to your taste.'

'Taste!' Mr Cliffguard shouted. 'It's not a matter of taste! It's a matter of art! You have ignored five hundred years of expertise! You have ignored the lessons of greatness!'

Jessica frowned slightly. 'I haven't ignored them,' she said. 'I just think I can do better.'

*

Dave was attracted to Jessica for two reasons. Firstly, she was very pretty. She wore her blonde hair in a simple and classic fashion, straight and tied in a single base knot. Her cheekbones screamed talent, and she was thin enough to annoy women and attract men. Her sense of style reflected her artistic prowess, and she tended towards expensive but understated clothing. Slim trousers and tailored leather jackets figured large in her wardrobe, and though the tones were advanced, nothing so common as a primary colour graced her palette. Jessica knew that at least half of being an artistic prodigy was looking the part.

Dave was also attracted to Jessica because, artistically speaking, she had 'it', whilst he most definitely did not. Though he told himself he was revolted by the concept of reflected glory, Dave very much wanted to find out what 'it' was, and determine how to get 'it'. He therefore had dual objectives in mind when he asked her out to the cinema, supposing that afterwards they could go to the pub and discuss the film. Jessica surprised him by not only accepting his offer, but also insisting they saw *Two Ways to Die* instead of one of the better reviewed literary conversions.

'Are you sure you want to see that one?' asked Dave.

Jessica raised a spectacular eyebrow.

'Sorry,' said Dave. 'I just didn't think it would be your cup of tea.'

'Cups of tea are for Granny,' said Jessica. 'Artists should expose themselves to a wide range of stimuli.'

'Of course,' said Dave, 'but what about the critics?

They don't seem to like it very much. I've read some really bad reviews.'

Jessica waved one of her beautiful hands. 'Critics are pointless,' she said. 'True artists should always judge for themselves.'

Two Ways to Die concerned itself with the actions of an ex-cop, now an alcoholic living in a dirty LA apartment. The ex-cop's brother – another officer of the law, but one still sufficiently alcohol-free to pursue his duties – was also introduced, and then promptly killed by a pack of Chinese gangsters, all of whom had tattoos of Betty Boop on their right shoulders. They killed him by tipping him into a deep-fat fryer at a Chinese restaurant.

This personal tragedy mobilized the alcohol-sodden ex-cop, who proceeded to beat up his old informants in an attempt to determine the identity of his brother's assassins. He eventually bloodied one of his informants with sufficient vigour to gain the intelligence he was after, and discovered that his brother had been engaged in corrupt activities, helping the Betty Boop gang to smuggle illegal Chinese immigrants into the country. His brother's duty had been to warn the gang of police-monitoring patterns, but in a fit of conscience, the unfortunate man had decided to 'go clean'. His employers had obviously killed him in concern over his steadily improving moral character.

'Goddamn,' said the ex-cop quietly, squinting with the pain of these revelations.

The film took forty minutes to establish its background plot, during which time Dave was hugely aware of the fact that his leg was touching Jessica's. For ambience, Dave had selected an old-fashioned red velvet cinema in place of a more modern affair. The owner of the establishment was a firm believer in intermissions as a method of increasing profits, and when the dusty curtain descended, Dave offered to buy Jessica a monstrously overpriced ice cream.

'I'm watching my weight,' she said. 'Creativity and puppy fat are infrequent bedmates.'

'Oh,' said Dave.

There was a short pause.

'I like your jacket,' said Dave. 'Is it designer label?'

Jessica looked at him. 'I prefer to think of labels as subservient to me, rather than vice versa,' she said.

'Oh,' said Dave again.

They waited for the curtain to ascend, which it eventually did. The ruined face of the alcohol-sodden ex-cop flickered back into existence.

Most of the action was saved for the second half of the film, in which the true greatness of the alcoholic ex-cop was brought dramatically to light. After a short fit of emotion over his dead brother's moral u-turn and subsequent demise, the inebriated hero set about recruiting other ex-cops to help bring the Betty Boop gang to justice. His allies were also great men who had fallen on hard times, thus reassuring the audience that they were worthy of approval (and not in fact the dregs of humanity, as they appeared to be).

'Cozmo, Frankie, Detoya, Marlon, Theo?' the ex-cop addressed his motley crew of enforcers.

27

'Some people are preying on this great land of ours. They're preying on the dream that is America.'

The assembled washouts grunted with anger.

'We're gonna make this right, boys,' the ex-cop announced. 'We're gonna set things straight.'

Following this pep talk, the squad of heroic ex-cops beat up some more informants, found out when the next shipment of immigrants was coming in, and then laid an ambush at the San Diego docks. The bloody gunfight that followed ended in the death of all the ex-cops but the hero, who was inexplicably spared by the Betty Boop gang and then thrown into the hold with their human cargo. Whilst in the hold, he made an inspired speech to the cowering immigrants about the free world, so impressing them that when the hatchway opened they rushed out en masse, suffering many casualties but eventually overcoming their evil oppressors.

'Goddamn you, America,' said the hero, holding a dying immigrant in his blood-covered arms. 'You can be a cruel old bitch when you wanna be.'

At the end of the film, having carried the day, the hero learned that the authorities planned to deport his army of illegal immigrants, sending them back to the lives they had been trying to escape. Resolving to give up alcohol and become a new man, he sailed away with them to the Far East.

Afterwards, Dave and Jessica sat at a small table in a small pub and discussed the film. Jessica sat opposite Dave, rather than by his side. He watched her mouth while she talked, which he could do with impunity because she was so entranced by her own opinions that she hardly ever looked in his direction.

'Clumsy irony,' said Jessica. 'Both conscious and unconscious.'

Dave, who was thinking about the camerawork, and how much he had liked the movement of focus during the gunfights, said, 'Mmmm.'

'The degraded images of the new world were poorly mirrored by the degradation of the legal system,' said Jessica. 'I'm sure the writer didn't realize that his awful script said more about the American dream than his use of the Betty Boop tattoos.'

'Mmmm,' said Dave again. He had also enjoyed the staccato bursts of gunfire, interspersed throughout the film like audible punctuation marks.

'And the title?' said Jessica. '*Two Ways to Die*? Western or Eastern? Brother or brother? Moral or amoral? Drunk or sober? It's a bit obvious isn't it?'

'Very obvious,' agreed Dave, trying not to look at Jessica's neckline. 'Er, which one?'

'All of them, Dave,' said Jessica, rolling her eyes. 'All of them.'

'Oh,' said Dave. He hadn't really been listening to Jessica's diatribe, but from the tone of her comments he realized that she'd come to agree with the critics.

'I suppose the reviews were right then,' he said. 'It wasn't very good after all.'

Jessica scowled at him, not liking the idea that she had conformed to a predominant viewpoint.

'I suppose they did pick up on *some* of the problems,' she admitted, 'but I don't think they really understood its deeper and more subtle flaws.'

'No, I suppose not,' said Dave helpfully.

There was a short pause in conversation.

'Which ones were they, then?' he asked.

'Oh for God's sake, Dave!' Jessica snapped. 'Weren't you listening to what I just said?'

'Yes of course,' said Dave. 'Sorry. I just thought you were talking about something else.'

Jessica shook her ponytail in despair. 'You mustn't let your mind wander,' she said. 'A true artist is always focused on the aesthetic.'

'I'll try,' said Dave automatically. He looked around for a subject that could lend him an escape. 'So, you're off to the Lightschool then?'

Jessica nodded and smiled the smile of the truly content. This was why she had agreed to go out with Dave. She liked to go on dates with people who truly adored her, or who were truly envious of her talent. She found each of these smells pleasant on a man, and Dave stank of them both. To Jessica, there was no greater aphrodisiac than admiration.

'And where are you going?' she asked, already quite aware of the answer.

'Oh, I'm not sure,' said Dave. 'It looks like I'll need to go through clearing if I'm to stand a chance of getting on an art course.'

Jessica nodded again. 'Maybe you should try graphic design?' she said, trying to keep the condescension from her voice.

'No,' said Dave. 'I think I'll keep trying for a place on an art course.'

'It's your decision,' said Jessica, shrugging her shoulders. 'If you really think it's worth it.'

'It is,' said Dave. 'I'm sure.'

Jessica took a sip of her gin and tonic. 'There's nothing *wrong* with graphic design,' she said. 'I mean, we can't *all* be artists, can we?'

'Well, I can,' said Dave. He felt dogged and desperate and more than a little bit drunk. 'I can become an artist.'

'You're quite positive about that? I would've thought graphic design was more up your street.'

'What do you mean?' said Dave. His voice was a little too loud for the air around him.

'Well, graphic design is much more vocational than art. It requires less conceptual thinking. Less abstract thought.'

'So?' said Dave. He was on his way to being angry.

'Graphic design would suit your talents,' said Jessica. It was as though she were speaking to a child. 'It's probably a better option for someone who's, you know, "technically competent".'

A flame of rebellion sputtered to life in Dave's soul, and an ambition was born from his frustrated desires. He vowed that one day he would be a success. One day, Jessica would admire his work and ask for his guidance. One day she would look at him with passion, rather than amused pity.

Dave set his jaw firmly.

'No,' he said. 'I don't want to be "technically competent". I want to be an artist.'

First Half

Chapter Two

A terrible lie

Dave examined his final set of sketches for the shampoo bottle. He frowned. It wasn't that he disliked his design. Not as such. It just didn't seem quite good enough. Quite brave enough. It wasn't completely obvious, to be sure, but neither was it as creative as he would have liked.

The typography he had used was hardly revolutionary, and the colours he had selected were predictable. In order to be a little different, Dave had tried to do something with the structure. His design had two layers, making it a bottle within a bottle, which as far as he knew had not been done before. The outer layer was designed in a material normally used for beach-balls. A squashy plastic that only came in bright colours or white. The inner layer was made of rigid PVC. Combining the two was difficult in manufacturing terms, and filling the space between the two layers with air was not something that existing machines could do. Dave thought that once they had a prototype in their hands, they would build new machines. He had designed the bottle as a kind of elongated rugby ball. The squishy, inflated texture that the two layers produced would force the average male to close the mental gap between bottle and plaything. They would be dying to throw it to someone. Plus, of course, the bottle would float in water, because of the air sandwiched between its inner and outer layers. Thus, he met his brief.

Carefully, above his finished sketches, Dave stencilled the following: *Preliminary sketches for a shampoo bottle aimed at young males, for use in communal bathing areas at gyms and sports facilities. Work commissioned by Drayten Finch Plc (household products and toiletries division).*

Dave knew it was a good answer to the brief. He knew he'd get at least a B for it, and quite possibly it would be selected by Drayten Finch for prototype manufacture. Regardless of this anticipated success, he didn't feel complete. He didn't feel like he'd created anything of merit. Or rather, he felt like he'd been manipulated into creating something of merit, rather than producing it on his own. He felt depressed, so he went home.

In his third and final year of a graphic design degree at Newcastle Institute of Arts and Media, Dave was still regarded as 'technically competent' by the only person that really mattered: himself. Though the graphic design syllabus called for some moments of creativity, their incidence was structured. Their timing set. The course was not based around lateral or random thought. It was based around the professional application of inventiveness. The ability to plan to a deadline. The ability to work in many different media. The ability to meet the needs of a client. The ability to work under pressure. The ability to change designs when the client changed the brief. The ability to be polite at all times and take rejection well.

Dave, ever the attentive student, had become very good at all these things, but was dissatisfied by the practical nature of his output. Mr Cliffguard had hobbled his expression in the past, and now the graphic design syllabus was imposing the same level of restraint. He didn't really understand the forces that moved within him. He just knew that graphic design did not give him peace.

On one occasion, Dave's desires had escaped. His class had been given a block of wood, four inches square, and told to increase its length by one hundred per cent within two weeks. The parameters of the project were very simple; no foreign matter could be added to the block, and any wood that was removed had to be put back on again in some form. Dave burnt the block and spread out the cinders in a line that was roughly double the length of the original piece. He was called in to see the Dean.

'Why did you do it, David?' asked the Dean. He was sitting behind a big white desk and scowling.

'Do what?'

'Why did you burn up the block?'

'Oh, that,' said Dave. 'Well, it just seemed like an interesting way of coming at the problem.'

'*Interesting*, David?' said the Dean. '*Interesting?*'

'Yes. I was just trying something a little bit different.'

'David,' the Dean said patiently, 'we do not appreciate ironic gestures here. If you want to be ironic, shocking, or otherwise comment on the nature of the graphic design syllabus, please leave the Institute and reapply as a fine art student.'

The Dean knew that with a D grade A level, no art foundation qualifications, and a reference that said he was 'technically competent', Dave was never going to get readmitted as a fine art student. After all, the Institute had rejected him for fine art when he'd rung around during clearing, as had everywhere else. They'd only admitted him to the graphic design course because of his obvious technical competence.

'I really didn't mean to be ironic,' Dave explained, 'I was just trying to be creative. That's all.'

The Dean put his hands on the big white desk and waited for a proper apology.

'I'm very sorry,' said Dave. 'I wasn't trying to cause trouble.'

The Dean pursed his lips.

'I'm very, very sorry,' said Dave. 'I really am.'

The Dean nodded sagely. 'We shall overlook it this time,' he said, 'but remember your place in the future. You are a designer, not an artist. You must show precision, detail and functionality in your work. We will not tolerate subversion in our designers. There is a time and a place for such things.'

Dave bowed his assent. Graphic design was not what he wanted, but he was aware that the Institute had saved him from an even less artistic fate when they allowed him onto the course, and his humble nature felt such a debt keenly.

'I'll try,' he said quietly. 'I promise I will.'

And from that point on, Dave was as good as his word. He kept his artistic urges in check. He repressed his frustrations and concentrated on producing the sensible and useful work that his tutors required. Though he was desperately unfulfilled, he knuckled down and clawed through his assignments. He was, by faculty reckoning, a good student, but he was not a happy one.

Dave sat on the bus traversing Westgate Road, being depressed and reading the advertisements. The conspiratorial tenements of Fenham loomed into view. Racks of blank stone, housing a number of financially-challenged Northumbrians and a significant proportion of the city's student population. Students who lived in Fenham didn't call it Fenham. They called it 'Nam'.

Dave's living room was occupied by Carlos and Stan, his flatmates. They were playing a digital golf game, which exuded from a small black box under the television. They each had a black controller in their laps.

'Please do not speak, Dave,' said Stan. 'I am near greatness.'

'Greatness,' whispered Carlos quietly. He was Spanish, and his accent lent the word a reverent, religious quality.

Stan and Carlos had, by Dave's estimation, clocked

about one thousand hours playing time on the golf game since its installation beneath the television at the start of the academic year. They were acknowledged world experts at it. Carlos had even sent some of their scores to a magazine in the States, which sent a letter back saying that they were sad, but very impressive, bastards. Dave knew just how important the game was to them. He stood quite still and waited for Stan to play his shot.

Stan performed a lengthy combination of strokes and clicks on the controller in his lap. It was like watching a very good touch typist at work. On the screen, the gaudily-clothed golfer (it was a feature of the game that you could select the player's outfits), took a mighty swing at the ball with his eight iron. The ball sailed through the air, tracked by a camera in the computer's mind.

'Please Lord, help us now,' said Stan.

'Dear Lord, please,' echoed Carlos.

And with a realistically wet thump, the ball landed in the centre of the green, just right of the pin. Stan rose from his chair and held a hand towards the TV in a gesture of acknowledgement. The digitized camera was scanning the digitized crowd, while digitized applause and cheering erupted from the speakers. Carlos was also clapping, next to the ghost of Stan that sat in the cushions beside him.

Depression deepening, Dave took the opportunity to get across the living room without interrupting play.

*

Dave was aware that he lived with Stan and Carlos mainly because they were fine art students. He liked them both anyway, he supposed, but because they were artists he had always been determined to like them more than the graphic designers on his course. He didn't want to be seen hanging around with the other graphic designers. He wanted to be seen with the artists.

Dave had first come across Stan and Carlos in the matriculation queue on his very first day at the Institute. The two art students had just met one another, and were debating the relative merits of Monet and Manet.

'Manet!' Stan was hollering. 'Always Manet! Foremost in both the alphabetical and artistic sense!'

'Bulls and shit!' said Carlos, whose English was rather embryonic at the time. 'Monet was greatest impressionist! Not his fault he's later in the encyclopaedia!'

'Have you *seen* Manet's *Olympia*?' asked Stan. 'Have you *seen* that painting? It's a bloody masterpiece!'

'Monet made waterlilies!' shouted Carlos, a finger raised resolutely in the air. 'I can say same thing of them!'

'But where's the psychological edge in Monet's waterlilies? They're just fucking plants.'

'Cathedral series also genius!' Carlos exclaimed loudly. He had not yet returned his finger to its post.

Dave listened in admiration as Stan and Carlos argued their way into friendship. Eventually, the two students agreed that the only way to settle their debate was to wait until there was a famous artist called Menet, whereupon they could accurately determine the relationship between alphabetical order and artistic talent. Once this conclusion had been reached, they fell silent.

Dave sidled over and tried to inject himself into their surroundings.

'Um, hello,' he said hopefully. 'I'm Dave.'

The two art students turned to regard him, their actions already a pattern.

'His name is Dave,' said Carlos, trying out the vowels for practice. 'Heees name eees Dave.'

'Indeed,' said Stan. 'Dave is his name.'

'Are you both artists?' asked Dave, feeling stupid the moment the words had left his mouth.

Stan and Carlos grinned.

'We are both artists,' said Stan solemnly.

'Artists of genius,' said Carlos.

'Although it remains to be seen,' said Stan, 'who is the greater genius between us.'

'Oh,' said Dave. There was a short pause while he gathered his courage. Stan and Carlos continued to beam at him, pleased to have an audience for their newly-formed double act.

'And what kind of art do you do?' Dave asked.

'Art of brilliance,' said Stan, nodding sagely.

'Brilliance and circumspection,' said Carlos, who had learned the second word in English class that morning.

'Right,' said Dave. 'Right.'

42

There was another pause whilst Stan and Carlos beamed at him some more.

'Well, I'd love to see some of it sometime,' said Dave. 'Your art, that is. I'd love to see some of it. As long as you wouldn't mind.'

'Ahhh,' said Stan. 'An art lover.' He turned to Carlos and nudged him in the shoulder. 'A lover of art.'

'You are artistic lover?' asked Carlos.

'Well, yes,' said Dave. 'I mean, well, no. I'm very interested in art, but I'm just a graphic designer really. I do love art though.' He was going slightly red.

'Of course,' said Stan. 'You are a man with soul and passion. It is evident from your shoes.'

Dave looked down, confused. He saw that his shoes were covered with paint. They were a hangover from his failure at A level. Spattered with his attempts at the canvas.

'Oh yes,' he said. 'I used to do a bit of art myself.'

'The shoes of enlightenment,' said Carlos carefully. These were all novel words, and he was enjoying them.

'Well, not really enlightened,' said Dave. 'As I say, I'm only a graphic designer.'

'Graphic design is a noble pursuit,' said Stan, noting the awkwardness in Dave's voice and leaping to his rescue.

'Nobell!' said Carlos, experimenting vocally. 'No-Bell. Nibble. Nobel.'

Dave grinned shyly. He liked Stan and Carlos. They made him feel good about himself.

'Listen,' he said. 'I don't know if you're doing any-thing after matriculation, but I'm going to the union. I don't suppose . . . well, I don't suppose you want to go for a beer?'

'Won't you be going with the other graphic designers?' asked Stan.

'I said I'd see them there,' said Dave, who had done nothing of the kind. 'I think they've already left.'

Standing in the kitchen doorway and listening to his two flatmates debate the correct angle for Stan's putt, Dave's misery redoubled. Since being refused entrance to the art world two and a half years ago, he had been trying to sneak onto the guest list by any means possible. Now he'd been reduced to hanging around by the bins outside the back door. With insight born of despondency, Dave realized that he'd become an art tart, a concept which Stan had explained one night in front of the golf game.

'Art, with its aura of creativity and originality, is a magnet for women,' Stan had said.

'Really?' said Dave.

'Indeed,' said Stan with great seriousness. 'Indeed. There is a whole breed of woman that lives to be near artists. To move in their circles. To be close to such ineffable work.'

'Ineffable?'

'Ineffable,' said Stan. 'These women are the art tarts. We must always be aware of them. They are often from wealthy backgrounds, and are southern, most commonly. They are fond of gin and tonic. They attend private views and eat sushi. They will kiss you on both cheeks.'

'They sound like a hell of an opportunity to me,' said Dave.

'Indeed,' said Stan again. 'Indeed they are. I myself have slept with over fifteen art tarts since my inauguration as a young artist at this bleak institution.'

Dave thought about this for a moment.

'Fifteen?' he said.

'Fifteen,' intoned Stan sadly. 'I wish them no longer. I crave an art bird.'

'An art bird?' asked Dave, wondering if Stan was going to burst into tears.

'Art birds are our kindred spirits,' said Stan, raising his eyes heavenwards. 'Practising artists who come from more impoverished backgrounds. Some have beaten the system and attend the great schools on their own merit. We can bed them as equals.'

'Bed them as equals,' repeated Dave, mesmerized by Stan's low voice.

'They are our destiny,' said Stan. 'But there are not enough of them to go around.' After a moment's more contemplation, he snapped out of his reverie and pointed at the screen.

'Hole three is a dog-leg to the left,' he said. 'I believe it is my honour.'

By living with Stan and Carlos, Dave was clinging to the coat-tails of his dream. He wanted to be with artists, even if he was not one of them. He wanted to converse about art, even if he was not allowed to produce it himself. And finally, in the absence of his own accomplishments, he wanted to reflect any glory that his artistic flatmates happened to emit.

The problem with Stan and Carlos was that they did not emit much glory. They were not really committed to furthering their creative abilities or the cause of art. They were committed to furthering the reduction of their digital handicaps and smoking weed. The perimeter of their daily activities stretched only to the gangster supermarket across the road, which stayed open all night to ensure the residents of Fenham were never short of beans or drugs. With such easy access to these two commodities and the comfort of their virtual golf club, Stan and Carlos needed little else to sustain their artistic lifestyle.

Dave made his way to the kitchen and did the washing up, which was the same colour as the walls. He could hear an argument breaking out next door. It was apparent that Stan's putt had been missed.

'Leftwards lean!' Carlos was screeching. 'Always leftwards lean on the eighteenth!'

'Spanish fool!' Stan shouted. 'How dare you advise me! You putt like an amateur!'

Dave found it worrying that his flatmates could argue so heatedly over an ethereal golf ball when they were both headed so firmly for third class degrees.

'I'm still hoping for a Desmond.' Stan would say to people.

'Desmond?' the confused party would ask.

'2:2!' Stan would say, waggling his eyebrows at them.

But in reality, both Stan and Carlos were unlikely to get anything but a Thora Hird.

Finishing the washing up, Dave went back into the living room, where a marijuana-induced calm had settled over the feuding parties.

'You coming to the Boat tonight?' Stan asked him. 'We're going to watch some art.'

Chapter Three

The circus performs

The Boat was where Dave, Stan and Carlos spent most of their Friday and Saturday nights. On the Boat they communed with a healthy if combustible mix of their fellow students and the local youth. The Boat wallowed magnificently beneath the Tyne Bridge, like the structure's massive genitals. The Boat was cool because it was a boat, but also a floating nightclub. And also, Stan and Carlos argued, an artistic installation in its own right.

Stan and Carlos were firstly appreciative of the Boat's location, facing the Riverside quay. They liked the way the redevelopment of Riverside had fleshed the water out with new bars, surrounding the Boat with an obsequious semicircle of lights.

'It's like they want to fuck the old girl,' said Stan.

Stan and Carlos also liked the interior of the Boat, which was composed of two levels. The upper level, a lounge bar, was full of faded armchairs and high stools, whilst the lower level was a nightclub, complete with a silver disco ball and revolving dancefloor. To add to the excitement of this slowly rotating contraption, the Boat itself listed at a queenly fifteen degrees, so that any navigation of the lower level was fraught with difficulty. If dancers concentrated on the tilt, the moving floor would catch them unawares, but if they focused on anticipation of the moving floor, the tilt would claim the top fifteen degrees of their beverage. Dave was a veteran of the Boat's dancefloor, but even he had trouble sometimes, and on several occasions had lurched purposefully towards a target only to find himself back where he started, covered in beer and facing the wrong way.

In addition to its status as a nightspot and artistic installation, the Boat enjoyed an unrivalled reputation as a metaphor for the British class system because of the way its two levels forced an artificial division of the clientele. All customers paid a notional one pound entry fee on the plank, but thereafter they peeled off to take their place on the lower or upper deck as status and wealth commanded. This was not a deliberate partitioning on the part of the organisers, but an unconscious decision by the attendees. Forced to decide whether they belonged in a lounge bar filled with pompous conversation and cocktail sticks, or a red-tinged hell of amorous glances and gyrating hips, clients normally did as their breeding suggested.

'Art tarts upstairs and art birds downstairs,' Stan often said.

Dave felt that to reduce people to such bipolar families was a trifle unfair, but even he had to admit that it was possible to predict the destination of a new entrant with an accuracy of around eighty per cent.

*

When they arrived at the quay, Stan and Carlos had still not explained what the evening's 'art' was going to consist of. However, they seemed unusually excited about it, and practically skipped from the bus stop down to the waterside.

'Come on, guys,' said Dave. 'At least give me a clue.'

'No, no, five times no,' said Carlos. 'You must be hungry, my friend. You must be hungry for the art.' He waggled his fingers in the air like a magician.

'But if I don't know what I'm looking for, I might miss it,' Dave complained. He was still smarting from his earlier realization, and the impishness of his flatmates was less endearing than normal.

'You are unlikely to miss it,' said Stan with a wink.

'Unlikely times two,' said Carlos.

'And anyway,' Stan continued, 'if we told you what it was, it would ruin the effect.'

'It would negate the work entirely,' said Carlos.

'It is performance art,' said Stan, 'and that is all that you shall know.'

Stan and Carlos had recently turned to performance art in a desperate attempt to drag their grades up to respectable levels. There was something of a vogue in performance artists running through the faculty, and they hoped to mine a vein of sympathy.

Carlos had arrived at the Institute fresh from Barcelona, where his vivid aerial landscapes, luminous cornucopias from the viewpoint of the sun, had been a cause of joy to many who witnessed them. The colours in these paintings, which ranged from lime to marigold, could almost be tasted in the darkness of the gallery, and the scenes were quickly bought by collectors, corporations, and even a church, for their uplifting nature. The money that Carlos made from these sales was used to pay for his education in Britain, where his parents hoped he would immerse himself in the London art movement and get a part-time job at Harrods. Unfortunately their grasp of geography did not quite do this strategy justice, so Carlos ended up in Newcastle.

Carlos took the change in climate very hard. Previously used to motes of light dancing in the evening air, he was now subjected to a grim curtain of twilight that descended sometime in the late afternoon, and a cold slicing winter that razed the world of colour. His work became muddy, the colours distorted. Soon he was painting great fields of black and grey rooftops, the light barely able to squeeze through the corners of his setting. His tutors quite liked these pieces, full of industrial soul and dark power as they were, but they just made Carlos miserable and one afternoon he burnt them all and was found sobbing in the paint room, covered in black number thirty-four.

Thereafter, Carlos concentrated his considerable talents on digital golf and smoking weed with Stan. He struggled with various new media, but could not find a form of expression that he liked. His dalliance with performance art was merely the latest in a long line of experiments.

*

Stan's art had always been theatrical in a sense. He was interested in action painting, fascinated by Pollock from the first moment he saw the great man's work. He spent a long time experimenting with new techniques in the Pollock mould; painting with syringes, painting in a rainstorm, painting with the lids of his paint cans. By the time he reached Newcastle, he'd started using everyday objects to paint images. The images he created were normally of the objects themselves, so the viewer had to reinterpret the painting and view it on both an internal and external level. People rather liked Stan's paintings for their tautological rhythms. Once he painted a giant vibrator using the vibrator itself, so the rubber veins and arteries repeated like a fractal through the canvas. It was generally thought to be his best piece.

Shortly after that, Stan went to a professional show and saw a doll's house in which every object had been minutely recreated from the most inappropriate materials available. There were perfect cardboard people, and TVs made from gold. The food was moulded plastic and the sofas fringed with fur. Stan stood before this little house of horrors and felt his heart sink into his shoes. Peering at twelve tiny Tampax stitched from Egyptian cotton, he realized that he'd been beaten to the punchline.

So Stan too had sought solace in front of the digital golf. Like Carlos, he continued to try new disciplines, but nothing really stuck. Performance art was his last chance. He thought it might be a bit shallow, and he didn't like the idea of a medium that depended so heavily on cultural context, but it was fun to be exploring something other than the undulations of an unreal fairway with Carlos.

Dave, Stan and Carlos crossed the plank and paid their obligatory pound.

'So, where are we best situated to view this great work?' asked Dave.

'Up top,' said Stan and Carlos together.

'Well, it must be unusual if you are both prepared to suffer the abuse of the upper deck for it,' said Dave.

The art students just grinned at him. Then they dodged across the revolving dancefloor to the stairs.

The upper deck was even more redolent with privilege than normal. Dave stared at the large number of women present, and felt the usual onrush of nerves. Carlos and Stan were in art tart heaven, and had already found elbows to touch and conversations to start. Trying to be as invisible as possible, Dave sidled over to the bar.

'Guinness please,' he said, and was surprised to feel a gentle touch on his arm.

'And a G and T,' said Jessica.

She looked sleek and triumphant. Her straight hair was still in a single knot, but now there was a streak of black running through it, a bold assertion of her style leadership. She was wearing a tight black T-shirt, which had 'T-shirt' emblazoned on it in grey lettering. Her trousers were expertly creased and her shoes were a parody of Dorothy's red lace-ups. She was still thin, and her high cheekbones were flushed with self-congratulation.

'Hi,' said Dave, paying for the drinks and turning as calmly as he could. 'Fancy seeing you here.'

Jessica kissed him on both cheeks. 'It's great to see you again,' she said. 'How are things with you?'

'Oh, fine,' said Dave. 'Fine really. Same as ever. Fine.'

Jessica's eyes flicked over his attire, and Dave suddenly felt very small and downmarket. He was dressed for the lower deck of the boat, wearing boots, an old golf shirt and the same jeans he had selected for their abortive date three years earlier.

'You're looking very good,' he blurted artlessly, his neuroses taking control of his mouth.

'Thanks,' said Jessica, failing to return the compliment. 'Are you here for the piece?'

Dave thanked God for Stan and Carlos. 'Of course,' he said, trying to sound knowledgeable. 'It must be bigger news than I thought if it's dragged the Lightschool contingent all the way up from London.'

'Not really. I was in Manchester visiting a show, and I heard it was on so I came up. I'm the only one from the Lightschool actually, though I do see a few familiar faces from "the scene".'

'Ah,' said Dave, nodding several times and trying to find some part of her where he could safely lay his gaze. 'And how is it down at the Lightschool?'

Jessica smiled rapturously. 'It's everything I hoped,' she purred.

'Good,' said Dave. 'Excellent. I'm really pleased.'

'And what about you?' asked Jessica, arching a perfect eyebrow. 'What have you been up to?'

Dave thought frantically. He was painfully aware of their last conversation, in which he'd told Jessica that he wanted to be an artist and that he didn't want to apply for a course in graphic design. His mind glazing in panic, Dave wondered how he could prevent her from discovering that the opposite had come true.

'Oh, not much,' he said. 'I've a few, er, projects on the go.'

'Really?'

'Um, well, just little things. Nothing to get excited about. Nothing that could compete with your work.'

He wanted her to disagree. He wanted her to accuse him of false modesty. But Jessica just nodded and smiled.

'Have you had anything displayed?'

'Oh no,' said Dave. He gave a short laugh, oddly loud and improper. It was a horrible question, designed to cause inadequacy. 'No, nothing so glamorous.'

Jessica waited for him to hand the query back to her. 'You?' he obliged, already knowing what the answer would be.

'Yes, a couple of pieces,' she confirmed. 'Only small galleries so far, but you know . . .'

Dave grinned like a corpse. He didn't really know what to say, although towards the end of the pause that followed, he began to think that he really should say something. Unfortunately, just as he was gearing up for his reply, Stan and Carlos reappeared. 'Come, graphic designer,' said Carlos imperiously. 'Come and see some *real* art.'

There was a brief hiatus in affairs, during which Jessica looked at Dave with a mixture of pity and delight, and Dave looked at the floor.

'Well,' he mumbled downwards, 'we must chat later.' He felt beaten and humiliated. Worthless and mundane.

'Yes, it would be nice to chat,' said Jessica. She had forgotten how satisfying a conversation with Dave could be. It was glorious to see him so unchanged, and his lowly status as a graphic design student had inflated her own sense of self-worth. She decided she would spend some more time with him later on. It would make her feel good about herself.

'I should do a bit of mingling,' she said, 'but then I'm all yours.'

Dave smiled as best he could, and then shuffled off behind Stan and Carlos. The three of them moved out onto the open-air deck that was attached to the lounge bar, adopting a position next to the railings. Jessica also moved outside and started talking to a French couple, whom Dave assumed were part of "the scene".

'Who's your friend?' Stan asked.

'Nobody,' said Dave, a little too quickly. 'Just someone from my sixth form college. Now at the Lightschool.'

'The Lightschool,' repeated Stan like a mantra.

'The Lightschool,' Carlos intoned sadly.

They drank their drinks in silence, waiting for some art to happen. Full of contemplative pathos, Dave turned his attention skywards. He discovered that from this angle the Tyne Bridge looked like a huge metal space station, hanging in the dark void above. If he blocked out all but the section he was focusing on and turned his head, he could make it orbit silently. The space station blinked its lights at him and spat a docking line outwards.

'Er,' said Dave, wondering if Stan and Carlos had put something in his drink.

But Stan and Carlos were making reverential noises, and Dave realized they were staring heavenwards as well. In fact, so was everyone else. The docking line wasn't a docking line. It was a climbing rope dropped from the edge of the bridge above them. It continued downward, fed out in body lengths, until it touched the roof of the lounge bar. Then it recoiled slightly, as though affronted by the taste of gin and tonic, and stopped.

Dave peered upwards at the bridge. A figure was now visible at the end of the rope. An astronaut in the emptiness of space. The figure busied itself with its hands, and the rope flinched. Jessica appeared at Dave's elbow again, keen to inflict her artistic authority upon him.

Stan, noticing that Jessica had rejoined their little group, addressed them as a body.

'Shall we speculate, children?' he asked.

Dave couldn't think of anything to say. He was transfixed by his astronaut, who had swung both legs over the railings, and who now stood on the edge of the bridge facing backwards. He had hardly even noticed the reintroduction of Jessica's presence by his side.

'Let us first discuss the nature of the upper deck on which we stand,' said Stan.

'For certain,' said Carlos. 'What do we think about the upper deck?'

Dave watched the astronaut push himself away from the railings of the bridge. In the dark air, the rope twitched and spasmed.

'To hint further,' said Stan. 'What kind of people do you see around you?'

Nobody lowered their eyes. They did not have to, they could still hear the murmur of idle gossip from the lounge bar, and the clink of wine glasses. They could also hear the thump of music from the lower deck. The rhythm pulsed in the soles of their feet.

'Brilliant,' whispered Jessica. 'The upper deck is the upper-classes. The artist is commenting on the inaccessibility of the upper-classes. There is no absolute barrier here. No actual segregation, but people arrive and they go where they belong.'

'Yes, yes,' said Carlos. 'Go on . . .'

'The rope is perhaps a form of birth?' said Jessica. 'The only way to gain access to the upper deck is through birthright? It is not possible to arrive by mortal means and simply walk upstairs?'

'That is certainly one reading,' said Stan. 'I believe you may have something. Dave, would you like to contribute?'

Dave was actually thinking of a much more personal metaphor, surrounded by members of the art world as he was. Through clandestine descent, the astronaut was about to explore a sphere of creativity that he'd never been part of. Dave had been trying to use the stairs for years, but the upper deck of the art world had always been closed to him.

He was never able to impart this observation. With a solemn grace that further enhanced Dave's impression of a deep space explorer, the body above them released its grip. The rope began to shriek as the abseiler starfished downwards.

'Oh shit,' said Carlos.

When the abseiler hit the roof of the lounge bar, he was tilted towards them, so thankfully only the top of his head was visible. His right arm hit a supporting metal ridgepole and appeared to disintegrate on impact, though the rest of his body passed through the roof with little resistance. Dave and his companions were all covered in a fine film of blood as the cloudy remains of the abseiler's arm hissed by. Dave felt a sharp pain in his shoulder as a meaty missile made impact, but the railings against which he stood kept him on his feet.

The body suffered greater harm on its way through the floor of the lounge bar. The head burst open without sound (which was yet to reach the scene), and the man's brain made a dash across the wooden floorboards, eventually coming to rest at the feet of an art critic from the local paper. Despite moving almost too quickly to detect, the brain remained intact throughout its journey, and was gelatinously identifiable to all those present upon the reinstatement of time.

As the body forced its way through the floor of the bar, the rough embrace of the floorboards tore its clothes and peripheries, so when it reached the coloured air of the lower deck there were only ragged flowers where its limbs had previously been. It burst into the nightclub like a falling angel, terrorized by heaven, sent on a screaming trajectory towards hell.

It was still quite early by the clubbing clock, and there were few enough dancers on the floor that the human meteor inflicted no further casualties during its terrible descent. In fact, it was moving so fast that most of the lower deck's residents didn't even register its presence until it struck home. The revolving dance-floor of the Boat was manufactured from wood over steel, and had seen the impact of too many heels to yield to a wet chunk of human flesh. The body, which had now lost enough velocity to be spared further out-rages, came to rest just off-centre, and spun sombrely under the auspices of the silver disco ball.

Dave watched the death of his astronaut in open-mouthed wonder. He found the whole process horribly beautiful. The lazy dismemberment of the falling body. The puffs of blood and eruptions of wooden sparks. The space station and docking line, hanging motionless in the aftermath. For the first time in his life, Dave felt complete. Filled with sensation. He wondered if this was how artists felt all the time.

Then the screaming started, and Dave was forced to take stock. Stan and Carlos had disappeared, and Jessica was equally conspicuous by her absence. Still in something of an aesthetic daze, Dave wandered through the panic and descended to the nightclub on the lower deck. Most people were rushing out over the plank, perhaps fearing more kamikazes were on their way. The revolving body had no dancing partners.

Dave looked up at the hole in the ceiling, through which he could see lounge chairs and overturned stools. He looked down at the floor, and the body. There was a bloodstained wallet lying nearby, apparently wrenched from the corpse's jacket by the wooden fingers of the roof.

Still in a trance, Dave picked up the wallet and put it in his pocket.

Chapter Four

Never the bride

At first Dave's shampoo bottle seemed a great success. Drayten Finch Plc thought it was 'very imaginative', and selected it for prototype manufacture. They even set up a full-size communal shower, of the type used by male sports teams, in their testing laboratory. Technicians gathered behind a one-way mirror and waited for a local rugby ensemble, bussed in from their Saturday afternoon game, to begin playing with the new design. Unfortunately their test subjects were so intimidated by these concentration camp surroundings that they performed their ablutions in terrified silence, trying desperately to shield themselves from the stare of the huge mirror before them. Several hid in the bath, establishing their modesty with flannels, and the bottle, which soon became slippy with suds, escaped their nervous hands and ended up on the floor. Nobody was prepared to bend over and pick it up, and the technicians pronounced Dave's efforts unsuitable for widespread distribution.

'Hard luck, David,' said the Dean, who'd heard about Dave's bottle on the Institute grapevine. 'It was a good effort, but perhaps you need to tone down your imagination a little bit.'

'Perhaps,' said Dave, staring at the Dean's right-hand shoulder.

'Always keep an eye on your tendencies,' the Dean advised gravely. 'Always keep an eye on those subversive tendencies of yours.'

'Oh yes, always,' Dave repeated vacantly, his mind nowhere near the Dean's words.

The failure of his bottle did not really matter to Dave. In fact, he gave it barely any thought whatsoever. He had witnessed something truly creative and he was feeling dwarfed by it. He couldn't think about anything but his astronaut. The beauty of the fall. The irony of the body's eventual destination on the lower deck, where perhaps it belonged. The feel of the blood, soaking through his shirt. The reactions amongst the audience. The emotions which the fall had generated. People who had seen it were going to counselling. People who hadn't seen it were wishing they had. Everybody was talking about it.

Dave felt inflated. He felt full of something. Something wanted to come out. He sensed, for perhaps the first time, the undeniable strength of his artistic subconscious. He was fat with potential.

That was why he had taken the wallet. He didn't care who the astronaut was, it was irrelevant to the way he felt. He just wanted to be part of the show. He had seen something and it had generated all these feelings within him and he no longer wanted to be just a bystander. He wanted to be *involved.* He wanted people to know he had the wallet. He wanted them to connect him with the event, which was something he could not hope to achieve. People would not connect him with the event because he was an artistic hanger-on, a graphic designer with ideas above his station. He desperately wanted to comment on what he had seen, to let himself be inspired by it, but he didn't think he had the right to try.

These feelings of artistic frustration were enhanced by the memory of Jessica, standing before him in arrogant state, confirming his place in the world. Her presence the night before, and her obvious delight in his failings, had reminded Dave of just how little progress he'd made in the last three years. He was horribly aware of the promise he'd made himself in that little dark pub. The promise to make something of his artistic career. To be so successful that even Jessica would admire his work. Since he'd last seen her, he had not taken a single step towards meeting his objective, and Jessica, knowing this, had laughed at him with her beautiful eyes. Thinking about Jessica made Dave more frustrated than ever. She threw the foolishness of his creative longings into sharp relief. Compared to her, he would always be 'technically competent'. He would never be an artist.

Dave tried playing the digital golf game to take his mind off things, but without Stan and Carlos to coach him, it was no fun. Dave was greatly impressed with everything his two friends did now. Even their feats of digital golf seemed impressive. But Stan and Carlos were no longer in Newcastle. They'd been arrested the day after their art claimed a life. Dave had at first assumed the police were there for him.

'Good evening, son,' the policeman had said.

'Er,' said Dave, wondering what the penalty for taking evidence from a crime scene was.

'Are your flatmates here, son?'

'Er,' said Dave again, trying to think of a good excuse for what he'd done, and failing.

'Are you all right, son?'

At that moment, Dave saw Stan and Carlos sprinting off down the road. He later realized they'd climbed out of the kitchen window.

'They've just gone out, officer,' he said.

The police caught Stan and Carlos at the house of a friend, playing on his copy of the digital golf game. They charged both students with manslaughter, and following bail, permitted them to return to their families and prepare a defence.

Stan and Carlos had received the inspiration for their vertiginous social commentary after a visit to a Newcastle bar called M1, where they'd been collecting material for a different piece of performance art altogether. M1 was the most expensive venue in Newcastle, renowned for its celebrity attendees, and it was in search of these individuals that Stan and Carlos had originally set out.

Their idea was a simple one, generated late one night after consuming a particularly efficacious bag of groceries from the gangster supermarket. They decided that they would smuggle camcorders into M1 and record the elite of Newcastle going about their nightly business. They would then splice these scenes into television footage of the celebrities they had captured. Through the purple haze that surrounded them at the time, this looked to Stan and Carlos like a clever way of examining the nature of mass-market celebrity. Viewers of the piece would see both public and private faces, the make-up on and off. The notion of fame would be laid bare.

'It will be art for the workers,' said Stan, holing a basic three-footer. 'Art *of* the famous, but *for* the workers.'

'We will mock the great tradition,' said Carlos, limbering up for a tee shot. 'We will be portrait masters with a difference. We will give them their heroes back cold.'

Stan leaned over and spoke in a conspiratorial whisper. 'We shall, of course, need disguises,' he said.

'Of course,' said Carlos. 'Disguises and guile.'

'Like two pimpernels,' said Stan.

'Scarlet,' said Carlos with satisfaction, releasing a meaty drive down the fairway. 'We shall call it *Scenes from a Scarleted World.*'

The first part of Stan and Carlos' scheme had progressed beautifully. Dressed in fine Spanish linen, which Carlos requisitioned from Barcelona, they breezed into M1 and began mingling with the great and the good of Newcastle. As the evening progressed, their trousers were loosened and their hidden camcorders withdrawn. There was sufficient wealth and hedonism awash in the room to distract their subjects, and very few people noticed what they were up to. Before long the two art students had collected ample footage for their work, and left discreetly, convinced they had avoided any repercussions.

Back at the flat and indulging in a celebratory game of digital golf, they were therefore shocked to hear the doorbell. They knew Dave was tucked up in bed, and all debts to the gangster shopkeepers had been paid. They were expecting no callers, and so they opened the door with considerable trepidation; a number of security chains safely in place.

'Hello?' said Stan quietly, speaking through the gap in the door.

'Hello?' said a deep voice beyond.

'Hello?' said Carlos.

'Hello?' said the deep voice again.

'Can we help you?' asked Stan.

'Please,' said the voice. 'Please don't do it.'

'Hello?' said Carlos worriedly. 'Do what?'

'Please don't,' said the voice. 'I love m'family. I'm a good man. Please don't.'

'Don't what?' asked Stan. His voice was fringed with hysteria.

'I'll pay ya,' said the voice. 'I'm a good man. I don't deserve this.'

'What? Deserve what?' said Carlos. 'What are you saying, strange person?'

'Please,' said the voice. 'Please let me in.'

'Let you in?' said Stan. 'Why?'

'So we c'n talk,' said the voice. 'I'm sure we c'n work something out.'

Stan and Carlos looked at one another in the darkness.

'He wants to pay us,' said Stan. 'He wants to work something out.'

'Maybe he is a patron of the arts?' said Carlos hopefully.

'Or a murderer,' said Stan.

'Or that,' Carlos agreed. 'He could be that.'

They pondered their predicament. They seemed to have little choice.

'All right,' Carlos said eventually. 'We are going to open the door now, but please be standing back, because you have scared us both greatly.'

When the door opened, Stan and Carlos were confronted with a sobbing Scottish bus driver, several feet taller than either of them but unmanned with distress. Between heaves of emotion the bus driver explained that he had followed them back from the nightclub in order to hear their demands. This confused the two students greatly at first, but after a long conversation, interspersed with encouraging pats on the back, they got to the bottom of things.

It seemed that in sourcing their celebrity images, Stan and Carlos had inadvertently captured the bus driver in a close embrace with a TV weatherman. As the father of two children and a member of a thoroughly homophobic community, the bus driver had kept this relationship secret for years, terrified of the impact it might have on his conventional working-class life. Given this extreme caution, he had been horrified to witness Stan and Carlos leaving M1 with their camcorders, no doubt ripe with evidence of his illicit affair. He had naturally assumed that they were planning to blackmail both him and his celebrity lover, and had followed them home to plead for mercy.

'It would end m'life!' wailed the bus driver dramatically, collapsing in a heap on the sofa. 'Gerald's career'd be ruined! Please! We're not hurt'n anyone! Please leave us alone!'

Once they understood their visitor's motivations, Stan and Carlos warmed to him immensely. They explained that their research had been of an entirely different nature, and after a short consultation in the kitchen, handed over all their footage for him to destroy.

'It was only an idea,' said Carlos magnanimously. 'We have many more ideas.'

'Absolutely,' said Stan. 'You poor man. You mustn't worry about us. You must put your family and gay lover first.'

The bus driver, astonished by this good fortune, broke down again. 'Oh God,' he sobbed happily. 'Thank ya boys. You've no idea how much this means. No idea at all. Thank ya boys. Thank ya both.'

Stan and Carlos waved him silent.

'It is our pleasure to help,' said Stan.

'Think nothing of it,' said Carlos.

'But I do,' said the bus driver, who was now

delirious with gratitude. 'I *do* think something of it. Can I do anything in return?'

'Hmm,' said Stan. 'What can you do?'

'I c'n drive a bus,' said the bus driver.

'No. No good,' said Carlos. 'Buses are predictable. They are boring. They have been done.'

'I c'n identify almost any kinda dog,' said the bus driver. 'Ma dad used to breed dogs.'

'No, dogs are no use,' said Stan. 'We have no artistic requirement for accurately designated dogs.'

'What else?' asked Carlos. 'What else can you do?'

A few minutes later, Stan and Carlos discovered that their bus driver was an abseiler, and it was a short step from this discovery to their proposal for a piece of performance art based around the Boat.

When they accepted the bus driver's offer of help, Stan and Carlos were too excited about their next idea to consider his suitability for the job. They explained that he would be required to start on the outer ledge of the bridge, directly above the Boat, and end triumphantly on the roof of the lounge bar. They did not enquire as to his skill, or his susceptibility to vertigo. Had they been more rigorous in their interview, they might have discovered that he was a novice who had only recently taken up abseiling to conquer his fear of heights. No one was more aware of this than the bus driver himself, but he felt so indebted to Stan and Carlos for not blackmailing him that no favour seemed too large. Besides, he decided, if he could descend ten feet without incident, then surely two hundred feet merely required a longer rope, not a similar increase in ability.

Stan and Carlos, convinced of a revival in their artistic fortunes, went out the following day and spread the word.

'Apparently,' said Stan, 'it's going to be a masterpiece.'

'A triumph,' said Carlos. 'Of a kind never seen here before.'

'We have it on good authority,' said Stan.

'From an impeccable source,' said Carlos.

'You must be there.'

'And you must bring companions.'

Half an hour into their enquiry, it therefore became obvious to the police that the incident they were investigating had been entirely orchestrated by two art students called Stan and Carlos. Everyone they interviewed from the upper deck had been asked to come, either directly or indirectly, by these two suspects. Even Dave had to admit that he was only there because of his flatmates.

Stan and Carlos' unfortunate bus driver, hanging high above his tiny metal target, had discovered that he was not quite over his fear of heights. He had also discovered that he was afraid of the dark and being above water. He was well on his way to developing a healthy fear of fine art students when he fainted and let go of the rope.

The police would have been unable to charge Stan

and Carlos with a crime if it were not for the camcorder films, which they found in the bus driver's garden shed, awaiting his next bonfire. Once the films had been matched with equipment belonging to the two students, there was proof of blackmail, which made Stan and Carlos directly responsible for the man's death. The police thought it impossible that the material they'd discovered could have been used for anything other than coercion, which they assumed to be the method by which Stan and Carlos had assured their victim's participation in the event. A warrant was quickly issued for their arrest, and an officer dispatched to knock on their front door.

Dave sat in his empty flat, marvelling at the creative energy of his absent flatmates. He emptied out the contents of the abseiler's wallet. Ten pounds cash. A reminder from the dentist that he was due for a check-up. A driving licence. A cash card. A photograph of his family. A gold American Express card.

Dave stared at this flotsam and felt like he would burst. Whatever was inside him, he had to get it out. He had to do something with it. He could not deny his urges a moment longer. So he wasn't the most talented artist in the world. So Jessica didn't think much of his abilities. So what? He had to express himself or he would explode. The results of his frustrations might not be artistically valid, but at least they would be medicinal.

Dave went upstairs to his room and found an old SLR camera. Then he rummaged through his laundry pile until he located the bloodstained shirt that he'd been wearing on the night of the accident. Then he went to work.

Chapter Five

In which Jessica does not achieve greatness

It was agreed by Jessica's tutors that she was, at best, an averagely talented student. The Lightschool tutors normally said this about all their students anyway, because as practising artists they competed for exhibition space with them, and didn't want them to do too well. However, in the case of Jessica, her tutors could condemn her to mediocrity with a clear conscience, because they actually meant it.

Jessica's basic problem was a lack of clear artistic direction, in place of which she displayed an unhealthy obsession with the latest fads and fashions. She seemed to be on the lookout for infamy rather than spiritual fulfilment.

'My art will be noticed, Daddy,' Jessica said over lunch in the capital. 'I'm going to make art that gets noticed.'

'That's good, angel,' said her father, 'but even if your art isn't a big success, your mother and I will still be very proud of you.'

Jessica looked at him like he was mad. 'What are

you talking about? Why on earth would you be proud of me then?'

Her father sipped his cappuccino carefully. 'Well, we think that what you're doing is very worthwhile. We're proud of you just for doing it.'

'Worthwhile?' said Jessica. She spat out the word like a piece of gristle. 'What do you mean?'

'Well,' said her father. 'It's very brave of you to pursue your dream. Not many people do so.'

Jessica drummed her fingers on the tablecloth. 'I see,' she said. 'And what do you think my dream is, exactly?'

'To be an artist,' said her father without hesitation. 'You've always wanted to be an artist.'

'An artist,' repeated Jessica, smiling at him. 'You think I want to be an artist?'

'Well, yes,' said her father. He was a bit confused. 'You've never wanted to be anything else.'

Jessica laughed girlishly, her charm back in place. 'Oh, Daddy,' she said, 'I don't want to be an artist.'

'You don't?' asked her father, completely bewildered by now.

'No, no,' said Jessica. 'I want to be a *successful* artist. One that people will *remember*.'

Jessica's art had always suffered in the pursuit of her ambitions. When she parodied Mr Cliffguard and her fellow classmates, Jessica had really been displaying her knowledge of artistic vogues and customs, not her innate ability as an artist. At the Lightschool this behaviour continued, as Jessica rifled the contemporary art scene for a mode that could propel her to stardom. Art, she believed, was awaiting the next big thing, and only a few lucky people would drive the paradigm shift when it came. Jessica was determined to be one of those people, and terrified that she would never be recognized as such. She therefore switched creative allegiances constantly, dropping one hothouse style for another and seldom working in an artistic field for more than a few months at a time. She was waiting for the big one. The one that would demolish the artistic landscape and leave only a few visionaries on their feet.

Jessica's tutors disliked this behaviour. They were used to artists who slowly decomposed within a specific genre, a process more romantic and introspective than Jessica's calculated bed-hopping. Her ambitions were felt to demean her efforts, and were considered improper conduct within such a neurotic institution. The Lightschool expected its students to be so tortured with artistic potential that they were almost incapable of social interaction. In modern art, mental impairment was believed to be a prerequisite for creative thought. Jessica displayed quite the opposite characteristics. She was bold and assertive, knowing exactly what she wanted to achieve and when she wanted to achieve it. Her tutors were united in their opinion. She was simply too confident to be any good.

The tutors also resented Jessica's assumption that she would recognize the next big thing when she saw it. They had never been able to predict the future, so why did she think she could? As a teaching institution, the Lightschool was so very contemporary that it sometimes struggled to decide exactly what contemporary meant. However, the Lightschool was determined that if Jessica had an idea what contemporary meant, it was going to be wrong.

Jessica, of course, completely ignored her tutors. She had never liked people who told her what to do, and retained a strong belief in her own abilities. She was going to be a successful modern artist, and if a particular train of thought was out in front, then she would make sure she was on it.

When Jessica arrived at the Lightschool, she dove headlong into minimalism, which was enjoying a resurgence at the time, and began producing minimalist sculpture by remoulding CDs into perfect rhomboids, squares and spheres. These objects were very carefully made and quite beautiful, though they felt threatening when the light on them waned.

'You have a good spatial eye,' said Jessica's tutor when he saw them. 'However, you should look a little deeper. Your work is too shallow, even for minimalism.'

He needn't have bothered constructing this criticism. The revival that minimalism enjoyed turned out to be as intangible as the genre itself, and Jessica abandoned it as soon as this became evident.

Towards the end of her first year, Jessica started to concentrate on size, having picked this theme up at one or two cutting-edge shows round London. She noticed that her fellow artists were often criticized if their work was excessively large or excessively small. Works that were too large attracted claims of wastefulness, whilst works which were too small were thought to be manifestations of low self-esteem. Jessica began painting childish landscapes in ever-increasing sizes, with the intention of drawing the viewer's eye to differences that were generated by scale rather than detail. Her tutor quite liked these studies, and offered some advice for improvement.

'Scale is an interesting topic,' he said, 'but perhaps you should explore a more complex base image. The landscapes you are using are too simple for the technique. They could lead people to believe that you are more interested in the idea than you are in the final effect.'

Of course, Jessica *was* more interested in the idea than the final effect, and her interest was typically shortlived. After a few months, the topic of scale began receding from the critical agenda. She dropped it straight away and moved on.

In her second year, driven by trends in the artistic press, Jessica took up the cause of abstract expressionism, and was commonly to be found in front of huge canvases covered in heavy oil paint. Her signature textures were angry and unsubtle, not because she actually wanted to paint that way, but because she had heard it was all the rage in Manhattan.

Jessica's second-year tutor was an old Lightschool

matriarch. She was confused by this change in direction.

'Abstract expressionism is all about process,' she explained patiently. 'It is an exploration of a theme. Repeating oneself to perfection. This is only one painting, and therefore you have only explored the paint once. You should look to produce a whole series of paintings. Then you'll know what you want to express.'

Again this advice fell on deaf ears. In the time it had taken Jessica to complete the first painting, abstract expressionism had re-entered the popular mainstream. Jessica found that once again she had come to the party too late. The vanguard of the movement were already in a cab on their way home. She moved swiftly on.

In her third year, after reading about the reinvention of pop art, Jessica decided to parody the British with a series of printed fake Churchills. She selected her subjects to be bald and decrepit, and then photographed them in the patent Churchill pose. They sat on her walls like an army, each wearing a bowler hat, smoking a cigar and raising the 'Victory V'. Her prints were in colour, and she repeated her favourites in lines. The old men spoke of symbolism, but also of anger and death.

Unfortunately, Jessica's third-year tutor was an extremely British artist from the days of the empire. He was eighty-seven years old and took the whole collection as a personal attack.

'I suppose there's some craft on display here,' he admitted grudgingly, 'but I find the work in poor taste.'

He was therefore gratified when Jessica ceased production of her Churchills and moved once again to fresh fields. Her decision was nothing to do with his comments. She had been watching a fair bit of television, and had noticed that pop art images were appearing less frequently on MTV.

Since the fake Churchills, Jessica had been concentrating on performance art. It was her last chance to pre-empt artistic fashion. Her last chance to make a mark. At the Lightschool, as at Newcastle Institute of Arts and Media, there was a general feeling that performance art was making a comeback. When Jessica boarded the train to Newcastle, she was treating the trip as a serious research exercise. She had heard whispers about a strange new piece of performance art, scheduled to occur that very evening. To Jessica, this sounded ideal. She was hoping to find something new. Something unusual.

The accidental dismemberment she witnessed did not disappoint her. That night on the Boat, Jessica found her new source of inspiration.

'As a matter of fact, Daddy,' Jessica said as they finished their lunch, 'I think I might have found something that people will remember me for. Something that will be *successful.*'

'Really, my sweet?' said her father, scribbling out a

sizeable cheque. 'Well, that's excellent news. What is it?'

'Oh, I can't tell you that,' said Jessica. 'I'm not sure what to do with it yet.'

'Oh,' said her father. 'Well, I'm sure it will be fantastic when it's done.'

'Yes, it will be,' said Jessica. She leaned over and kissed her father on the cheek.

'Goodbye, angel,' he said, tweaking her nose with affection. 'I'll call you as normal this weekend.'

'Goodbye, Daddy,' said Jessica. 'Give my love to Mummy.'

'I will,' her father promised. 'And I hope your new idea is a success.'

'Oh, it will be,' said Jessica. 'It's only a matter of time.'

The police had not kept Jessica for more than a few hours after the accident. She had been unable to provide any information they had not already gleaned from other sources, and was allowed back to London after giving a brief statement. It never occurred to her to call Dave before leaving. Her mind was on more important matters. She was thinking about herself.

Back at the Lightschool, Jessica spent days mulling over what she had seen, wondering how to use the power of the accident for her own ends. She was particularly interested in the dramatic irony that had been authored. She liked the fact that the falling body had been returned to its proper societal stratum in death, and it amused her that the planks of the upper deck had failed to hold the weight of the abseiler's metaphorical birth. She became extremely preoccupied with the class system as subject matter, and started thinking about a piece of her own to examine it.

Her initial thought was to script identical dialogue for people with strongly working-class or upper-class dialects, film both sets of individuals speaking the words, and then display this footage in a suitably challenging format. A giant map of the British Isles was one idea she toyed with, envisaging a huge piece of green baize filled with holes for TV monitors and her subjects speaking within. She thought it might be fun to disrupt the locations of her contributors, so a conflict was generated within the observer between what their eyes and ears were telling them was the real background of the individual, and the expectations generated from the subject's placement on the map. Then she thought it would be fun to display her map on the gallery floor, so that people could locate themselves within a class region while observing.

Her second idea was to display the class monologues on a wooden class tree, with monitors showing posher individuals hanging higher up the foliage. Again, Jessica thought she could have some fun with this visual format. Could she move a few people out along the branches to show how they had skirted the system? Could she place a couple of upper-class monitors on the floor to indicate the rotten apples they had become? And finally, could she place some monitors beneath the gallery floorboards, signifying the working-class roots of society that were too often precluded from view?

In the end, Jessica decided on a much simpler creation. She obtained an ordinary magazine-stand from a bankrupted newsagents and installed it within her studio. Her plan was to place the working-class monitors on the top shelf and the upper-class monitors in the middle. In this way, she hoped to point out how working-class imagery and drama had become something of an illicit thrill, whilst upper-class lives increasingly decorated the desirable mainstream. The supposed shoppers were the massed ranks of the middle-class, represented by the viewers in the gallery.

Confident that she had the kernel of a good idea, Jessica began to look for locations in which to film. Her father was still supplying a handsome monthly allowance, so she could go where she wanted. With the falling abseiler fresh in her mind, and keen to revisit the scene of her inspiration, Jessica decided Newcastle would be a good place to start.

Chapter Six

Reflected glory

Dave cleared out Stan's room for his working space. The walls were whitewashed, which suited him fine, and any external light could be blocked out by an old, opaque set of blinds. There wasn't really much furniture left in the room anyway, because Stan's parents had arrived in a huge old transit van and packed away their son's shame in the back. Dave moved the bed and chairs into Carlos' room, and was left with a workable space. The rent was paid up until the end of the academic year, so he calculated that his efforts had a life span of twelve weeks, which was better than nothing.

Getting the photography blown up was hard. He needed materials, and ideally a screen-printing press. The only press he knew of was in the Institute's cabbage-green basement, and should therefore have been available to him. However, it was guarded by Big Ken, a gigantic hulk of a man who had been employed on the same salary for thirty years. Big Ken hated both students and the end products of their labours, and regarded it as his duty to refuse the production of anything he didn't immediately see the merit of. Big Ken never really saw the merit of anything.

'Can I produce two A1 copies of this please Ken?' the student would ask.

'Fuck no,' Big Ken would say, cracking his knuckles and peering myopically at the hated *objet d'art*.

The standard procedure for using the printing press was to obtain faculty reinforcements in the form of a senior member of staff to convince Big Ken that the project had either artistic or graphic merit. Big Ken would then grumblingly oversee the proceedings. Dave could not follow these channels, as his project was extra-curricular, and obtaining staff assent to circumvent Big Ken would be impossible. He was also quite sure that Big Ken would not approve of the abstract nature of his work-in-progress, so there was no hope of conspiring with the huge Geordie.

Dave did what he had to do. He bought a Newcastle United ticket for a vastly inflated sum on the black market and descended to Big Ken's printing hideout.

'Hello?' he said, knocking nervously on the laminate door. 'Ken? Are you there?'

A series of terrible noises erupted within.

'Hello?' called Dave again. He pushed slightly on the door, which swung open to reveal a lumberjack shirt.

'Aye man?'

'Hello, Ken,' said Dave. 'How are you?'

'Rubbish,' said Ken. He scratched a pocket of hair on his neck. 'What yer want?'

'Nothing really,' said Dave. 'I just thought I'd pop round and say hi.'

'Fuck off,' said Ken.

'Right,' said Dave. 'Absolutely. It's just, well, before I go, I need to ask you a question.'

'Don't like questions,' said Ken.

'I understand,' said Dave. 'I'll be very quick, and then, I promise, I'll be off.'

'Right,' said Ken. 'What's yer question, like?'

'Well,' said Dave. 'It's about the Magpies.'

Big Ken stiffened. The logo of Newcastle United – the Magpies – was the only thing he had been seen to print willingly. He was a lifelong fan of the team.

'I was wondering how much a ticket would cost these days.'

'Fuckloads,' said Ken. 'S'fucking disgrace.'

'Really?' said Dave. 'Only I've been given a ticket to today's game, and I was wondering how much I would get if I sold it.' He produced the hallowed square of white card, which was licked at the edges with silver.

'Gahhh,' said Big Ken. He followed the ticket's trajectory, his eyes watering with desire and despair.

'The thing is,' Dave said, 'it would be nice for a proper fan to have it. I mean, what with the cost these days, real fans don't get to see many matches do they?'

Big Ken shook his enormous head in time with the ticket. 'S'fucking scandal, like,' he said miserably.

'I don't suppose you're free this afternoon?' Dave asked. 'You're a fan aren't you?'

Big Ken eyed Dave with suspicion. 'Have to watch

the equipment,' he said. 'What you playing at, boy?'

Dave cursed his inexperience with bribery. He was new to such artifice, and the subtleties of it eluded him. 'Look,' he said, 'I'll be honest. I don't really need the money, so I'd be happy to sell the ticket to a proper fan. You should go. You're a fan, but you never get to go. It's not fair.'

Big Ken swayed slightly in space. He was peering at Dave with confusion.

'Fuck off,' he said in disbelief. 'How much you want for it, like?'

'Oh, whatever you've got will be fine,' said Dave. 'After all, it didn't cost me anything, did it?'

Big Ken cleared his throat loudly. 'Got two pounds forty,' he said.

'Right,' said Dave. 'Well, that's fine.' He held out the ticket.

'Fuck off,' said Big Ken once again. He was staring at Dave's hand in astonishment. 'What about me equipment?'

'Oh, I don't expect anyone will miss you,' said Dave. 'If you like, I'll tell people you went home sick.'

'Sick,' repeated Big Ken. With shaking hands he handed over his two pounds forty.

'Enjoy the game,' said Dave. 'I hope it's a good one.'

'All good,' said Ken. He carefully folded up the ticket and wedged it in a dirty shirt pocket. 'Greatest team in the world.'

'So I hear,' said Dave. He turned awkwardly to leave. He didn't like pulling the wool over people's eyes. He was an honest individual at heart.

'Cheerio then,' he said, making his way up the basement stairs. 'I hope the Magpies win.'

'Aye,' said Big Ken. He turned back towards his lair, but paused with his hand on the door. 'Lad?' he said.

Dave stopped on the stairs and turned round. 'Yes?'

'Fucking cheers man,' said Big Ken, and he shut the door behind him.

Dave was ashamed of his actions. He was ashamed of his trick. However, he had to get his photography enlarged. He was embarked upon something now, and if he didn't see it through to the finish, he might never know peace.

Back upstairs, Dave hid in the cafeteria until Big Ken had departed the Institute grounds. Then he returned to the scene. The basement had no lock (with Big Ken in near permanent residence there was no need for one) so Dave let himself in and went to work.

By the end of the day, he had a result he was happy with.

The second problem was the mannequin. Dave tried all the usual places: old store clearouts; car boot sales; flea markets. He couldn't find a male mannequin torso without defects. Eventually he decided there was nothing for it but to approach Vincent.

Vincent had been Dave's drinking partner during his first week at the Institute, but Dave had soon come to the conclusion that he would die if he continued to go drinking with Vincent, so he had started hanging around Stan and Carlos instead. Dave still saw Vincent from time to time in the pub, molesting women and pints of lager. He had no idea what Vincent was studying, and doubted that Vincent did either.

Vincent had apparently been born with the God-given ability to stay vertical and conscious regardless of the quantity of alcohol he consumed, and he was still to be found charging through bushes and climbing over parked cars long after his peers had succumbed to either gravity or biology. He had been arrested several times, though he was now on sufficiently familiar terms with the local constabulary to escape severe punishment.

When he was drunk, Vincent liked to steal things, but not for Vincent the obvious traffic cones and road signs; he perpetrated far greater feats of robbery. Once he had made off with a cello after an inebriated evening at the concert hall. On another occasion he liberated an entire dinner service from his favourite Indian restaurant. Perhaps his greatest achievement was the theft of a horse from the constabulary stables themselves.

Dave knew that a mere mannequin was easily within the realms of Vincent's abilities. He simply had to be convinced that it was an appropriate target. And Vincent offered the added benefit of secrecy, because he would have forgotten what he had stolen by the following morning. There was no danger of him realizing that Dave the graphic designer was attempting 'high' art.

Dave called Vincent up and asked him if he wanted to get a beer.

Six beers later, he found himself slumped by a cash machine in the centre of Newcastle. Across the street he could just make out Vincent, who was kicking a lamppost in an attempt to make it go out. Vincent had only drunk twice as much beer as Dave, so he was still relatively sober.

'Vince?' called Dave pitifully.

'Definitely went out last week,' Vincent muttered to himself, staring up at the lamppost in concern.

Dave opened his mouth to call again, but a variety of foodstuffs seized their chance to escape. 'Blug,' he said.

When he looked up from his dinner, Dave saw Vincent charging at the lamppost with his head down, looking for all the world like a maddened bull. He struck the centre of the lamppost with great force and the light above them blinked out.

'Ha,' said Vincent from the floor, rubbing his forehead absentmindedly.

'Vince?' called Dave again.

'Yes?' said Vincent, hopping to his feet and wandering over.

Dave stared upwards, his eyes struggling with the concept of focal length. 'Needfavour,' he said. Words wandered through his mind like bars of soap. He had trouble holding onto them.

Vincent smiled down at his prone companion. He liked Dave, and was always happy to go out drinking with him, mismatched though their tolerance levels might be. Vincent had known Dave was a nice person from the moment he met him. In Dave he sensed an honest soul. A genuinely nice guy. His friend certainly had some issues to resolve, some frustrations and desires that he kept hidden from the world, but Vincent was pleased to see that he never took these out on other people. Dave was kind, tolerant, and nice. Perhaps a little too nice for his own good.

'Come on, Davey boy,' he said, pulling Dave to his feet. 'My, noodles for dinner, was it?' He plucked a curly adornment from Dave's lapel.

Dave nodded. 'Goomate,' he slurred, steadying himself on Vincent's shoulder.

Vincent smiled at him. 'You're a good lad too, Davey boy,' he said, clapping his friend on the back. 'Now, where next?'

Dave attempted to aim one of his arms at the boutique across the road. 'Betcha,' he said. 'Betcha canna.'

'That's a shop, mate,' said Vincent, following the trajectory of Dave's waggling limb. 'S–h–o–p.'

'Nnnnn,' said Dave. 'Manna. Manana. Manniky.'

'Mannequin?' Vincent hazarded.

Dave nodded frantically, and was very nearly sick again. He took a deep breath and marshalled his vocabulary. 'Betchacantnikkit,' he said.

Vincent's eyebrows raised slightly, and he turned to survey the boutique anew. 'Is that right?' he said, almost to himself.

Dave nodded woozily, and seeing an appropriate bus come round the corner, he stumbled into the road to flag it down. His work was done, the idea was planted. Vincent had a lot more drinking to do before the night was out, but Dave's challenge would remain in his mind.

As the bus pulled off, Dave saw Vincent seating himself in a pub across the road from the boutique. He had bought six pints of beer, and he was staring at the mannequin like a kestrel.

Dave's bus pulled out of sight.

The following morning, Dave awoke to find the mannequin sitting on his settee. It was handsomely attired in Gucci apparel, and Vincent was asleep in its lap. Trying to ignore his raging hangover and absent stomach lining, Dave disrobed the mannequin and hid it away. Then he awoke the hapless cat-thief with a fried breakfast and a cup of tea. As predicted, Vincent's recollection of the evening was heavily truncated. He remembered the incident with the lamppost, but thereafter his memory was blank. The absence of his booty was made irrelevant by the fact that he could not remember stealing it in the first place, and this helped assuage some of Dave's guilt about manipulating his friend's actions. Dave re-assured himself that Vincent would have stolen something anyway, and that he had done no harm in ensuring it was a mannequin.

As for Vincent, the fact that he could not remem-ber what he'd been doing the previous evening was hardly worth mentioning. He was quite used to such reality gaps, and the patchy nature of his past did not bother him in the slightest. He ate his breakfast with relish and then went to the pub.

When he had finished his work in Stan's room, Dave felt better. It was out. Whatever it was, it was out. He felt finished. For the first time in his life, he had created something on his own, in exactly the way that he wanted. He hadn't followed the advice of others, and he hadn't let himself be swayed by the conventions and habits of a discipline. Dave was proud of his work, and the strength of his self-appraisal surprised him. Perhaps, he thought, his impulses really were worthy of expression. Perhaps, if he tried hard enough, he could be more than just 'technically competent' after all.

Dave was falling asleep in front of his completed work when the phone roused him. 'Hello?' he said.

'Hey, Dave. It's Jessica. Is it true?'

'Er,' said Dave.

'Is it true, Dave?' said Jessica.

'Er, how did you get my number?' said Dave, realizing that he could not have given it to her on the Boat.

'Student directory,' said Jessica. 'Is it true?'

'Is what true?'

'Were your flatmates responsible for the work we saw, Dave? Everyone is saying they were. Is it true, Dave?'

'Yes,' said Dave. 'Yes, I suppose it is.'

She sighed. 'What amazing guys. Their work has really inspired me, you know. I want to do my own piece in the same mould. I'm coming up to Newcastle and I'd really like to see their house. I'm sure it would be really inspirational for me. Can I come round?'

'I suppose so,' said Dave. 'But there's not much to see really. They've sort of taken it all with them.'

'Well then, you can tell me all about them,' said Jessica. 'I'll come round and you can tell me all about them.'

'I suppose,' said Dave again. He was a little confused by the way Jessica was talking to him. She almost seemed to be treating him as an equal.

'How did you end up living with those two anyway?' asked Jessica. 'They don't seem much like you.'

That was more like it, thought Dave. 'Just lucky I guess,' he said.

'Very lucky,' said Jessica. 'Look, I've got the address. I'll pop round when I'm up there, OK?'

'OK,' said Dave.

'Bye, sweetie!' said Jessica, and she hung up.

After this conversation, Dave was unable to rediscover his sleepy contentment. In fact, he failed to drop off until late into the night. Instead, he soaked the sheets with thoughts of Jessica. As usual, she had dismissed him as a creative lackey, focusing on those she thought worthy of her attention. Dave fumed as her comments reinvigorated his frustration. For the first time in his life, he had completed something of which he was proud, but even if he'd told her about it, she wouldn't have cared. Dave wanted Jessica's endorsement more than ever before. Of all the critics he wished to silence, she was the most vocal. Her rejections were the most absolute. Dave wanted to show Jessica that he had some creative talent. There was an artistic work of his own in Stan's room, and he was convinced it was worthy of her admiration.

Dave dropped off dreaming of Jessica's approval. They were walking through a park together, and her head was on his shoulder. She was whispering things in his ear, but he couldn't make out the words.

Chapter Seven

Dave the artist

Towards the end of their final year at Newcastle Institute of Arts and Media, students were expected to find a job. If they couldn't actually find a job, they were at least expected to decide what area they wanted to be employed in, and begin 'putting out feelers', as the careers adviser liked to say. Dave got a job in advertising purely because the careers adviser mistook him for a fine art student. Had she realized that he was a graphic design student, she would have steered him towards an office boy role in one of the smaller and less glamorous design agencies on her list.

The Institute's careers adviser was a wretched woman called Miss Roly. She had always been rather large, which made her surname all the more unfortunate. As a child she had been teased mercilessly for the combination of her girth and nomenclature, and had developed a comprehensive dislike for her fellow man. Turning towards the natural world, she hoped to find peace with the less vicious vertebrates, but her determinedly awful science grades conspired against her, and she ended up as a laboratory assistant to an eminent immunologist. This unpleasant man, though a vastly respected intellect, was consistently mean to both her and the test subject monkeys for which she cared. One day, in a fit of outrage over his most recent abuse, Miss Roly released two monkeys into the toilet within which he was answering a call of nature. The monkeys climbed up the sides of the cubicle and, recognizing the bald pate of their tormentor, urinated copiously over his indisposed form. After the immunologist had made his damp escape, the laboratory staff spent several hours attempting to recapture the monkeys, who were enjoying themselves immensely, having discovered how to temporarily blind people with liquid soap.

The university for which Miss Roly worked did not want to sack her in case the media got hold of the story and exposed the farce that had taken place in their supposedly first-rate primate facility. They transferred her to personnel recruitment, where they supposed by definition she could only do harm to people they did not yet employ, and who could therefore not sue them. Miss Roly was appalling at this job as well. Her miserable experiences with the human race had motivated her to bring all interviews to a close as quickly as possible, before the interviewee could start to make fun of her, and as a result she seldom selected the right candidate for the job. Several of the people she appointed turned out to be from the wrong academic field, and when the administration found out they'd employed a gynaecologist to teach dental surgery, they decided that enough was enough.

In desperation, they wrote Miss Roly a series of glowing references and she got a job as the careers adviser for Newcastle Institute of Arts and Media on significantly improved pay.

In her new position, and still adverse to human encounters, Miss Roly had developed a strategy for disposing of her students in record time. She had noticed that the fine art students were always scruffy and covered in paint (from their artistic endeavours, she supposed). They could therefore be identified at a moment's notice. The fashion design students all wore dark Italian denim, black leather boots and white linen shirts. Plus they often had tape measures hanging around their necks as accessories. They were instantly identifiable as well. The graphic designers looked fairly normal, so she simply assumed they comprised all the other students in the populace.

Miss Roly's technique, which was based on the use of these stereotypes, was devastatingly simple. She would open her office for a three-day period, categorize her charges the moment they walked in the door, and from that point on treat them accordingly. This allowed her to save the time that would have been taken up finding out which course they were on, and she was thus able to bring each interview to a close all the more rapidly.

In the further pursuit of interview brevity, Miss Roly had shortened her career advice to minimum length. For the graphic design students, she had a variety of design agencies and architectural firms who might require someone to make the tea, and she would give them a few names and a pamphlet on how to write a covering letter before sending them away. Similarly, she would present the fashion students with a list of fashion houses, and ask them to pick five to contact. Then she would give them the same pamphlet and send them away as well. The art students presented her with more difficulty. She knew there was more than one career path they could follow, but to keep things short and simple she had devised a tree diagram of questions that would present the choices to them quickly and efficiently.

Question 1: Do you want to carry on with your art?

If the subject answered no to this question, she sent them to the job centre, pointing out that their degree was now useless. This often allowed her to eject them within several minutes of their arrival. If they answered yes, she went on to question two.

Question 2: Do you want to be a professional artist?

If the subject answered yes to this question, she gave them the number of the Northeastern Artist's Association, who were supposed to provide help for young artists on the make, but who actually never answered the phone. Then she sent them away. If the student answered no she progressed to question three.

Question 3: Do you want to teach art?

When they said yes, she gave them the UCAS application book, explaining that they would need to complete their teaching qualification at a different educational establishment (this was preferred by employers), and sent them packing.

Nobody had ever gone through Miss Roly's procedure and then answered no to question three. Not, that is, until Dave.

When he walked into the interview room, Miss Roly immediately concluded that Dave was a fine art student. He looked slightly haunted, which was one of the two fine art student expressions (the other one she often described as 'pompously self-important'). He was also covered in flecks of paint from the amendments he had been making to his work in Stan's room. She avoided his gaze and waved him into a chair.

'Do you want to carry on with your art?' she asked, staring resolutely at her desk.

Dave completely misinterpreted this question. He assumed she must have found out about his clandestine use of Big Ken's printing press. Perhaps, he thought, it would be better to declare his hidden passions to the Institute? If he was to be punished, he supposed they would look more kindly on a frustrated artist than a thieving graphic design student.

'Yes,' he said shyly. 'I'd like to if I can. It's meant a huge amount to me to finally make something on my own. I'm really very proud of it. I realize I wasn't really supposed to . . .'

'Do you want to be a professional artist?' Miss Roly asked brusquely, not looking up.

Dave thought quickly. He decided that it would be presumptuous to pretend he actually *was* an artist.

The Institute had been teaching him as a graphic design student for three years. To ignore this and try for a new career would be impolite.

'No,' he said. 'No, I don't think I could really claim to be a proper artist. I know that I should also use my technical skills. I should also design things. Things with a functional use. It's just that I'd like to keep producing art as well. As a hobby. I wouldn't ever assume that people would buy my work.'

'So really, you want to teach art?' said Miss Roly, waiting for him to agree.

Now Dave was just confused. 'Er, I wouldn't possibly presume to teach art,' he said nervously. 'I'm only just discovering it myself.'

Miss Roly was breaking out in a cold sweat. This interview had lasted about twice as long as she typically liked, and her usual system of questions had failed her. She cast about her desk for some way to get rid of her tormentor, and her eyes alighted on the application form she had been sent by an advertising agency. It was the first of its kind she had ever received. The agency was looking for talented art students who might be interested in an apprenticeship. The role was described as 'junior creative, responsible for assisting senior creatives and general office tasks'. Miss Roly didn't know what any of this meant.

'Here then,' she said, thrusting the letter towards him like a crucifix. 'Take this and let me know how you get on.'

Dave took the letter and retreated. It was obvious

that Miss Roly was angry with him, and he didn't want to enrage her further.

'OK,' he said. 'Thanks very much for the chat.'

When Dave got home, he found his front door ajar. With a sinking feeling he wandered upstairs, hoping that they hadn't taken too much. In the doorway to Stan's bedroom he found Jessica sitting on the floor. She was staring at his artistic catharsis.

'Well,' she said, 'haven't you been a busy boy?'

Jessica was staying at a friend's house in Jesmond, which was at the other end of Newcastle from Fenham, and not just in terms of geography. It was nicer, its streets leafier, the taxes higher. In Jesmond the student flats often had window boxes, whilst in Fenham they sometimes didn't have windows at all. Stan had frequented Jesmond during his art tart phase. He claimed there was a greater concentration of art history students in Jesmond than anywhere else in the UK. Art history students were notoriously susceptible to Stan's charms.

When Jessica had taken the taxi from Jesmond to Fenham, she was expecting to find Dave at home. Instead she had been unlucky enough to encounter Dave's next door neighbour, Vartak.

An illegal Polish immigrant, Vartak had moved to Newcastle following the Second World War, where he'd successfully evaded the authorities for so long that they had become fed up and stopped looking for him. Now he was over eighty years old and extraordinarily senile, often found patrolling the streets in preparation for German attack, or shouting at invisible enemies in Polish.

Jessica thought that Vartak was a prime example of the embittered class struggle that must have so mobilized the artistic tendencies of her now-heroes, Stan and Carlos. Having paid her taxi fare, she approached the old man, who was muttering next to the dustbins.

'Hello,' she said, hoping she would be able to film him for her forthcoming piece on class stereotypes. 'Can I ask you a question?'

Unfortunately, Jessica was a dead ringer for a young social worker who had pursued Vartak's expulsion from the UK with great vigour in the late nineteen forties.

'*Bitchbag!*' screamed Vartak, pulling a rusty bayonet from his trousers and rushing at her.

After being chased up and down the street a few times, Jessica thought she'd better get away from the old man before his heart gave out, so she leapt over Dave's garden fence and found a Jessica-sized hole in the slats that made up his front window. Once inside, she hid upstairs until Vartak forgot about her.

Whilst upstairs she found Dave's installation.

Dave had taken his pictures of the Tyne Bridge at night, from below. Jessica realized that he'd taken them from the upper deck of the Boat, which meant he must have crept on at night because she'd heard it hadn't reopened for business yet. The photos were of the centre section of the bridge. It looked spooky, she thought. Like a floating power plant or something (she didn't realize he still saw it as a space station). He had blown up the photos and printed them onto transparent Perspex, and from the quality of reproduction she thought he must have used a screen-printing press. The colours had almost entirely gone from the photos now that they were so large, and the metal edges were dulled, as though interstellar fog had impaired the reach of the camera.

Dave had erected his huge photos of the bridge, three in all, as a triptych about a foot away from the bedroom wall. Behind them he had placed light boxes, rather like the ones used to look at film negatives (in fact, they were exactly that, Dave having bought them from the local photography shop). The light shone through the Perspex prints irregularly, making them look as though they had internal power sources, and enhancing the impression that they were images of a celestial object.

A large vitrine on a painted white plinth stood in the centre of the room. It was lit from beneath (the local hardware firm had grudgingly delivered Dave's requirements), and inside stood the torso of the mannequin, dressed in Dave's still-bloodstained shirt. On a small stand at the bottom of the case was pinned the gold American Express card. It was arranged to look like a badge of honour, or a plaque, erected in tribute to a valiant pioneer.

Jessica's first reaction to Dave's work was one of immense professional jealousy, caused by the fact that she really really liked it. The work was a potent monument to the events they had both witnessed on The Boat. The irony of the attempted attack on the class system was doubly emphasized by the gold card, and the atmosphere of the location was superbly captured in the lighting and photography. She also realized that the work was slightly contentious, containing evidence from the crime scene that the police were surely not aware of. Jessica had lost track of Dave after the fall. She assumed he must have stumbled upon the hapless victim's wallet during this period and concealed it until the police had ushered them all out. His use of the American Express card would cause something of a fuss if the work was ever shown, but Jessica was wise enough to know that without causing some fuss, no art these days stood any chance at all.

Once the initial feelings of envy had passed, Jessica began to reevaluate Dave. It seemed she had misjudged him. He obviously had some talent, though his personality got in the way of its expression. Before he had seemed like a fawning idiot, but now she repainted him as an idiot who was really rather sweet. His northern ways and bumbling manner were suddenly just idiosyncrasies of a young artist. His failure to verbalize opinion was a sign of shyness rather than dim-witted uncertainty. Jessica was aware of Dave's ongoing attraction to her, and now wondered if he didn't deserve a little more attention himself. She decided that she would be very nice to Dave when he got home.

In changing her opinion of Dave, Jessica was

doing what she always did when faced with artistic genius. She was manoeuvring into a position where she could be associated with it. She told herself that Dave's installation was too good to remain locked away. That it deserved to be seen by the public. To be appraised and commended as a piece of art should be. What her subconscious was advising of course, was that there was benefit in being the one who discovered the work and brought it into the world. If she wasn't the artist who had produced the installation, then at least she could be the one who recognized its value.

Consciously, Jessica was not aware of such calculation. She was merely convinced that Dave was a close friend, and that helping him to display his installation would be an act of purest altruism. Sitting on the floor she waited, cuckoo-like, for him to return to his nest.

When Dave saw Jessica in front of his installation, he experienced a peculiar cocktail of emotions. There was some pleasure at the fact she'd seen his art, a lorryload of worry concerning what she'd say about it, and a swamp of brackish anger left over from the last time they'd spoken. After a brief mental struggle, everything sank into the anger.

'What are you doing here?' he said. 'How did you get in?'

From her seated position, Jessica eyed Dave thoughtfully. His paint spattered clothes, his slightly hopeless hair. The artistic furrow in his brow. Yes, she had definitely misjudged him.

'Your window was open,' she said. 'And an old man was hassling me.'

'That's Vartak,' said Dave. 'I hope you didn't upset him. He gets upset very easily.'

'Yes, I noticed that,' said Jessica. 'He was very aggressive.'

'Maybe he was protecting the house from unwanted visitors,' said Dave.

'Hey! You invited me round here, remember?'

'Actually,' said Dave, 'you invited yourself.'

'Well perhaps,' said Jessica. 'I'm sorry if I was a bit pushy.'

Dave was slightly taken aback by this hint of apology. It was most out of character.

'Well,' he said. 'Regardless of whether you were invited or not, you shouldn't have just let yourself in. There are private things in here.'

This was Jessica's cue. She stood up and moved over to Dave, placing her hand on his arm. 'Private things like this?' she said, gesturing at his installation.

'Yes,' said Dave, looking down at the hand on his arm. 'Private like that.'

Jessica turned back to him and cocked her head to one side. 'Do you really think something this good should stay private?'

Dave started. 'Good?'

'Very good,' said Jessica.

'You think it's good?' said Dave in amazement.

'I think it's better than good,' confirmed Jessica. 'I think it's brilliant.'

Dave let out a short breath, which was all he dared.

Amongst the confidence and beauty of Jessica's face, he could see admiration. She liked his work! She liked his art!

'I suppose I am quite pleased with the way it's come out,' he said, attempting to sound nonchalant.

'You should be more than pleased,' said Jessica. 'You should be proud.' She gave his arm a little squeeze.

'I suppose,' said Dave. 'It's not bad for someone who's just "technically competent", is it?'

'It's not just not bad,' said Jessica, looking right into his eyes. 'There's nothing bad about it.'

Dave flushed at her gaze. He'd done it! She finally appreciated him as an equal! He felt faint with jubilation, and didn't want her to leave. Now that Jessica had confessed her admiration of his work, he wanted more. He wanted to hear her compare it with her own, and compare it with that of others.

'Cup of tea?' he asked hopefully.

'That would be nice,' said Jessica, her hand still in place on his arm. 'Do you have any Earl Grey?'

When Dave came back upstairs with the tea, he found Jessica staring at his piece. There was a thoughtful expression on her face.

'You know, this is really too good to sit up here,' she said. 'You should exhibit it.'

'I doubt the Newcastle police would see the artistic merit,' joked Dave.

'I didn't mean in Newcastle.'

'You didn't?'

'We'll talk about it later on,' said Jessica. 'I thought I might stay the night.'

Dave coughed tea all over the carpet.

Chapter Eight

Mergers and acquisitions

Dave's experiences on the sexual battlefield were very limited. His intelligence network, which had never really been up to scratch, fed him poor information throughout adolescence, and he remained unable to crack enemy codes. On the few occasions when direct action had been called for, he'd opted for a suicidal charge over the top, which always seemed to end in the emphatic defeat of his forces. In recent years, his troops had become demoralized by lack of action, and Dave now suspected that the whole regiment would have to repeat basic training if they were to be relied upon in combat.

Because of his tactical ineptitude, Dave had not really enjoyed the sexual dynamic of Institute life. He was unusual amongst his peer group in this regard, because his friends had perpetrated enough sexual escapades to fill a Mills and Boon novel. Stan and Carlos had been subject to the heaving bosoms of the art tart sorority wherever they went, and though their symbiotic relationship with the digital golf game reduced the frequency of such adventures, they had

always done very well when the fancy took them.
Vincent had also collected an impressive tally, though
his strategy was rather different. He would drink until
he could barely see, and then leer at every woman he
could find until one of them leered back. When
Vincent awoke the following morning he invariably
discovered that the woman beside him was extremely
hungover, as well as being far less attractive than he
remembered. He tended to deal with this situation by
offering to make coffee, and then running off to the
pub as soon as he was clear of the bedroom. Once they
realized that Vincent had abandoned the house in
panic, his erstwhile partners were often equally grate-
ful for the chance to slip out unnoticed.

Dave had always envied his friends their sexual
exploits. Whether they focused on quality or quantity,
their conquests were far in excess of his own. He had
been a participant in only two such events during his
undergraduate years, and neither had gone as
planned.

The first of Dave's studenthood liaisons had been with
a media studies student by the name of Amy. This
flame-haired vixen dragged him back to her flat within
three drinks of their introduction, where she stripped
to her underwear and threw him into bed.

'Tear off my knickers!' she shouted, beating at his
face in passion.

'OK,' said Dave breathlessly.

He reached down and grabbed the tendril of
gossamer that clung to Amy's right thigh. Then,

tensing his muscles, he pulled with all his might. Unfortunately, the tendril turned out to be a lot stronger than gossamer, strengthened as it was by a backbone of unbreakable elastic. Amy's grunts of excitement turned to screams of pain as the knickers formed a vicious tourniquet and sliced through her flesh. Dave was hurled against the far wall in the ensuing mêlée, and badly sprained his right ankle as he crashed to the floor. He spent the rest of the evening applying lotion to Amy's brutalized hindquarters, enduring her accusations of deliberate assault.

The second of Dave's assignations had occurred at the Institute's annual ball. He'd been feeling unusually confident in his tuxedo, and was entertaining fantasies of a Bond-like dash across the marquee, when he was approached by a singularly attractive woman in a long black dress.

'Would you like to buy me a cocktail?' she asked, flicking decadent eyelashes at him.

'OK,' said Dave.

The conversation that followed, though rather one-sided, went well. Before Dave knew it, he was being manoeuvred towards an alcove where the electrical equipment was stored. Once safely inside, he was taken firmly by the collar and drawn closer.

'Kiss me, David,' the woman purred.

'OK,' said Dave in amazement, leaning forwards with his mouth open.

The kiss was long and passionate, and grew more passionate as the woman moved backwards, pulling

Dave towards the humming stack of generators. Not quite believing his luck, he slipped his arm around her and touched the bare flesh of her shoulders. It was at this point that he knocked over a half-full pint glass, which had been left on one of the generators earlier that day. Realizing the danger and stepping back in alarm, Dave witnessed his beautiful companion drop like a stone as she received a large electric shock through the base of her dress. By the time the fire brigade had arrived to put out the marquee, he had dragged her to safety, but she did not regain consciousness for several hours, and it seemed appropriate for him to be absent once her good health was confirmed.

Given his disastrous sexual history, Dave was extremely nervous when dealing with members of the opposite sex, and this was particularly true of Jessica, whose approval he had lusted after so desperately for so long.

'I'm sorry about the food,' he said as they sat down to dinner. 'Spaghetti bolognaise is the only thing I can cook.'

'That's OK,' said Jessica. She smiled at him across the kitchen table. 'I wasn't expecting an artist *and* a chef.'

Dave spilled parmesan into his lap. Jessica's attentions were making him nervous. 'Oh, I'm not sure I could be called an artist.'

'Well, if you say so,' said Jessica. She sucked on some spaghetti and it shuddered through her lips. 'If you want to be modest.'

'It's not really a matter of modesty,' said Dave. 'The thing upstairs was just a one-off. It's not like I'm a practising artist.'

Jessica took a sip of red wine. Her throat moved with dark shadows. 'You mustn't undersell yourself,' she said firmly. 'Your piece is the equal of anything I've seen at the Lightschool.'

'Um, thanks,' said Dave. He took a gulp from his own glass, which was significantly depleted. He had been calling upon it for courage.

'Don't thank me,' said Jessica. 'I'm only telling the truth.' She pinioned an olive with her fork and held it out to his mouth.

'Thanks,' said Dave again, pulling off the olive with his fingers. He wasn't capable of taking it in the manner with which it had been offered. It was simply too much for his nerves.

For pudding, Dave served up some ice cream. Embarrassed by Jessica's compliments, he tried to turn the conversation her way.

'Do you go out in London much? When you're down at the Lightschool?'

'Sometimes,' said Jessica. 'We go clubbing, or to new bars in Soho.'

'That sounds fun,' said Dave. 'Have you been to any good places recently?'

'One or two,' said Jessica. 'There's a new bar that shows art in the toilets. They rotate the pieces each week.'

'Really?' said Dave. 'Is the art good?'

'It's OK,' said Jessica. 'Nowhere near as good as your installation.'

Dave cleared his throat awkwardly and looked away. 'And what about the people on your course?' he asked. 'What are they like?'

'Oh, nice enough,' said Jessica. 'As artists go.'

'Any names I should watch out for?' asked Dave. 'Anyone who's going to be famous?'

Jessica smiled at him and spun her spoon in the ice cream. It made a little pile of shavings.

'On the basis of what I've seen today,' she said girlishly, 'they should be watching out for you.'

This pattern of conversation continued throughout the evening. Wherever a conversation began, Jessica found a way to bring it back to Dave's art, and specifically, the installation upstairs. Under her blowtorch of flattery, Dave almost forgot the old Jessica. The Jessica who'd shunned and dismissed him. He forgot everything except the way she was this evening. The way she was looking at him, and the way she smiled.

'So, are you going to let me take your installation down to London and display it for you?' Jessica asked eventually. She had just poured him a fifth glass of wine, and the lights were turned down.

A tiny alarm-bell went off inside Dave's head. A remnant of past concerns. He didn't quite understand why it was ringing, but it warned against surrendering his art into Jessica's care.

'Oh, I don't know about that,' he said, trying to pinpoint the source of his doubts.

'I would be very happy to,' said Jessica.

'Well, that's very kind,' said Dave, 'but I'm not sure I could ask such a big favour.'

He wanted to display his art more than anything, and to have it alongside Jessica's work was a dream come true, but once she took it from him it would disappear, and so would she. For the first time in his dealings with Jessica, Dave felt in control of the situation, and if she took his art to London with her, he would lose that control.

'I'm just not sure that . . .' he began again.

Jessica walked over to his chair and perched on the armrest. She moved like a cat.

'Dave,' she said seriously. 'I'm only trying to give your work the audience it deserves.'

Dave gulped. He had drunk too much wine, and Jessica's proximity was overwhelming his reason.

'Well . . .' he said.

Jessica leaned closer. Her top stretched tightly over her breasts, and the creases in her trousers flattened against her slim thighs.

'I would really like to,' she said, her eyes dripping with suggestion.

'Well . . .' said Dave again. His heart was racing. His troops, who had not been on parade in a while, were desperately searching for their uniforms and trying to marshal resources.

'I would *really* like to,' said Jessica, her lips brushing his.

'Well, you see . . .' moaned Dave. His command centre was in disarray. There were lots of generals shouting at each other. They all had opposing ideas about the enemy, but he couldn't make any of them out.

Jessica's wonderful mouth encircled his. He was infected by her wine-dark breath, and her tongue moved through him like a snake.

'Hmmm?' she asked again, with Dave hanging from her mouth like a supplicant.

Dave's military strategists threw in the towel.

'OK,' he mumbled through her kiss.

Chapter Nine

Branded goods

Once she had permission to take his installation to London, Jessica decided that she didn't really want to kiss Dave any more.

'Mmmm,' she yawned dramatically. 'I'm suddenly as tired as a dog. Where's the spare room?'

'Spare room?' asked Dave, her kiss still hovering above him.

'Yes, you know, the spare room,' said Jessica. 'You must have some spare space now your flatmates have left.'

'Of course,' said Dave. He paused slightly and wondered whether to debase himself.

'What?' asked Jessica.

'Well, there is a spare room,' said Dave, 'but I was wondering . . . well . . .'

Jessica laughed at his embarrassment. 'That's very sweet of you, Dave,' she said, 'and obviously I'd quite like to, but I think we need to keep this relationship on a strictly artistic footing, don't you?'

'Artistic footing?' said Dave.

'Yes, we need to recognize each other for our

119

artistic talents, rather than our bodies. I'm not sure I could take your installation to London with me if we slept together, it just wouldn't be appropriate.'

Dave nodded miserably.

'Silly boy,' said Jessica, tweaking his nose. 'You know I'm right.'

'I suppose,' said Dave. 'I'll get some spare sheets from the airing cupboard. You can have the room that Carlos used to sleep in.'

'That sounds fine,' said Jessica. She padded over to the sofa and made herself comfortable. 'Let me know when it's ready.'

Twenty minutes later, Dave had constructed a passable bedchamber amongst the lonely detritus in the room once occupied by Carlos.

'Good night,' he said in the hallway. 'I hope you sleep well.'

'I will,' said Jessica. She pecked him on the cheek. 'Thanks for dinner.'

'No problem,' said Dave. 'Glad you enjoyed it.'

'We'll talk about your piece tomorrow,' said Jessica. 'We need to make arrangements.'

And with that, she shut the door in his face.

Dave went downstairs to do the washing-up.

In the morning, Jessica was all business.

'Pleasant night?' asked Dave.

'Fine,' said Jessica, taking the coffee he'd made without a word of thanks. 'Now, let's talk about your installation.'

'OK,' said Dave. Overnight, despite some mis-
givings, he had decided to commit his work to Jessica's
custody. He would let her take his installation with her,
and he would hope she had his best interests at heart.
Not only was it the only way to get his art shown, it was
the only way to guarantee he would see her again.

'Let's talk about the installation,' he said.

Jessica's plan, which she laid out over breakfast,
was simple. Dave would dismantle the installation
whilst she collected footage for her piece on class
stereotypes (she was now determined to include
Vartak amongst her subjects). She would then borrow
a car from her friend in Jesmond and take Dave's work
down to London. Jessica's friend in Jesmond was
always keen on trips to London so she could go shopping. She would be happy to donate her vehicle to the
cause.

Jessica had already worked out what to do with the
installation once she got it to London. She was going
to sneak it into the Lightschool's undergraduate
show.

The Lightschool undergraduate show comprised a
piece from each student, normally completed in their
final year, when they were supposedly at the peak of
their powers. Once their work had been graded,
students took it outside the establishment to an
external gallery, where a broader audience (and a
wider selection of dealers and critics) could pass
judgement. This year, the Caesar Gallery in east
London had been selected as the external space in
question. The Caesar Gallery was relatively cheap to

rent, and located in an area that was impoverished enough to have an 'artistic' feel to it, but not too dangerous to take a taxi to. There were also a lot of good public houses nearby where the students could loiter and court the interests of the trade.

Jessica knew that a fellow student called Clive had been appointed to liaise with the gallery's curator, and given that she had been sleeping with Clive on and off for about a year, she was fairly confident that she could slip an extra exhibit into the show once it left the Lightschool. In magnanimous tones, Jessica explained this strategy to Dave.

'OK,' said Dave miserably, thinking of the favours headed Clive's way.

'Good,' said Jessica. 'Now, you know we can't show it under your name because of the gold card. If someone realizes the card is authentic, the artist will be held responsible. It'll have to be anonymous.'

Dave was secretly glad to have a *nom de plume* to hide behind in case the installation was found lacking. He assumed that if his work was well received, he would be able to step out and make himself known once any fuss had died down.

'Anonymous,' he agreed.

Jessica smiled at him. 'I should title it as well,' she said. 'I'm a bit more familiar with naming conventions.' She patted him on the knee.

'I suppose,' said Dave.

'I'll let you know what I come up with,' said Jessica.

'I suppose,' said Dave again.

'Right then,' said Jessica.

By the end of the morning, both Jessica and Dave's installation were gone. In addition to Dave's pride and joy, Jessica left with plenty of film for her piece on class stereotypes. Once Dave had calmed Vartak down with a can of brown ale, she not only managed to film him grumbling outside his house, but also captured him patrolling the street, shouting at the owner of the local pub in Polish, and buying endless tins of ravioli from the gangster supermarket across the road.

Dave tried not to think about his work once it had gone. It was only the end of the second term. He'd have to wait three months to see if Jessica could slip it into the Lightschool undergraduate show. He also tried not to think about the title she'd sent him on the back of a postcard, which he disliked.

'*Untitled: Attempts to deconstruct the system fall short (1),*' she wrote.

'It can't be untitled. It's got a title,' he said on the phone. 'It can't be both.'

'Yes it can,' said Jessica. 'Trust me.'

'And there aren't any more of them,' said Dave. 'Why is there a one in brackets?'

'Just trust me,' said Jessica mysteriously. 'This is how we title art.'

Dave reflected that he wasn't part of 'we', so he supposed he'd better follow her advice. He still thought the title was a bit poncey though.

To take his mind off the whole business of Jessica and

his installation, Dave turned his attention to the letter that Miss Roly had given him. It was from a large advertising agency called Laurent Création, which was asking young artists to prostitute themselves for the promise of minimal wages and experience. Even taking into account the degree of exploitation that applicants could expect, this letter was still extremely unusual. The position of junior creative person within any decent advertising agency could easily be filled by accepting one of several thousand individuals begging for the job.

Creatives normally came in pairs comprising a copywriter (who wrote text and scripts) and an art director (who visualized the work). There were many other people involved of course: film producers, model makers, recruiters of celebrities and so forth, but such individuals could be employed on a project-by-project basis. The creative teams were the salaried employees, the ones who had to take briefs and brain-storm them into ideas for advertisements, normally in very short spaces of time. Despite the high pressure, low pay and general abuse, aspiring creative teams were quite happy to accept a temporary position polishing the shoes of senior teams, just in order to 'get on the ladder'. In short, creative assistants were in low demand and high supply. Sending out letters to recruit them was not necessary.

Nonetheless, a recruitment letter had been sent, and by none other than Philippe Laurent, the sole founder and artistic overlord of Laurent Création.

*

In the mid nineteen-nineties, Philippe Laurent had set up his agency for two equal and complementary reasons. Firstly, he was tired of working for other people, and secondly, he scented opportunity. Philippe could see the end of the century coming, and he knew that advertising was about to change.

In the last few years of the millennium, Philippe Laurent led the charge away from mere salesmanship and towards post-modernity. His agency made advertisements about other advertisements, knowing that the audience would see the connections. It made films devoid of meaning, concentrating on form and finish and style. It appropriated, amalgamated and absorbed the best elements of popular culture, re-presenting them to the nation in bite-sized ad form. Philippe Laurent, sitting at the helm of this post-modern enterprise, believed that in the era of saturation, message was irrelevant. He believed that in an economy of overstretched markets, what you said to people no longer mattered. The *way* you said things was now one hundred per cent of the battle.

As Laurent Création marched into the new century, the agency's understanding of polish and tone appeared to catch up with even the sources it drew upon. Laurent Création's ads became leaders of fashion, forerunners of style. Somehow, the agency seemed to know which jokes, treatments and techniques were going to be popular before they became so. It almost seemed to have an aesthetic hotline to the future.

This artistic precognition was no accident.

Philippe Laurent had followed in the footsteps of another advertising man, the legendary Charles Saatchi, to become a collector of modern art. But unlike Saatchi, Philippe made duplicitous use of his hobby. He believed that modern art was the best place to track aesthetic vogues and fashions, and he never missed a chance to steal a bit of the zeitgeist from the little wooden galleries that he visited. There was rarely a heavyweight private view that Philippe Laurent did not attend, and whilst Saatchi and the other collectors walked out with peoples' paintings, Philippe walked out with their ideas.

Philippe's recruitment letter was a direct extension of this guile. He believed that by employing a fine art graduate as an office run-around, he could diffuse some of their advanced social and stylistic judgement throughout his agency. He wouldn't have to pay them much, and he would receive up-to-the-minute creative advice in return. It was, to Philippe, a no-lose situation.

Of course, Dave didn't know any of this. He simply read 'junior creative, responsible for assisting senior creatives and general office tasks' and decided that any job with the word 'creative' in the title would be more than acceptable. He was sick of being practical. He wanted to use his newly-uncovered creative talents.

Philippe's recruitment letter called for a copy of the applicant's favourite advertising campaign, and a short explanation of why they liked it so much.

Dave started to think about advertising.

Chapter Ten

The future

Jessica received a 2:1 as a direct result of her trip to Newcastle. Her tutors, when examining her final degree piece, found themselves faced with work which was somewhere on the dividing line between a 2:1 and a Desmond, but the town of Newcastle made the difference.

When Jessica got back to London, she began working on her magazine rack of stereotypes as planned. However, as she spliced film and listened to her class monologues, she became more and more obsessed with Vartak. Her footage had yielded a series of craggy profiles, and a wonderful variety of facial expressions and language. The old man, flipping between realities, was one moment convinced the Tsar's forces were advancing towards him, and the next discussing the clemency of the weather in Newcastle compared to that of his homeland. On several occasions during filming, he had repeated his confusion of Jessica with the social worker from the forties, and threatened her with his bayonet. Jessica felt that there was more to

Vartak than one face in her stereotypes display. She watched the Vartak film over and over, and listened to his guttural Polish monologue again and again. Jessica decided that Vartak, and not class in general, would be the subject of her final show.

First she painted his portrait. Despite her tendency to adopt the most recent artistic vogue, Jessica was an excellent painter, and she did his unique character justice in her work. The portrait was painted in thick Van Gogh style with layers of rich oil. She emphasized his features, not comically but accurately. She exacerbated the colours of his face. She did what most good portrait painters do. She made him look like himself, but more so.

Then she painted a twee English scene in water-colours. A landscape of rolling green hills and oak trees. A romantic image of Britain. The style of the painting was meant to emphasize the preposterous notion of such a place. It was painterly, the brush strokes loose. Parts of the white canvas were left unpainted. The painting was naïve. The linear per-spective slightly off. The line of the scenery abutted the horizon at just the wrong angle. The painting was a mockery of the British dream.

Finally, Jessica printed a still of Vartak's house from the video footage she had taken. Then she air-brushed the old man out of the frame. She photocopied the image and blew it up, and photo-copied and blew it up again. The end result was a grainy, dirty portrait of Vartak's residence. The real Britain. The one Vartak had found when he arrived in

Fenham. Jessica's repeated replications of the image generated a stark and striking contrast. Greys had been drained from the picture. The house stood quietly in black and white.

Jessica hung these three images in her studio space. The portrait of Vartak was the centrepiece, with the unreal Britain on the left and the ever-so-real Newcastle on the right. Over speakers, Jessica played Vartak's rambling commentary, which isolated to sound alone and without companion expressions sounded almost like a battle between different characters for supremacy.

Jessica's tutors liked the way she had used painting and printing techniques to emphasize the unobtainable Britain and the obtained Britain, and they found the portrait disturbing and emotional. The soundtrack they at first assumed to be the work of an actor, though they had to admit that it was an excellent counterpart to the images. The point of the work, that life does not turn out how we expect, and that to dream of the future is inevitable but futile, they felt was well communicated. The technical quality of the work was worth a 2:2 on its own, but debate as to whether the grade should be higher centred around the history of the artist and the apparent spontaneity of her piece. After three years of watching her hop between disciplines, the Lightschool tutors doubted Jessica's sincerity.

Jessica had named her work in what she felt was the contemporary style. She called it *A million men in a million corridors (3)*.

'Where are the other two?' said one of her tutors. 'Where is the history behind the work that shows she is serious?'

'This is a silly name,' said another. 'Does she really believe in what she is doing? Is she making fun or is she genuine?'

'Jessica must realize,' a third stated gravely, 'that art is more than fashion. She must realize that her work has a mind of its own. She must stop imposing her ambitions upon it.'

Jessica's supporting portfolio, though of average quality, saved her. Her artist's statement was long-winded and pretentious, and said nothing that the tutors had not already received more eloquently from the work itself. The sketches she attached were rudimentary, and did not speak of lengthy preparation or research. However, in order to be complete she had also attached her note of thanks to Vartak. The tutors were forced to conclude that Vartak was a real person who lived in Newcastle. It followed directly that Jessica had been to see him.

Jessica's tutors were all successful academics from London. None of them had been further north than Potters Bar.

'Anyone who goes as far north as Newcastle in search of inspiration deserves at least a 2:1,' wrote one of them in his final report.

'The artist must have searched high and low to end up where she did,' wrote another. 'I no longer doubt her sincerity in exploring her topic of choice.'

'I amend my conclusions,' wrote the third. 'In

seeking out this man, Jessica was obeying the whims of her art. I can think of no other reason why she would choose to visit Newcastle.'

A consensus was reached. Jessica got her 2:1 and began to make preparations to move her work to the Caesar Gallery for the external show.

'Have whatever you'd like, darling,' said her father at their post-graduation lunch. 'Have absolutely anything you'd like.' He fingered his menu awkwardly.

'Is something wrong, Daddy?' asked Jessica.

'No, no,' said her father. 'Nothing's wrong. I just thought you might need a bit of cheering up. That's all.'

'Why on earth would you think that?'

'I must say, I'm very proud of you for getting a 2:1,' said her father. 'Very proud of you. Would you like some nice wine, by the way?'

'Daddy, what's wrong?'

'Well,' said her father, playing with his fish knife and choking back emotion. 'As I say, I'm very proud of you, I really am, but I'm a bit worried about how *you* feel. I thought you might be a little bit disappointed.'

Jessica raised her eyebrows. 'Disappointed, Daddy?'

'Well, I thought maybe you had your sights set higher than a 2:1,' he mumbled. 'I thought you were probably expecting a First.'

Jessica laughed. 'Oh, Daddy,' she said. 'Don't be silly. I wasn't expecting a First. A 2:1 is fine.'

'Oh,' said her father with relief. 'Well, that's good. That's very good.'

Jessica chuckled. 'They were never going to award me a First,' she said. 'A 2:1 is all I was expecting.'

'Well, that's very mature,' said her father. 'It's very mature of you to accept that.'

'I knew I would be marked unfairly,' said Jessica. 'My work is much too progressive for the Lightschool. They would never award it a First. Most of them couldn't even understand it.'

Dave also received a 2:1. He spent his last term pottering around his still-empty flat and sketching more designs for household objects. He walked a 2:1 in comparison to Jessica, because all his tutors agreed that he was extremely technically competent. They didn't give him a First because he wasn't creative enough.

'There is always a balance, David,' the Dean preached to him at the graduation ceremony. 'There is always a balance between function and form.'

Dave did not offer any resistance to the Dean's comments. He ate his vol-au-vent in silence.

'I consider you one of my successes,' the Dean remarked happily. 'I consider you a student who I balanced.'

Dave bit a sausage off a stick. He was hardly listening to the Dean at all.

'When you came to me, you were slipping, David. You were slipping towards the aesthetic.'

Dave took a gulp of poor Chardonnay.

'But I righted you, David. I put you on the straight and narrow.' The Dean slapped Dave on the shoulders. 'Well done, boy! Well done for using my advice so well!'

Dave said goodbye to the Dean and went home.

Dave was depressed during graduation. He was depressed because Stan and Carlos were no longer around, so he had to go drinking with Vincent, which was both expensive and dangerous. He was depressed because he had not heard from Jessica, and with every passing day he grew more desperate for news of his installation. He was also depressed because he had not been able to create anything he was pleased with since *Untitled: Attempts to deconstruct the system fall short (1)*. He wondered if that was it. Maybe his allocation of creativity was used up for ever? Maybe he had to go back to being 'technically competent' and be happy with that?

Finally, Dave was depressed because he hadn't heard anything from Laurent Création, and look as he might, he could not find a similar position within any other advertising agency. He'd rung a few agencies up, but they'd told him there were a thousand art students in line just to sharpen the creatives' pencils, and he'd have to have a 'contact' if he wanted to jump the queue. It looked as though the position at Laurent Création was unique. Dave had even tried approaching Miss Roly to see if there were any other opportunities she might have letters for, but she had completed her obligatory advice giving for the year, and had re-barred the doors to her office.

Then, in his final week at Newcastle Institute of

Arts and Media, Laurent Création wrote to Dave and asked him to come down to London for an interview.

Dave had thought very carefully about his response to Philippe Laurent's recruitment letter. Eventually he'd selected a series of magazine advertisements by a new telecommunications company as 'his favourite advertising campaign', and had sent them in as requested. He liked the advertisements for their arresting nature and visual impact, which, deciding he'd better be honest, is what he wrote in his letter. Unbeknownst to Dave, his favoured campaign was one of the most reviled in the history of advertising. Consumers hated it, the trade press had vilified it, and several national newspapers were now getting in on the act. Dave, who did not read the newspapers very much, was unaware that he had sided with a pariah.

The campaign that Dave had championed was being seen as evidence of the moral decline of British advertising. It used nationalism, one of the last great taboos, to promote cutting-edge mobile phones. One execution showed a Catholic teenager on the streets of Armagh. The boy was holding one of the featured handsets and sat in front of an IRA mural urging the return to hostilities. There was also a Protestant version of the ad, featuring a blonde girl in front of a Union Jack. She too was holding one of the phones, and she had an old RUC badge sewn onto her jacket. The strapline was the same in the case of each image, and stoked the bonfire of controversy even further. *Hello World* read the adverts, proclaiming not only the function of the mobile phones themselves, but also the politics of the children who held them.

Not content with the potential of Irish unrest, the campaign went on to make use of Afghani teenagers and young American GIs. These diametrically opposed youths displayed the phones in front of shelled buildings and the doorways of desert lairs. In another set of executions, young Palestinians and Israelis faced off, clutching mobile phones in one hand and khakied-up guns in the other.

Rather unsurprisingly, the advertisements offended everyone. The nationalist groups involved saw them as exploitative, the general public saw them as tasteless, and politicians thought they were disruptive and explosive. The response was immense. Journalists decried the moral standards of the media and commercialism, magazine editors were hauled over the coals for allowing the advertisements to run in the first place, and advertising agency chiefs quickly condemned the advertisements as unrepresentative of their industry as a whole. The agency that had actually produced the ads was forced to make a public apology, and suffered massive staff and client defections. The general consensus was that it was a very bad campaign.

There were two people in Britain who recognized the brilliance of the advertisements. The first was the managing director of the commissioning company, who had seen sales rise over fifty per cent since their inception. The second was Philippe Laurent, who understood the advertisements for what they were; a brilliant piece of cult generation. He knew sales would go up, because while the advertising stood for all kinds of awful things, the target audience for the brand were anti-everything and would appreciate the furore it had caused. Philippe also suspected that in the future, when the dogma of nationalism held less sway, the work would be seen as revolutionary. He had seen similar studies at private views over the last few years, and recognized the need for young communities to explore the forces that divide them.

Dave also liked the campaign, but he did not understand why it was so good. He simply knew that the images in the advertisements appealed to him. He found the composition as striking as the subject matter, and he enjoyed the degree of portraiture that the photographer had been permitted. The ads were offensive certainly, and contentious, certainly, but they were also pleasing to the eye and the sense of self. Dave liked them on an aesthetic and intellectual level that he found hard to articulate. A fact that was reflected in his badly worded covering letter.

Philippe Laurent, scanning through hundreds of letters he had received from all over the country, saw the cut-out magazine advertisements and added Dave's name to the list of interviewees without even reading his poorly worded attachment. He never noticed that Dave had declared himself a graphic design student rather than a fine artist.

Chapter Eleven

The fall of Caesar

Jessica had even fewer problems getting Dave's installation into the Lightschool undergraduate show than she had foreseen. Clive, the student representative for the show, was all too eager to please his occasional bedmate.

'Of course darling,' he said, lighting a cigarette in Jessica's dishevelled bed. 'Of course we can add another piece of yours.'

'It's not mine,' she said. 'But I think it should be displayed somewhere, and we have the extra space don't we?'

'Of course, darling,' said Clive, blowing smoke rings. 'Bags of space. I shan't tell anyone whose the extra piece is. Your secret is safe with me.' He winked.

'It's not mine,' said Jessica again. 'I want you to put it in under the name "Anonymous".'

'Darling,' said Clive, kissing her nipples. 'Whatever you say.'

The Lightschool tutors weren't so stupid that they didn't notice the clandestine addition of Dave's work, but they were so nervous about the overall quality of the show that they decided another exhibit couldn't do any harm. The curator of the Caesar Gallery agreed. He was worried about the show too.

Jessica's class at the Lightschool had started out with promise. A diverse group of individuals with unique characters and talents, they were expected to produce excellent work by the end of their third year. The general feeling was that the class had not lived up to its promise. Ironically, this was due to difficulties caused by their diversity and the uniqueness of their characters and talents.

Wendel Morris, for instance, had come to the Lightschool to work on his fabulously intricate cityscapes. He was forty-five, and regarded by the other pupils as the token mature student. For Wendel, the Lightschool represented a second chance at life, and he took his work very seriously. Each cityscape was months in the making. His were beautiful, figurative, classical paintings. Pretty paintings. They were a labour of love for Wendel, and when he saw his fellow students working for three days in mediums such as video, and getting comparable marks, he became resentful of the sacrifices his work demanded of him. He began to get careless, to speed things up a little. By the time the final show came round, some of the precise joy had gone from Wendel's paintings, and he was deeply insecure about his art, his age, and his appearance.

'Tell me,' Wendel once asked Jessica, 'how do you produce your art so *quickly*?'

'Oh, it just comes,' said Jessica. 'I don't have to do anything special.'

'I wish I could make art quickly,' said Wendel. 'I always thought inspiration was supposed to take a long time.'

'Well,' said Jessica, 'when it comes to inspiration, you've either got it or you haven't.'

'I suppose you're right,' said Wendel, turning back to his rapidly worsening skylines.

One of the students whose approach had so upset Wendel was a video artist named Mickey Cunningham. Mickey worshipped the terrifying nature of life, and spent his time in pursuit of the extremes that could inspire his efforts. He leaped off bridges and jumped in front of cars in order to generate artistic insight, always carrying a portable camera to record the results of these antics. Unfortunately, Mickey's attempts to experience the ultimate rush were slightly too successful. He was killed halfway through the third year, having strapped himself to the top of a London Underground train carriage. He was hoping to obtain creative energy from the suicidally claustrophobic roaring tunnel ceiling, but when the camera was recovered it seemed that he had only managed to record the fatal problem of the tunnel's insufficient distance from the train roof to which he was strapped. His final show was posthumous, and featured footage he had taken of himself diving into the London Aquarium shark tank, where he caused several of the sharks to die of fright.

As unofficial leader of the class, Jessica was asked to provide Mickey's eulogy. She dressed in a black suit for the occasion, and looked proud and forlorn and austere.

'Mickey was an innovator,' Jessica proclaimed from the front of the chapel. 'He was never afraid to experiment, to go beyond the conventional.'

The congregation stood silent, awaiting her words.

'And I understood his compulsion,' said Jessica, 'because I *also* practise innovation. I *also* try not to conform.'

She looked reverently at the shiny oak coffin, savouring the moment. 'Goodbye, Mickey,' she said finally. 'I shall continue the work that's begun.'

Along with neurotic Wendel Morris and deceased Mickey Cunningham, the Lightschool's third artistic disaster was a foreign student from Japan by the name of Uri Kunioshi. Uri was a cartoonist from Tokyo. One of the best. His work was calligraphic, ornate, and entirely in Japanese. He also sprayed far-eastern caricatures onto his canvases instead of portraits. Uri did not speak any English, and refused to learn on the basis that the new language would 'scar his art'. This made it rather difficult for him to follow his tuition, and his work did not really progress much during his time at the Lightschool. He also took a lot of drugs and met a lot of western women, which didn't help him to preserve his Japanese identity. His work had taken on a bitter and sarcastic tone by the end of his time in London.

'It's a shame about Uri,' Jessica announced from her soapbox, 'but I'm not sure he had greatness inside.'

The fourth under-achiever was Nedrina Burchill, who was obsessed by evil, a preoccupation she shared with a long line of greats. Since primary school Nedrina had been drawing the baddies on TV, and in her time at the Lightschool, she was mainly to be found watching tapes of war crimes tribunals, from which she would sketch the protagonists. Her final year show included a series of guns, which instead of steel and enamel were manufactured entirely from pieces of bone. The tutors found Nedrina's work rather disturbing, and though it piqued their interest, they tended to avoid its assessment.

'When you think about it,' said Jessica, 'Nedrina's art is really rather mundane. After all, there's nothing less sinister than deliberate menace. If you want to be scared by a piece of art, then go and look at Bacon.'

Of all their student failures, perhaps the greatest disappointment to the staff was the collapse of Sarah-Jane. This talented girl from a middle-class background had been ushered into the Lightschool because of her fabulous abstract designs. She generated coloured oblongs on flat black backgrounds, and the results were really quite beautiful. Sarah-Jane was talked of as having a 'Mondrianesque' sense of space and colour. One painting was described as a 'Broadway Boogie-Woogie for the new century', but like Mondrian, Sarah-Jane was famously obsessive in the composition of her work, a trait which deepened throughout her years at the Lightschool. Soon her class were calling her 'the dirty modernist' because she had refined and focused her abilities for painting coloured oblongs, and only coloured oblongs, to the extreme. The day before the final show, Sarah-Jane was found painting and re-painting the coloured oblongs in her latest piece, which she had been working on for over a year. The painting was actually hanging in the gallery by this time, but she wouldn't let it go until she felt it was perfect. Sadly, the continual amendments she made hampered both her productivity and the eventual quality of what was produced.

'You might want to redo that one,' said Jessica towards the end of their third year. She had wandered uninvited into Sarah-Jane's studio, carrying a cup of coffee with cream.

'Yes, I was worried about that one too,' replied Sarah-Jane. 'It seems less complete than the others.'

'Quite right,' said Jessica. 'You must trust your eye. You must trust your judgement. There's no point in stopping until you are happy.'

She took a sip of her coffee. 'In fact,' she added thoughtfully, 'even when you are happy, you should question your judgement again.'

Despite their predominance of failures, there was one mild success that the Lightschool staff could celebrate. Their formulaic pencil sketcher of nudes had apparently blossomed into an unusual and inventive translator of this old-fashioned material. The student was John Green, who had entered the Lightschool with the help of a scholarship, and had recently been drawing with a wonderful wobble to his style. John's previously exact figurative lines had become an interesting parody of themselves, veering away from their intended task. His shading was also messier, and its boundaries could not hold it. The end result was a noisy but evocative style, almost impressionism with a pencil. Everyone congratulated John on the dramatic and effective change in his technique, unaware of the fact that he had developed the early stages of Parkinson's disease, which guided his hand in strange directions.

'Your nudes are quite fascinating,' said Jessica to John. 'Tell me, how do you recruit your models?'

'F-f-f-f-f-friends m-m-m-m-ainly,' said John, whose condition had produced a stutter.

'Tell me, John,' said Jessica. 'Am I your friend?'

'Of c-c-c-c-c-course,' said John.

'Then you should sketch me,' said Jessica. 'You should sketch me as your best work.'

'Oh,' said John. 'Well, I'm not sh-sh-sh-sh-sure about that.'

'Nonsense,' said Jessica. 'You'll do it brilliantly. Anyway, I won't take no for an answer.'

John Green's nude of Jessica was pretty much the highlight of the Lightschool undergraduate show. Everything else was worrying average – the category into which Jessica's piece on Vartak was bracketed.

Dave's installation, the tutors decided, was a bit obvious in parts, but they liked the figure in the case with his American Express card, and the bloodied shirt was agreed to at least partially convey the aura of a martyr, or a victim of industrialization. This, they felt, was supposedly the point of the piece. The tutors also felt that Dave's work tried hard at something fairly simple, unlike Uri's most recent Eastern abuse or Sarah-Jane's hugely over-engineered oblongs. They preferred the atmosphere Dave had generated with his sections of the Tyne Bridge to Wendel's hurried cityscapes.

In short, the tutors thought Dave's installation was OK. Not great, but OK. The show needed an installation, they decided, and its addition allowed them to idly speculate on the identity of 'Anonymous', which took their minds off the rest of the work.

'So who is it, Clive?' they asked the student representative. 'Is it a second year who cannot wait? A recent graduate who wants to cause a fuss?'

'I cannot say, man,' said Clive, blowing smoke rings. 'I have been sworn to secrecy.'

When the show opened to the trade, professional opinion was similar to that of the Lightschool tutors. Dealers and critics thought it to be unadventurous and rather disappointing by the establishment's usual standards. They decided that Dave's installation was an attack on the systems of commercialism, capitalism and westernization. The figure covered in fake blood obviously represented a martyr to these causes, and the structure in the background referenced the corporate machine, the inventiveness of man, and the identity of the west.

The critics basically thought that Dave's work was OK as well. They thought it was an old idea that had been executed in a vaguely interesting way. Nobody offered to buy it. Jessica's Vartak triptych was found to be similarly underwhelming, and nobody offered to buy her work either.

Jessica, as usual, did not let the opinions of others get in the way of her own beliefs. She was proud of her piece on Vartak, and decided that the system was just not ready for such a sophisticated social critique. She also retained her faith in *Untitled: Attempts to deconstruct the system fall short (1)*, and was sure she had been right to transport it to London and sneak it into the gallery. She put off calling Dave to report the critical reaction to his work, and hoped that someone who could understand its power would eventually attend the show.

Someone did, though not quite in the way that Jessica had hoped.

Chapter Twelve

The grey market

The offices of Laurent Création were near Embankment. The lobby was constructed almost entirely from glass, with glass armchairs for guests and a glass coffee table for magazines to rest on. The walls were also glass, and from the lobby Dave could see creative people doing creative things in creatively spacious offices all around him. He sipped his cup of tea from its pure glass cup, which was difficult because it had become as hot as the beverage inside it, and he kept burning his fingers.

Dave had worn his suit for the occasion, which was a grey affair from Burtons menswear. As in all new situations, Dave was extremely nervous, and convinced that the events of the day would go against him. This conviction was enhanced by his surroundings, which made him feel ugly and inappropriate. There were three other businessmen waiting in the lobby, all dressed in perfectly-fitting wool suits cut from muted blues and greens. Their shirts were pristine powdery white and their ties were understated. Their hair was silver at the temples but not in the middle. None of

them seemed fazed by the bank of smiling receptionists, who were uniformly and perfectly
beautiful. There was a Scandinavian blonde and a
demure brunette and a Bohemian redhead and
a coloured Amazonian temptress. These four women
sat behind a glass reception desk, through which their
legs were quite apparent.

'Yah?' the blonde receptionist had said when Dave
arrived at the front desk, twitching her head and
nearly blinding him with her hair.

'Um, hello,' said Dave, shielding his eyes from her
sparkle. 'I'm here for an appointment.'

'Who with, honey?' asked the Amazonian
temptress.

'Oh,' said Dave. 'Yes, I've got the name here in my
bag.' Turning away from the desk so his actions
wouldn't be misconstrued, Dave got down on one
knee and began rummaging through his knapsack.

'Laurentcréation?' he heard the brunette say
behind him. 'Yessir. Yes. Itsringingforyounow.'

Dave resurfaced to find himself facing the redhead instead of the blonde. He was not sure whether
he had shuffled along in his deliberations, or whether
the receptionists had rearranged to confuse him.

'Bill Bones. I'm here to see Bill Bones please.'

'Have a seat,' said the redhead. 'I'll call him
straight down.'

Dave looked over at the businessmen in their
expensive suits. None of them looked back.

'Over there?' said Dave.

'That *is* the waiting area,' said the redhead. 'If you'll just be seated then someone will bring you a drink. Mr Bones will be down in a few minutes.'

Bill Bones was conducting all the interviews with Philippe Laurent's list of candidates. He was a long-standing employee of the company, and though he'd been writing ads for fifteen years, he had only enjoyed the first two.

Early on in his career, after producing some groundbreaking scripts for a large life assurance firm, Bill had become known as the man who could write advertisements for the 'older audience'. This demographic had always been an extremely lucrative source of business for advertising agencies, but nobody, particularly not the rising stars of the creative world, wanted to write ads for old people. When he arrived at Laurent Création, an unspoken agreement to use Bill for these campaigns was quickly reached.

Incontinence pad briefs, gardening tool offers, firms offering holidays in British beach resorts. They all began to come Bill's way. He did a reasonable job with them, but they started to get him down. Pack designs for impotency cures, mail drops for re-mortgaging firms, posters for bingo halls. Bill was submerged in empty-nester products.

In the course of his years on these clients, Bill changed. He became more attuned to the mind-set of his audience than perhaps was healthy. He began to get cantankerous and moody. His hair turned grey in the space of three years. He grew long and bushy sideburns, and started wearing shiny acrylic ties just to clash with the office trends. He drove an old Volvo, happy in the knowledge that it would look out of place in the agency car park, which was rife with Porsches and Jaguars. He was rude to people on the phone, an invention he didn't approve of, and he practically refused to use a computer at all, condemning them as a menace. He didn't meet women, had very few friends, and worked alone. He spent holidays in Scotland and evenings at the dogs. He liked soap operas.

Bill had been given the task of interviewing the graduates because no one else wanted it. He was only thirty-eight, but when he came down to the lobby to collect Dave, he looked ready to retire.

'Burtons menswear?' he said, pointing at Dave's suit.

'Er, yes,' said Dave, blushing a deep maroon.

'Thank God,' said Bill, shaking his hand. 'Someone normal. You should have seen the wankers I've had in here so far.'

The interview was conducted in a small glass room on the second floor, which was bordered on the left by a huge glass atrium. Dave could see creative heads moving about in the offices below.

'Tea? Coffee?' asked Bill.

Dave, whose fingers were still tingling from the dangerous glass vessel he had been handed in the lobby, answered without thinking. 'Have you got any proper mugs?' he asked.

Bill looked enormously pleased. 'Mugs coming up,' he said. 'Never could stand those poncey glass vases they use downstairs. Tea or coffee?'

'Strong tea with two sugars, please,' said Dave.

'Builder's bottom then,' said Bill with an approving nod.

Bill had already interviewed seven applicants before Dave, and had been disappointed by each of them. These outstanding fine art students, each recently graduated with commendations of one form or another, had uniformly annoyed him.

'I am interested in the link between fine art and consumerism,' said one. 'I have been taking photographs of famous products and reassembling them as collage in the gallery space.'

'So you've been taking pack shots and turning them into art?' said Bill.

'Yes,' said the hapless candidate. 'The gallery space forces a re-examination of the packaging images, many of which have come from art in the first place. It's a way of looking at the origins of an idea.'

'You cheeky bastard,' said Bill, somewhat missing the point. 'That's illegal, that is. They could have you for that.'

That particular candidate had been rated very poorly within Bill's interview notes.

Bill liked Dave already for his down-to-earth demeanour and appearance, so in keeping with his own view of the world, and so opposed to the excesses of the advertising world in general. However, he felt he should really ask the young man for an explanation of his work before forming a final judgement.

'So,' he said once Dave's tea had been procured. 'What area does your work focus on?'

'Oh, my work is fairly practical,' said Dave. 'I do a lot of design projects. Typography proposals, consumer items, that kind of thing.'

'Very useful,' said Bill approvingly. 'But don't you artists always have to be creating something deeply conceptual and stylistic?'

'Oh, I'm not really an artist,' said Dave, assuming that Bill had seen his application letter, in which he gave his degree as graphic design. 'I'm a graphic designer, remember?'

'Indeed,' said Bill. He had decided that he hated artists, partly due to the way that seven of them had wound him up that day, and partly because he loathed his art-obsessed creative director, Philippe Laurent.

'So,' he said. 'You never do any art at all?'

Dave thought about *Untitled: Attempts to deconstruct the system fall short (1)*. He'd heard nothing on the matter from Jessica, even when he'd sent her a note to say he would be coming to London. Art had caused him nothing but pain. He regretted every one of his urges.

Dave made a decision. From now on, he would be happy with his lot. He would no longer pretend he was an artist. 'Art doesn't get you anywhere,' he said firmly. 'I try not to waste my time with it.'

Bill was delighted, and grinned ear to ear with encouragement.

'Indeed,' he said happily, sipping his own mug of builder's bottom tea.

When Bill took Dave upstairs to see Philippe Laurent, they found him on the phone. Philippe Laurent had a transparent Perspex phone to go with his glass desk. He was wearing a tailored suit in super-rich black, a linen shirt with no tie, and a pair of catlike steel spectacles. When he saw Bill outside his office door, he cupped the phone receiver between his head and neck and gestured them both in.

Dave and Bill sat down on a black leather sofa facing Philippe's desk. Dave noticed that unlike every other office in the agency, Philippe's did not have glass walls. Instead its partitions were solid and distinctly opaque, offering the creative director some degree of privacy.

'So they're going to take it tonight?' Philippe was saying excitedly. 'That's amazing! Can anyone bid for it before then?'

He listened to the receiver for a moment, his long gallic hair shivering with excitement.

'Right,' he said. 'I'm coming over. I'm not letting Charles or Virginia beat me to this one. If the police carry it off, it'll be big. The media attention alone will demand some recognition. I'm coming over to see it now.'

Philippe put the phone down. Bill stood up and gestured for Dave to do the same.

'Philippe?' said Bill. 'This is Dave. I've selected him as the best candidate from the shortlist you prepared. Would you like to see what you think of him?'

Philippe Laurent hardly even glanced in Dave's direction. He was throwing things into an expensive briefcase. 'No, no,' he said, unplugging a mobile phone from a recharger on his desk. 'I'm sure you've picked the right one. Anyway, I have to do something urgent. Very urgent.'

He pushed past them both to the door.

'Welcome to the team!' Philippe Laurent shouted backwards, leaving the office at a run.

Chapter Thirteen

In which Jessica is reborn to greatness

Marcel White was a cultured man. He was interested in film, contemporary literature, and art. As a student, Marcel had attended Cambridge, where he studied natural sciences and indulged himself in an understanding of the artistic world. After Cambridge, he met his wife, and under the influence of her father, who was a police commissioner, he turned his substantial talents towards fighting crime. His massively impressive background in the sciences made him perfect material for a forensic analyst, and this was the course he had steered. Rising swiftly, Marcel soon became the northern director of the metropolitan forensics division, with additional duties reporting to special branch and several other government agencies.

Marcel tried to visit at least one new collection each time he was in London on business. When he stepped into the Caesar Gallery and found himself before Dave's installation, he knew exactly what he was looking at.

'Gracious,' said Marcel to no one in particular.

The name on the American Express card would

have given things away eventually of course, but it was the cleverly evoked atmosphere of the night in question that immediately caught Marcel's attention. On that night he had been called to the Boat from his home on the outskirts of Newcastle, rushing to the aid of a police force who had little experience with the traumatized bodies of abseilers. He remembered the peculiar aesthetics of the scene all too well. He had examined the flayed remains with his usual diligence and craftsmanship, but the motherly arches of the Tyne Bridge, watching over his grisly task, had filled him with unease. The job itself had been routine, the bus driver had clearly died on impact, and his body contained no trace of chemical agents. The angle of the fall was commensurate with an unintentionally speedy descent, and there were witnesses who could testify that the man had not released his grip until he was below the edge of the bridge, so there was no chance of anyone assisting him from above. Marcel had pronounced accidental impact as the cause of death, and went home, full of dread at the feelings he was leaving on the dark river. He thought Dave's installation was a perfect recreation of the emotions surrounding that night, and wondered for a while who the talented 'Anonymous' might be.

'Quite brilliant,' said Marcel, standing alone in the gallery.

Then he came to his senses and called Scotland Yard.

When the police arrived the next day to dismantle the installation, which had been confirmed by the bus driver's family as containing evidence taken illegally from a crime scene, they were met with several fronts of opposition. There were multiple reasons to oppose the dismemberment of Dave's work, and multiple parties to field them.

The Lightschool staff felt that there was a point of principle involved in refusing the police access to the installation. Art, they claimed, was sacred, and should not be subject to manipulation. It had not been explained to them why the reclamation of the offending work could not wait a week until the show ended. An alarming precedent, they said, would be set if the desecration of the piece was permitted.

The Lightschool students agreed with this stance and decided to close ranks. They also relished the thought of something to protest against, and led by Jessica, who was delighted that her discovery was finally gaining some attention, they set up a constant vigil around the installation to prevent its removal under cover of darkness.

The curator of the Caesar Gallery, concerned for the future of his exhibit, quickly made enquiries as to its fiscal status. The insurance agents told him that as the work was now deemed to be illegal, they could not honour any claim that might surface as a result of its confiscation. Justifiably outraged that any possible sales proceeds could be lost, especially when people were just starting to show an interest in the piece, the curator added his voice to the dissenting throng.

'*Artistic immunity! Artistic immunity!*' shouted the

protestors, united as never before behind their wall of makeshift placards.

After a twenty-four hour stand-off, the police lost their patience and mounted an enforced removal of Dave's installation using armed officers and tear gas. Unfortunately they were slightly too late to pre-empt the involvement of the local media, who had heard about the impasse and arrived at just the right moment to witness the finale. Cameras winked and videotape span madly as scuffles broke out with the police on the floor of the gallery. Several other works were damaged in the confusion, and as the officers made off with their prize, protestors began screaming into microphones and weeping over their raped exhibition. The more substantial media networks were not far behind their regional cousins, and they soon arrived to gather material. The story ran on prime-time national news, featuring hurriedly sourced clips from old Newcastle news reports detailing the death of Carlos and Stan's unfortunate abseiler. Thus a connection between the two events was forged in the national consciousness.

Overnight, the art world changed its mind about 'Anonymous' and *Untitled: Attempts to deconstruct the system fall short (1)*.

Now that the installation was linked to another artistic event, its true interdisciplinary genius was obvious to all. It was a record of performance art, but it was also a comment on performance art using conventional materials. And not only that, but it was a demonstration of the power of performance art within contemporary society, as evidenced by the involvement of the police and the media. Dave's work was deemed multi-layered and complex. The art world couldn't get enough of it.

One group of critics cited the work as a new form of portraiture, using the atmosphere and trappings of the final moments in a person's life to reflect them, rather than the more conventional representation of their bodily form. Another body of thought speculated that the artist was commenting on the pointlessness of individualism, the uselessness of identity in the face of uncaring fate. And yet a third group of commentators hailed the installation as a comment on snuff movies and the pervasive nature of violence within the modern world.

The important thing, all the critics agreed, was that they couldn't agree. This fact, indicating that the work could be read in many different ways, was what made it so good.

The installation also met certain other criteria for status as a modern masterpiece. It sent up art itself by using a mannequin, thus mocking the eighties' and nineties' preoccupation with these objects, which were often employed as a soulless surrogate for the self. In addition, having been appropriated and destroyed, it was more alive in the public consciousness than it was in the real world. Several art collectors, including Philippe Laurent – who arrived late on the scene – attempted to bid for remnants of the piece as it was dismantled, but in the end the police took everything except the floorboards on which the installation had stood. One collector even wanted to buy these floorboards, but was refused by the Caesar curator, who was happily calculating how much he could charge for that space in the future.

There was also the attention of the media to interpret. Now that the piece had been immortalized by its public deconstruction, its title seemed horribly portentous. Nobody doubted that the author of *Untitled: Attempts to deconstruct the system fall short (1)* had orchestrated the involvement of the law from the beginning. The Lightschool contingent who had dismissed the work at its inception excused themselves by saying that the piece had clearly not been 'finished' by the artist until it had been dismantled in the eyes of the world. They said they had been wrong to judge it before the involvement of the police and the media, that it was rather like examining a half-painted version of the Sistine chapel and pronouncing it lacking.

The use of the name 'Anonymous' was also believed to be a finely calculated and brilliant move – an integral feature of the work itself. The need for celebrities in art had long been established, and the creation of celebrity was regarded as an artistic execution in its own right. The cult of 'Anonymous' that developed following the confiscation was again assumed to have been ingeniously anticipated by the author of the work. Several commentators claimed that the artist had achieved 'true interdisciplinarity', by using not only performance and material art, but also mainstream media and national awareness in the fabric of their execution.

When the rapturous critics had stopped talking about how good the work was, their focus turned to the identity of 'Anonymous'. There was only one possible candidate. She had asked Clive to sneak the work into the gallery. She had led the student protest when the integrity of the work was threatened. She had, a journalist discovered, been in Newcastle on the evening when the subject of the work had lost his life. She had also been back to Newcastle since, it was revealed, supposedly to research her final examination piece.

Jessica carefully denied any suggestions that she might be 'Anonymous', but then, said everyone, that's exactly what you would expect 'Anonymous' to do.

Dave was back in Newcastle by the time he saw the news. He was celebrating his new job with Vincent, who was celebrating the fact that it was Wednesday.

'I hope I'm OK at it,' said Dave. 'I hope I can do it all right.'

'You'll be fine, Davey boy,' said Vincent. 'Have a bit of faith in yourself.'

'I suppose it'll be fun to work in advertising,' said Dave. He took an uncertain pull on his lager.

'It'll be brilliant,' said Vincent. 'There'll be women and parties and fast cars.' He necked half a pint in a mouthful. 'Just you wait and see.'

'Oh, I don't think it'll be as glamorous as all that,' said Dave. 'I think I'll just be helping out round the office. The job doesn't pay much, after all.'

'Life's what you make it, Davey boy,' said Vincent,

releasing a professional burp. 'There'll be plenty of cash. You'll just have to make sure that it's yours.'

'I'll try,' said Dave quietly. He noticed Vincent had finished his beer. 'Do you want another?'

'Grand,' said Vincent. 'Get two, and I'll drink the rest of yours while you're gone.'

Dave smiled and made his uncertain way to the bar. It was quarter past six, and he had already drunk rather more than he was used to.

'Two lagers please,' he said to the barman, craning his head to peer at a TV suspended from the ceiling.

The TV was flickering with images. It showed a young news reporter outside a building. There were people shouting in the background.

It was a news report about a protest.

A protest about art.

A protest about *his* art.

'There you go, mate,' said the barman, handing Dave one pint of lager and placing the other on the countertop.

Dave gave the barman a note without even looking at it. His eyes were fixed on the screens. He was watching students kick and scream as his installation was carried off in pieces. He was watching critics speak of its greatness. He was watching his art become famous.

At the end of the report, Jessica appeared in front of the camera.

'So you deny that you are responsible for this work?' the reporter asked.

'Of course,' said Jessica. 'I was merely responsible for its introduction to the gallery.'

'But you deny that you are "Anonymous"?' said the reporter determinedly.

'If anyone was to declare themselves as "Anonymous" then, "Anonymous" would cease to exist,' said Jessica, smiling cryptically at the world. 'If I really were "Anonymous" then I certainly wouldn't tell anyone.'

Dave dropped his pint glass in horror. Jessica had played him for a fool. She had appropriated the one thing he was proud of in his life, the only thing he had created, and she was taking the credit. Everybody was going to assume that she was 'Anonymous', and there was no way he could prove that she wasn't. He had no evidence that the installation was his.

Vincent had been too drunk when he stole the mannequin to remember that he had stolen it in the first place. That had been the whole idea. Dave had specifically arranged for Big Ken to be absent when he made the screen prints, so the gigantic Geordie couldn't back him up either. The hardware shop which had supplied the vitrine and stand were hardly likely to remember that they had done so. They probably did adhoc requests in wood and glass all the time. And as for Stan and Carlos, they'd been in custody when his creation had come into the world. They knew nothing of it whatsoever. He hadn't even kept the postcard Jessica had sent him announcing the name of his work, or the remainder of the bus driver's wallet. He'd destroyed all the leftover evidence to protect himself from suspicion in case things went sour.

Dave felt the pit of his stomach fall away. Jessica had stolen his art and there was no way he could get it back.

'*You bitch!*' he screamed at the television. '*You fucking bitch!*'

Second Half

Chapter Fourteen

The flat line

Laurent Création's director of research was a troubled-looking man by the name of Julius Parker-Benbow. Julius had been a mathematical child prodigy and a photo of his sixteen-year-old face, smiling upon receipt of an Oxbridgian First, was to be found on his office wall. In fact, so intellectually precocious had the young Julius been that most of his abilities were burnt up by the time he was twenty-three. His university shed him from the advanced research unit without a second thought, and he made his way to London in search of gainful employment.

It was in London that Julius met Philippe Laurent, who had only just formed his embryonic agency. Both men were drinking in a rather grubby pub in Soho, favoured by admen and frustrated academics alike, and Julius found the young Philippe to be a sympathetic audience. Infuriated by the linear nature of commercial enterprise, Julius spent most of their conversation bemoaning the lack of challenges available to him in the city. He claimed the identification of variables in the money markets a simple matter, and the apparent complexity of high finance an illusion. A man of his abilities, Julius complained, should not be expected to deal with such tawdry conundrums on a day to day basis. He was greatly offended by the simplicity of the problems that the merchant banks had offered him, and made frustrated gestures as he talked, spilling beer on his corduroys.

'The world,' he explained to Philippe, 'is simply a set of equations. The colour of the sky is an equation, as is the colour of the sea. The taste of a peach is an equation. So is the heat of the sun. These are *interesting* equations. They are *true* equations.'

Philippe smiled. 'Truth is beauty,' he acknowledged.

'Exactly,' said Julius. 'My point *exactly*. Our lives are made of numbers. Terribly complex, beautiful, powerful numbers. I don't *want* to understand boring financial systems. I want to understand the numbers in *life.*'

'You say life is made from numbers,' said Philippe, 'but what about art?'

'Also numbers,' said Julius. 'Just like everything else.' He peered contemplatively into his pint glass.

'All art?' said Philippe. 'All art is made from numbers? You're telling me you can work out whether a piece of art is good or not using numbers?'

'Absolutely,' said Julius. 'I appreciate the task would be complex, you'd need a lot of equipment, but it's possible. Feed in the visual preferences of the human eye. The patterns people want and the ones they don't expect. The proper lines of perspective. It's theoretically possible, though no one would ever do it.

It would take all the fun out of judging art for yourself.'

'But what about cultural trends?' Philippe asked. 'What about the effect of society on art, and art on society?'

'Still numbers,' said Julius. 'It's all numbers.' He made an expansive gesture with his arms.

'Advertising?' said Philippe. 'Numbers too?'

'Absolutely,' said Julius. 'Complicated numbers, but numbers nonetheless.'

At the end of the evening, Philippe offered Julius a job. He explained that he had recently been commissioned to write an advertisement for McGoverns, a chain of supermarkets, highlighting a special offer they were running on a particular brand of tea. The offer was going to be in place for a week, and the client wanted an advertisement to run on the radio throughout this period. Philippe disliked the client, who did not think that 'creative' advertising worked, and who had therefore asked for very straightforward copy. He also disliked the drink of tea, and the unhealthy preoccupation the British had with it. However, the supermarket was one of the first real clients that his youthful agency had managed to obtain, so Philippe put some thought into his response. In the end, he came up with two different advertisements, the first of which met their request for straightforward promotional copy, and the second of which he actually liked.

The straightforward advertisement was a simple

affair, highlighting the value of the deal and stressing its limited lifespan. It was voiced by an appropriate celebrity and set to the McGoverns corporate music.

Here at McGoverns we're dedicated to saving you money.
That's why we're offering two boxes of Green Meadows tea
bags for the price of one. Yes, that's right! Two boxes instead
of one – a fifty per cent saving!
Hurry down and get them before time runs out!

The advertising department of McGoverns were quite happy with this execution, feeling that a factual approach was the most appropriate for the job in hand. However, the account man who was presenting the work persuaded them to have a look at Philippe's second execution as well.

Philippe's second execution was a different affair altogether. It was a short song, familiar to the British through their love of tea and its place in the national history. Philippe had adapted the lyrics for his purpose, but the tune remained as old. It was sung as it would have been on wartime radio, surrounded by crackly static and brought to life by a thin, nasal voice:

Tea for two, and two for tea,
two for one, that's one for free,
tea for you and tea for me,
come see . . .

The details of the offer were voiced over as this

little ditty ended: *Green Meadows teabags. Two for the price of one, all this week at McGoverns.*

McGoverns, deciding it was better to humour their agency than argue the toss, agreed to run a split-copy test. Their preferred straightforward copy went out in the north of the country, and Philippe's 'creative' execution appeared in the south.

In the north, sales tripled, which was what the supermarket had expected for such an offer. In the south, where Philippe's version of the ad had run, sales went up by a factor of ten. The client never questioned Philippe's creative judgement again.

Philippe's challenge to the mercurial brain of Julius was simple: find out why the second ad worked better than the first, and then tell me, so that I can write advertising that works this well all the time.

'The numbers of creativity?' said Julius. 'You want to know the numbers of creativity?'

'Yes,' said Philippe. 'I want you to derive the perfect advertising for me.'

'It will be complicated,' said Julius. 'It has never been attempted before.'

'That's OK,' said Philippe. 'I'm in no rush.'

'It will be difficult. It will be very difficult.'

'Well, if it's too hard, you can always go and work for the banks instead.'

Julius Parker-Benbow, who loved a mission of quantification, was a salaried employee of Laurent Création within a week. His brief, extended across the agency, was to isolate and quantify the best way to compose 'creative' advertising. Julius loved a problem that no one else could solve.

Dave regarded Julius, along with Bill Bones, as one of his two friends within the agency. Dave had never made friends easily, and found it particularly difficult to do so with those who were supremely handsome and confident. Laurent Création was ripe with such individuals. The agency rang with laughter and good looks, and everybody seemed to have purpose and drive. Most of Dave's colleagues were terribly self-assured, smartly dressed, and fabulously good at small talk. Dave was none of these things, and felt completely out of his depth around them.

Julius, however, was a kindred spirit. The research director displayed none of the brash certainty that typified the other Laurent Création employees, and seemed just as nervous around them as Dave was. Julius spent his time in the research department, peering out at the agency with frightened eyes. He only ventured forth at lunchtime, when he and Dave would take a meal together in the glass agency canteen.

'Found out how to write the perfect advertisement yet?' Dave would always ask him.

'Written any good advertising yet?' Julius would always reply.

It was their private joke. Julius had never really worked out how to compose the perfect advertising campaign, and in over a year of being a creative assistant, Dave had never been asked to create anything. Despite a ten-year difference in their ages, the two were drawn together by the enormity of their frustrations.

A decade previously, when Philippe took him on, Julius had flung himself at his appointed task with dangerous enthusiasm. He developed innovative statistical techniques to examine the effect of advertising storylines, hoping to uncover some proportional link between drama and success. He showed people lists of company names and asked them to pick the ones they liked. Then he showed people images from the companies' advertising and asked them if they had changed their minds about which ones they liked. Then he used probed association and other subconscious techniques to see which companies they *really* liked.

'A creative correlation,' he whispered to his data, 'There must be a creative correlation.'

Julius strapped feedback cameras to the heads of the public to find out which bits of advertisements they looked at. He showed them scenes featuring breasts, and celebrities, and shocking images, and consulted his equipment to see if they had looked at these things for a disproportionately long time. Then he used enormous and ungainly databases to see if sales could be connected with the appearance of smiling faces or beautiful scenery. He even tried artificial intelligence, wiring up tangled neural nets in an attempt to author a machine that could tell him just how good advertising was and why.

'A pattern of appeal,' he muttered to his constructions. 'Where is the pattern of appeal?'

*

None of Julius' techniques had worked. After ten years at Laurent Création, he could fit what he knew about how to write the perfect advertisement on a piece of A4 paper. He knew that sometimes it was good for advertising to be funny, and sometimes it wasn't. He knew that sometimes advertising was more effective if it took a bit of working out, and sometimes it wasn't. Likewise, he knew that babies, shocking images, celebrities, the colour red, reams of product detail and slow camera movements could all contribute positively to the effect of an advertisement. Unfortunately, he knew they could all contribute negatively as well. In fact, he hadn't found a single thing which, when included in an execution, would always be uniformly good or uniformly bad. Nor had he detected a single style of advertising which always worked. Sometimes funny was good. Sometimes clever was good. Sometimes stylish was good. Sometimes none of these were any good.

There were some tiny glimmers of hope, a few basic rules that could be followed. Bigger letters in a headline were good up to a point, after which they became too big and made the headline look silly. Music was better if it was attuned to the current pop trends, and when advertising male products, the use of women within the drama was most effective if some of their clothes happened to fall off. However, Julius felt a bit of an idiot presenting these findings to Philippe and the creative department, who regarded such guidelines as common sense. They didn't want to know how to make their advertising more uniform. They wanted to know how to fan the flame of creativity. They wanted a formula for inspiration, an algorithm for originality. Julius could not give them one.

After ten years of failure, Julius now hated advertising and advertisements and working at Laurent Création, but his obstinate scientific training demanded that he complete his task. He would be the man who discovered how to write the perfect advertisement, or he would not be a man at all.

'I had a thought the other day,' Julius said to Dave in the canteen. 'A thought.'

Dave nodded sympathetically.

'I've decided to re-examine my data at the sector level,' said Julius.

'What, you mean like food? And clothing? And banks?' said Dave.

'Exactly. Exactly that. I'm wondering if the rules are vastly different for every single sector,' said Julius. 'Perhaps the Holy Grail is different for each type of advertising, or each target audience that sees it.'

'Target audience?' said Dave. 'You mean like "women with kids", that kind of thing?'

'Yes, like that,' said Julius. 'Perhaps there is a perfect advertisement for each demographic group?'

'Or each person?' said Dave.

Julius looked like he was going to cry. 'Do not say such things,' he whimpered.

'Never mind,' said Dave quickly. 'At least Philippe

is still sponsoring your work, even if you haven't quite cracked it yet.'

'Philippe is a bastard,' said Julius sadly. 'He thinks it cannot be done and he likes to see me fail.'

Philippe Laurent had indeed suspected that the task he had set Julius was impossible, but he had decided to cover the outside chance of success. If there *were* components to creativity, Philippe reasoned, it was better that he have access to them than anyone else.

Anyway, the formulae that Julius produced were an important tool for brow-beating clients, who were straightjacketed by their shareholders into universal accountability. Julius, with his derivations and his integrations, could convince them they were not spending their millions on unconsidered artistry. When Philippe wheeled Julius into a meeting, the combination of his Oxbridgian credentials and impenetrable scientific vernacular would quieten the most argumentative client within minutes. The cost of employing him was easily offset by the substantial client meddling he prevented.

Given their differing mind-sets, the relationship between Julius and Philippe had, quite predictably, soured over the years. Julius came to realize that his work was not really expected to succeed, and he was further insulted when any quasi-conclusions he did come to were put in a drawer and forgotten about. In the absence of tangible findings, Philippe treated the scientist as window-dressing and continued to ignore all his efforts.

*

'Philippe is a bastard,' said Julius again.

'Bastard,' Dave agreed, frowning at the guts of his sandwich.

Like Julius, Dave had also suffered at the hands of Philippe Laurent. In over a year of working at Laurent Création, and despite his best efforts, Philippe had never spoken to him cordially. In fact, of the few hundred words Philippe had directed Dave's way, the majority had been insults.

'Is this the best you can do?'

'Am I speaking slowly enough for you?'

'Do you honestly think this is good enough?'

'Can you manage not to fuck up a coffee?'

'Brush your hair, you look like a vagabond.'

'Oh for Christ's sake, I'll do it myself.'

Dave didn't really understand why Philippe treated him with such hostility. He had run many errands for the creative director during his sixteen months of employment, but none to Philippe's apparent satisfaction.

Of course, Dave didn't know that Philippe had eventually got round to looking at his CV. He didn't know that Philippe had been expecting him to be an artistic protégé, sowing advanced stylistic and aesthetic seeds throughout the department. By the time Philippe realized the mistake Bill Bones had made, it was too late for him to get rid of Dave. The papers were signed, the contract was binding. Philippe decided that it would be more trouble than it was worth to sack the graphic design graduate he had ended up with. It would be easier to treat the boy badly, pay him a pittance, and make him leave of his own accord.

In the pursuit of this strategy, Philippe could not afford to expel a single word of praise for Dave's efforts. In fact, he went further, and perpetrated his concerns amongst others.

'He's just a graphic designer actually,' he would say to those who asked where Dave had come from. 'He lied in his application letter. I was hoping to get a young art graduate. You know, someone who could be of use *creatively*. That idiot Bones liked him and offered him a job. I suppose you can use him for any little things you don't want to do yourself. Just don't give him anything important to do, for God's sake.'

The employees of Laurent Création were not naturally cruel people, but they had not been encouraged to look upon Dave kindly.

Bill had been wise enough to spare Dave the details of Philippe's disappointment, (he himself had been made *very* aware of them in a short meeting with Philippe some months previously), and so Dave was ignorant of the professional contempt in which his colleagues held him. All he knew was that he never seemed to be able to do anything right. Nobody trusted him with tasks of importance.

'So, what have you been up to this week?' said Julius, counting the grains of sugar on the glass tabletop.

'Oh, I've been keeping my head down,' said Dave.

'There's a pitch on. Philippe gets even crabbier when he's working on a pitch.'

'He hasn't asked you to help out?'

'No,' said Dave with a sigh, 'he said it was far too important for that.'

Dave was as familiar with the feeling of underachievement as he was with that of isolation, but it still hurt that he wasn't able to express himself. It still hurt to be considered a liability. At Laurent Création, Dave lived out a life that was painfully familiar. Once again, his creative abilities were considered surplus to requirements. Once again, he was given mundane tasks to complete. Once again, he was unhappy.

Faced with a comparable working environment, anyone else would have upped and left, but Dave was conditioned to such treatment. Having been whipped into submission by both Mr Cliffguard and his Newcastle Dean of faculty, Dave was well prepared for similar abuse at Laurent Création. He ignored the depth of his feelings and tried to prove his worth in the only way he knew how. He put his head down and soldiered on.

Every time Philippe made a complaint about his output, Dave tried harder to impress. Every time Philippe criticized his work, Dave took his employer's words to heart. He was trapped, once again, in a web of his own making. Dave was convinced that if he applied himself, he could earn the respect of both Philippe and his colleagues. He couldn't see that their minds were already made up.

*

'Well,' said Julius. 'We are indeed a sorry pair.' He raised his can of Coke. 'Here's hoping the last day of the week will look up.'

Dave nodded and raised his own. 'To finally finding out how to write the perfect advertisement,' he toasted.

'And to finally getting to write one,' said Julius.

The cans made a hollow sound as they collided.

Chapter Fifteen

Honest, decent and true

Philippe Laurent looked down at the brief on his desk. The brief, which invited his agency to pitch for a piece of business, was causing him a problem.

The piece of business in question was very, very large. It was also very prestigious. In fact it was so prestigious that no one but the creative director could be seen to have written the advertisements for the pitch. This was the problem that Philippe faced. Although writing advertisements was technically his job, he hadn't really had to do it for a while, and he was in no particular rush to start up again.

'*Merde*,' said Philippe, drumming his fingers on the clear glass tabletop.

It wasn't that Philippe didn't think he could produce work of a high enough quality. In his time, he had produced some hugely memorable advertising. It was simply that he hadn't written anything particularly memorable for a while. Not personally, anyway.

Philippe was often remembered for his work on a children's charity called St Clarice. Agencies sometimes did work for charities on a non-profit basis because their efforts were immune to criticism (who would criticize such altruistic output?) and besides, it was good public relations to have a charity or two on the client list.

When Laurent Création had been assigned the St Clarice account, the client was in some degree of despair. After years of televized tragedy from Africa, the Middle East and the Balkans, St Clarice's efforts to rehabilitate homeless and abused British children were receiving little attention. They struggled to be heard amongst the clamour of celebrity telethons, and their footage of grubby orphans could not compete with the shadowed eyes and tattered rags of the foreign youngsters on the nine o'clock news.

Studying this competitive situation in an attempt to form his thoughts, Philippe realized that the reason people were prepared to send money overseas was that they were ashamed. They saw the walking dead, and they glanced guiltily at their microwaves, their convertibles, their roast beef and Yorkshire pudding. They pledged because they were privileged industrial suburbanites. They pledged because they felt guilty.

'Foreign horrors sell,' he explained at the first client meeting. 'We'll just have to make people realize that there are equivalent disasters in their own country.'

'Well, I don't want to damage anyone else's income stream,' said the client. 'Those charities are doing great work.'

'If you don't mind me saying so, that's a very dangerous attitude. They are your competitors. They are taking money from your pockets.'

'But the money is going to good causes.'

'But it's coming from *your* pockets.'

'I suppose you're right,' said the client. 'It just seems a bit churlish to begrudge them their success, that's all.'

'It's not churlish,' said Philippe. 'It's business.'

Following this conversation, Philippe wrote a series of short TV ads using some of the St Clarice children. He showed one boy, who had been beaten and violated by his parents, staring defiantly at the camera. Behind the camera an interviewer, or a St Clarice worker, obviously hovered. The room in which the boy stood was sick with bare wires and scabby paint.

'Do you remember the drought in Cambodia?' asked the unseen adult.

The boy didn't appear to understand what he was being asked. He just stared at the camera as if it was going to rape him.

In another film, a girl in a detention centre peered out at the camera from behind cold black bars.

'Have you heard of Bosnia?' asked the reporter.

The girl just snarled back.

In the third execution, two twins clutched each other in a dirty grey cot, and were unable even to look at the camera, so terrified were they of the adults before them.

'Do you know where Eritrea is?'

The twins started crying.

In each film, no answer to the question was articulated beyond fear or anger or resentment. The viewer was left in no doubt that these children were not part of the civilized world.

At the end of each film a voice spoke. 'Children also suffer in Britain.'

Then the end frame came up, a black page with the St Clarice logo and a phone number. Above the phone number were four words: *Help our children too.*

Contributions to St Clarice doubled that year, and Philippe won an industry award in the category of charities and public announcements.

Another of Philippe's famous campaigns was for a medium-sized family car called the Ferrano. The spawn of a poorly managed South American automotive firm, the unfortunate Ferrano had very few positive features to speak of. It was marginally slower than all the other cars in its class, had a comparatively unappealing interior, and was less economic in terms of fuel consumption. Its design was less outgoing than that of its rivals, and it came in a less flattering range of colours. It also lacked extras, whilst its peers had them in spades.

At the time of Laurent Création's introduction to the account, the Ferrano was favoured by northern mothers, who were able to get the cars at a low price because the British manufacturing plant was situated in the north, and the local market was flooded.

Northern mothers also felt loyal to the miserable machines because so many of their husbands were involved in the Ferrano's construction. Southern families scorned the Ferrano, particularly in the affluent suburbs of London, and to spot one south of Nottingham was, at the time of Laurent Création's appointment, a unique achievement.

Philippe and his team researched the Ferrano desperately, trying to uncover some gem of information that could inform their work. No matter how many magazine articles and test results they read, they could not find an iota of praise for their client's embarrassing creation. The task appeared hopeless. The machine was a liability.

Then, when Philippe was close to resigning the account, a young account executive came up with something. In a pile of leftover industry data, she happened upon a Ministry of Transport report dealing with road accidents. In this sombre document were detailed the dead of the British roads, and next to the dark columns of names were listed the circumstances of their demise. The young account executive had found something for Laurent Création to talk about. No one, it seemed, had ever been killed in a Ferrano.

'Eureka,' said Philippe, staring fixedly at the columns of numbers.

The reasons for the Ferrano's zero mortality rate were simple, and completely unconnected with the car's safety features (which in keeping with the general theme of the vehicle, were marginally inferior to those of other models). The donors of this admirable safety statistic were in fact the afore-mentioned northern mothers, who tended to live in small rural communities, and conducted their perambulations at correspondingly rural pace. The circumference of their exploits was normally limited to the children's school, and perhaps the local shops. They never had to face the trauma of London traffic at the weekend, and the horrors of the A40 on a dark and slippy night were unknown to them. Thus did they avoid the motorized hands of fate that reached for many of their BMW or Honda driving counterparts.

Philippe, ever the opportunist, knew that human nature was to assume that such correlations were causal. If you told people that sperm counts were dropping, and that potato consumption had been rising at a mysteriously similar rate, they would find some way to link the two together. He decided to tell people that no one had ever died in a Ferrano. They would jump to their own conclusions.

'We will own the concept of safety,' he told the client.

'But the car isn't very safe,' came the response.

'Don't worry about that.'

'But how can we claim something which isn't true?'

'Just leave that to me.'

With help from a young art director he had just employed, Philippe composed a series of arresting posters, each pointing out the uniqueness of the Ferrano's zero mortality rate.

'*Not dead fast*,' screamed the first.

'*No undertaking*,' shouted the second.

'*Go from zero to one hundred*,' hollered the third.

In the bottom right-hand corner of these posters was the Ferrano logo, which the viewer's eyes would gravitate towards in search of an explanation.

'No one has ever died in a Ferrano,' claimed the sub-copy proudly.

Alongside these posters, Philippe ran a thirty-second TV advertisement. It was filmed across Europe, and featured short little images of small roadside shrines. Each shrine was decorated with the personal artefacts of the motorist it commemorated, and hanging from the central crucifix were their car keys. The film was careful to capture the marque of car that each dead person had been driving, focusing in on the branded metal key rings as they wobbled in the breeze. The only brand not featured was the Ferrano.

'No one has ever died in a Ferrano,' said the end frame.

Philippe's campaign was a roaring success. Neurotic crash survivors and concerned parents rushed to buy the tinny contraptions, naturally assuming them to be the safest cars available. Other car manufacturers complained that Philippe had misrepresented the data, but Philippe pointed out that no safety claims had actually been made. The outraged competition then responded by producing campaigns demonstrating the safety of their own vehicles, but Philippe didn't really mind; he knew his ads could only work once anyway.

Eight years after the campaign, the Ferrano continued to sell well throughout the UK, and was still considered one of the safest cars on the market, despite the fact that just as many people had now died in it as any other model. This was even more ironic considering that the makers of the Ferrano had improved the car's safety features tenfold since Philippe's original advertisements, urgently trying to justify his positioning of their product.

The Ferrano and St Clarice campaigns had been high points of Philippe's creative output. Since their completion he had managed to avoid having to write any advertisements at all. This lack of productivity was not a symptom of ill-health or creative under-nourishment. It was simply a perk that came with the position of creative director. Philippe's agency employed a large number of talented creatives to produce work that he could sign off and take some of the credit for. He wasn't expected to write advertisements himself. For most clients it was enough that the head of the agency had approved their campaign. They didn't dare demand any more of his time than that.

Each Monday morning, Philippe would receive the work of his staff and pass comment.

'Fine,' he would say. 'OK, fine, acceptable, do that one again, throw that one away and start again. Quite good, rubbish, fine.'

As he talked, piles of advertisements would be sorted and filtered for action.

'Fine, fine, appalling, dreadful, fine.'

Sometimes in these meetings, client issues would be raised.

'The client was wondering,' an account executive would say, 'whether we could put a pack shot in at the end of the film?'

'Tell them they can have a pack shot when they make something people find attractive,' Philippe would respond. 'Tell them their product is too ugly to appear in an advertisement.'

'The client has asked,' another account executive would mention, 'if we have considered the use of a jingle?'

'Jingles are irritating. Tell the client they don't need a jingle. Their products are already irritating enough.'

These Monday morning meetings were Philippe's preferred way of dealing with client requirements. He liked them to know that he had looked at their work, but didn't want to write anything for them himself.

However, the present client, the client that Laurent Création were about to pitch for, was different. They were too prestigious, too global, and spent entirely too much money to accept anything less than the personal attentions of the creative director. Four of the biggest agencies in London had been selected to pitch for the account, and Philippe had to admit that the calibre of the client merited the competition they had aroused. To his annoyance, Philippe found he was in danger of actually having to write some advertising.

*

Philippe was not unusual in disliking his creative obligations. Most advertising creatives looked upon the actual composition of advertisements as a painful and difficult occupation, which detracted from the more relaxing pastime of attending industry award ceremonies and debating the merit of each other's work. In defence of their attitudes, they pointed out that the process of creating advertising was a great deal more tortured than the process of creating work in other fields. In advertising, they argued, as in no other creative sphere, the full horror of the deadline was realized. The deadline was an eternal shadow, a date on which the success or failure of their work was to be ordained. They watched the deadline lumber over the mental landscape towards them, overturning ideas and pushing past inspiration. The deadline could crush entire careers in its meaty paws.

A novel could take months, they would point out, perhaps even years. Painters and sculptors could ferment for decades in a single discipline, pondering a single idea. Only journalists, they conceded, would ever feel the deadline's hot breath in the way that they did, and journalists could sometimes fill their space with photos, or rearrange editorial, thus delaying its dreadful advance for another day.

In advertising the deadline was immutable, and often preposterously short and brutish. A week to create was unusual. A day all too common. An hour not unheard of. And one never knew the creative task one would be set. There was no way to prepare, no defences to assemble.

Most creatives developed strategies to deal with the deadline's proximity. Some sought a state of constant artistic readiness, surrounding themselves with books and magazines, leaving TVs on in office corners and internet search engines on starter's orders. They opened dictionaries at random in the hope of plagiaristic brainwaves, or mused on the patterns of dried-up old coffee. Others, when confronted with the deadline's hairy figure, sought refuge in serene and poetic environments. A quiet broom cupboard, or an alcove on the roof of the agency building. In these mental cocoons, they pretended not to hear the muffled thumps of the deadline's approach.

A few creatives had developed very bizarre tactics indeed. Philippe knew of one team who would wait until the deadline was knocking on their office door, and then go down the pub and drink until they had a good idea. If they had one they would go back to the agency and attempt to render it coherently, and if they didn't have one they would keep drinking until they passed out. Another team famously avoided focusing on the deadline's approach until they were due to present work to the account managers, and would then rely on raw panic as the primus for their ideas, drawing them out as they talked through them.

Philippe was no less terrified of the deadline than his employees, and had long ago developed his own strategy for dealing with it. He had started up his own agency so that other people had to meet his deadlines for him. This strategy had worked very well for him so far, and he hadn't really had to write anything of note since the famous Ferrano and St Clarice campaigns. He had no intention of breaking this happy record now.

Reaching a conclusion, Philippe looked up from the brief on his desk.

'Marcy?' he called to his secretary. 'Marcy? Are you out there?'

Marcy, a frightening woman who had been with Laurent Création since its inception, and who played rugby, appeared in the office doorway.

'What?' she said. She was the only person in the agency who could speak to Philippe as an equal.

'I want everyone to have a go at this brief,' said Philippe. 'We need to give it our best shot.'

Marcy nodded her gigantic head.

'Quite right too,' she said. 'Don't see why you should have to do it all yourself. Get those lazy bastards working.'

Philippe handed her the brief. 'Get copies done,' he said. 'Send one to every creative team in the agency.'

'It'll take a day in internal post,' said Marcy, with a look that implied she would speed up the internal post if she could get her hands on the people responsible. 'It's five-thirty now, so it won't go out till Monday. That means they won't get it till Tuesday.'

'You're right,' said Philippe. 'The deadline's too tight to waste a day.' He thought about asking Marcy to carry it round, but changed his mind, knowing that she would consider it a major imposition.

'Get copies now, and then find someone to take it round on Monday morning,' he said. 'Use Dave. Even he shouldn't be able to make a mess of that.'

Marcy took the brief and stomped off to the copying room. Philippe sat at his desk and reflected on the benefits of success. He was damned if he was going to write any advertising himself. He had plenty of people to do that kind of thing for him.

Chapter Sixteen

Thank alcohol it's Friday

The Credit Risk and Peanut was one of those pubs whose continued solvency was entirely dependent on the building next door. Though the pub was in a state of some disrepair, it derived a passable living from the traffic supplied by the Laurent Création offices, which it abutted on the city side. Without this patronage, a large brewing chain would almost certainly have swallowed the horrible establishment whole, no doubt converting it into a far nicer place to drink.

Given the high incidence of alcoholism within the creative arts, any pub in close proximity to an advertising agency was known to be on to a winner. As an added bonus, because employees of advertising agencies worked more varied hours than other professional groups, the establishment was saved from loss of profits through over-capacity. This problem bedevilled pubs that had formed symbiotic relationships with firms of barristers or bankers, who had a tendency to rush the bar at five-thirty, but who normally wanted to be back in suburbia by nine. When Laurent Création set up shop on his doorstep, the landlord of the Credit Risk and Peanut had been handed a remarkably profitable clientele.

Despite this good fortune, the proprietor was not a man at peace. Laurent Création could always relocate, he reasoned, to be replaced by sober civil servants or young entrepreneurs who preferred to drink in Kensington vodka bars. Worse, if its current tenants departed, the Laurent Création building could be converted into a large and healthy gymnasium. Even assuming the agency stayed put for many years, another less grubby drinking house might move in on the area. All these dreadful possibilities plagued the landlord of the Credit Risk and Peanut, and curdled his grey sheets at night. He was well aware that the attentions of his patrons were as fickle as summer, and so he missed no opportunity to squeeze revenue from them whilst times were good. He also refused to upgrade the unpleasant interior of his establishment, believing (quite rightly) that the decaying ambience generated by the sticky floorboards and crippled furniture would drive his customers further into their cups.

Each Friday, the human contents of Laurent Création would trickle into the Credit Risk and Peanut as their phones fell silent and their creative obligations were met. Once in the pub, everyone attempted to distance themselves from the trauma of work by talking about work with the people they worked with. Dave normally drank with Bill Bones (who was such a mainstay of the landlord's turnover that he had his own pewter tankard behind the bar) and Julius, who would treat himself to a few before he went home to his family. The trend of the evening's conversation was fairly predictable. Julius would start things off, depressed because yet another experiment to define the components of perfect advertising had failed. Bill would counter that at least he didn't have to work on incontinence trousers and chair lifts, and Dave would contribute his own musings on what it was to be a creative assistant who wasn't ever asked to create anything. By the end of the evening they would all have resolved that they were not going back to Laurent Création the following week, and would then go their separate ways until Monday morning.

Arriving at the Credit Risk and Peanut on this particular Friday evening, Dave was confronted with the usual tableau. Julius was slumped miserably in his seat, and Bill was patting him on the back in commiseration.

'So Julius, discovered how advertising works?' joked Dave, hoping to lighten the mood.

'Yes,' said Julius, crumpling onto the table in despair.

'Really?' said Dave.

'Really,' said Julius. 'I tried a new approach this afternoon. It worked. It actually worked.' He let out a sob of emotion.

Bill stopped patting Julius on the back and looked up at Dave gravely. 'This afternoon, Julius isolated the perfect subject matter for any advertising.'

'Well that's good, isn't it?' said Dave. He wondered

why his friend was not jumping for joy. 'What have you found?'

'Kittens,' mumbled Julius into the woodwork. 'Bloody kittens.'

'Kittens?' said Dave.

'Kittens,' said Julius again, peeling his long face off the table and turning it heavenwards.

Bill raised his eyebrows in Dave's direction. 'Apparently an advertisement with a kitten in it cannot fail,' he said.

'One kitten, or indeed multiple kittens,' said Julius, still staring upwards like a madman. 'However, I have yet to determine whether factors such as recall, brand consideration and intent to purchase are proportionately linked to the density of kittens within an execution.'

'You must be joking Julius,' said Dave. 'Surely you're joking?'

'I wish I was,' said Julius. 'You think I don't know how stupid I sound? But it's there. It's irrefutable. I tested and retested the data. I used every possible analysis. No execution on the entire database that contains reference to kittens or a visual representation of a kitten has ever failed to increase sales.'

'So kittens generate a positive return on investment?' said Bill, the trace of a smile playing at his lips.

'Absolutely,' said Julius. 'Would you like to see a graph?'

'No, that's all right,' said Bill. 'Can I get you another drink?'

'I'll get them,' said Julius. 'I need to drown my

sorrows.' He rose unsteadily to his feet and turned to address the world. 'A lifetime's work, and what are my conclusions? Use more fucking kittens.'

He staggered off to the bar.

'Poor bugger,' said Bill to Dave. 'Go and help him carry the drinks, will you?'

When Dave got to the bar, Julius was paying for the beer, which had mysteriously come to ten pounds, a mathematically impossible feat for three identical drinks. Julius however, was too miserable to notice. He was also too miserable to realize that he had been holding ten pounds in his hand while the publican's hungry eyes were performing calculations.

By eleven o'clock Julius had parted with five more ten pound notes, and had consumed most of Dave's beer as well as his own. He was suicidally drunk, and Dave and Bill felt it was time to bundle him into a cab and send him back to the loving bosom of his family. Julius blew raspberries at them from the back window of the taxi as he trundled off into the darkness.

As on most Friday nights, Dave and Bill were the only employees of Laurent Création still present at the sounding of the bell. Most of their colleagues had long since excused themselves with dinner parties in Camden, theatre tickets in the West End, or expensive soirées in Soho. As on most Friday nights, Dave and Bill had no such functions to attend.

'Fuckit,' said Bill, staring into his empty tankard. 'I'm going to lose some money. You coming?'

This was what Bill always said at the end of Friday

evening, a sentence that preceded his drunken attendance at the Silver Dollar, an establishment from which he seldom emerged with a profit. Dave had been with him once or twice, but tonight the thought of jostling with angry Japanese women for a place at the roulette table was extremely unappealing. Besides, Julius had embezzled so much of his beer that he was still largely sober, and his spirits were low. He didn't really feel like having company.

'No thanks, Bill,' he said. 'I might try and catch a late film in Leicester Square.'

Dave often attended the late night performances in Leicester Square. He liked the anonymity of the place in the small hours. The huge billboards appealed to his sense of the outrageous, and the smoky auditoriums reminded him of churches, the sinning masses in quiet worship of the gods before them. Most of the cinemas also charged a lot less after midnight, and given Dave's pitiful salary, this was a prerequisite for his attendance.

Wandering the paving stones, Dave gazed upwards at the monologue of fame. The square was fat with lost foreigners and London youth. The remnants of a red carpet lolled from one cinema entrance like a huge dead tongue, and crackling cans of drink and burger organs lay around the place. Clearly there had been a premiere earlier.

Dave had a patented method of choosing a film, which was to isolate the poster he liked best in aesthetic terms, and then quickly buy a ticket before factors like the cast, title or plot could change his mind. His aesthetic criteria were fairly arbitrary. It could be the way the colour had drained in reproduction, or the use of light in the space around the poster frame. It could be anything that drew his eye. He found that this method normally steered him towards films that were at least interesting, if not actually good.

In his census of the billboards on this night, Dave came across a poster that looked very familiar. The film was called *Two Ways to Live*, and a family of memories accompanied the images above the title. The ruined face of the cliché sodden ex-cop was a little older, but still recognizable from Dave's first and only date with Jessica. Chinese imagery was scattered around the poster in a pleasingly random way, suggesting that this sequel would tell the story of the ex-cop's journey to the Far East, taking up where *Two Ways to Die* had left off.

Thinking dark thoughts about Jessica, Dave paid his money and found a smudged red seat near the back of the cinema.

Two Ways to Live was generally felt to be a slightly more accomplished film than its predecessor, concentrating as it did on the clash between eastern and western cultures. The first scene of the film saw the newly inspired and alcohol purged ex-cop arrive in China with his deported companions; those who he had saved so dramatically at the end of *Two Ways to Die*.

'You are great man,' said one of the deportees. 'Welcome to share in my home.'

'The American hero,' a second agreed, 'is welcome anywhere in Shanghai.'

The ex-cop squinted out towards the horizon and stood with his legs far apart. 'I thank you kindly,' he soliloquized. 'For America doesn't seem to need its heroes any more.'

Following this exchange, the ex-cop moved in with the family of the first deportee, which allowed the more touching aspects of his character to surface. In one scene, he tried to learn Chinese, and bought a bag of fruit at five times the normal price. In another he was seen practising meditation (at which he was clearly not good) in a rose garden.

Once the audience had been reminded what a good man the hero was, a turning point arrived in the plot. He was approached by members of the Shanghai police force, who were investigating the death of an American girl. The dead girl had been employed by the American Ambassador, and a tattoo of Betty Boop had been found on her right shoulder, marking her as part of the gang that the hero had thwarted so bravely in the first outing. The Shanghai police asked if he would be good enough to repeat this feat over.

'Please to help us,' said the Police Commissioner. 'We do not know what to do.'

The ex-cop frowned and narrowed his eyes with machismo. 'Why should I help you?' he said angrily. 'What makes you think I will help?'

'You are a policeman,' said the Commissioner.

'An *ex*-policeman,' said the ex-cop.

'Here in Shanghai, we have a saying,' said the Commissioner. ' "Men do not take strength from badges, they take strength from other men." '

The ex-cop squinted manfully into the night. 'Goddamn it,' he said finally. 'I guess I'm a policeman after all.'

The hero's return to law enforcement (and his subsequent pursuit of the dead girl's masters) led him inexorably towards the world he had abandoned in his flight eastwards. The plot darkened, and there were moments of weakness with alcohol, particularly after a bloody gunfight in which he killed three more members of the Betty Boop gang (whom he had traced using clues on the dead girl's body). The plot then became blacker still when he discovered a cargo container full of murdered immigrants at the Shanghai docks. This grim discovery, clearly a message aimed at dissuading the hero from further investigation, drove him back to the bottle, and within the space of two scenes he was recognizably alcohol-sodden once more.

Drunk, suicidal and unshaven, the hero abandoned his investigative duties and became an ex-cop for the second time in as many films. The audience, who were used to his tantrums by now, knew that this was a necessary step he had to take. He could not rise phoenix-like to victory until he had sunk back into the ashes from whence he came.

'This world,' the ex-cop muttered from the barstools of Shanghai. 'This goddamn little world.'

The inevitable process of the hero's redemption began when the American Ambassador, employer of the dead girl from the consulate, appeared on TV at her funeral. Watching the broadcast with his Chinese hosts, the hero was stunned to discover that they recognized the man. It seemed the Ambassador had interviewed them before their abortive shipment to America, the events of which had been chronicled in the first film. Upon making this discovery, it was immediately obvious to both cast and audience that the American Ambassador had been the head of the Betty Boop gang all along, running an extensive immigration racket with the help of his corrupt consulate staff.

'Goddamn,' said the hero, squinting with passion and rage.

Following his discovery, the newly-incensed hero climbed back on the wagon, had a shave, and tracked the Ambassador down at his palatial weekend retreat. Storming the walls with a knife between his teeth, he clinically did away with various bodyguards and then burst into the villain's lair.

The two faced off, circling each other cautiously.

'You will die screaming, like your brother,' snarled the Ambassador, baring his chest to expose a body-wide Betty Boop tattoo.

They fought by hand (the hero's bullets were apparently exhausted), and just when it looked like the despicable Ambassador had the hero at his mercy, he was crushed by a huge statue that had been disturbed in the fighting. It fell on him as he was about to deliver the killer blow, suggesting the gods were watching over the redeemed hero once more.

At the end of the film, the freshly-shaven and clear-eyed hero was commended by the Chinese government and offered a permanent place in the Shanghai police force. He refused their kind offer, and with firm jaw pointed resolutely westwards, claimed that it was time to return to his own people. The final scene of the film showed him practising his meditation in a rose garden overlooking Los Angeles, content at last with his place in the world.

In contrast to the critics, Dave didn't enjoy *Two Ways to Live* as much as *Two Ways to Die*. A different director had been used this time around, and he thought the use of light to emphasize the moods of the players was much less subtle. He was also critical of the action in the sequel, which did not flower as delicately as that in the first outing. And he didn't like the score, which was harsh and pointed. Not finely tuned as a counterpoint to the action, as it had been in *Two Ways to Die*.

Dave left the cinema and plodded down to Trafalgar Square. Still dwelling on Jessica, he wondered what she would have thought of the film.

'Probably would have liked the continued use of the iconic American motif,' he muttered angrily, 'as long as the critics praised it first. Stupid thieving bitch.'

Because he was so preoccupied with Jessica, Dave was less surprised than he should have been when he got to Trafalgar Square and saw her face on the side of a bus.

Chapter Seventeen

The greatest show on earth

When the art world decided she was 'Anonymous', the artist responsible for the seminal interdisciplinary work *Untitled: Attempts to deconstruct the system fall short (1)*, Jessica began to make a lot of money.

Everything she did found gallery space, and most of her back catalogue was subsequently bought by high profile collectors. Pieces began to migrate overseas, and a few were even sold in New York, making her part of an exclusive club of successful modern artists from London. She was asked on to talk shows, and appeared in outrageous articles in the tabloid press. As a spokeswoman of new British art, she was also interviewed by hard-hitting documentary makers, who quizzed her on the concept of modernity, the power of the media, and the nature of western capitalist aesthetics.

'Why shouldn't artists be rich and famous?' Jessica said to the camera. 'What could be wrong with that?'

'You don't think it could compromise your work?' the interviewer asked.

'I don't see why it should,' said Jessica. 'My work is mine and mine alone.'

'But what about the old masters?' said the interviewer. 'Many great artists completed their best work *because* of isolation and poverty. They did it for love, not money.'

'And many others were bankrolled by the church or the state,' said Jessica. She waved a braceleted hand in dismissal. 'There have always been well-paid and well-known artists. I am hardly the first and I certainly won't be the last.'

'But don't you think the sheer *degree* of acclaim you have received is unusual? Don't you think it *must* affect your work?'

'Poppycock,' said Jessica. 'Nobody assaults pop stars with these questions. Nobody asks film directors to keep a low profile. If I am famous, it is because my work deserves it. If I am popular, it is because my work has touched a nerve.'

In all her interviews, in all her public appearances, acknowledging Dave's contribution to her success had never crossed Jessica's mind. In fact, she hardly thought about him at all. She had forgiven herself for the appropriation of Dave's work as quickly as others had assumed her own brilliance in creating it. It was fate, she reasoned, that had dealt her this hand, and it was fate that wanted her to play it. She was more likely to further the cause of modern art than Dave would have been, so it was probably for the best that she had been credited with his work. After all, she was the real artist, and he was just a graphic designer. Things had worked out the right way.

Jessica also reminded herself that she had been part of the process by which Dave's installation had become such an icon of the artistic world. Without her intervention to get the piece into the Caesar Gallery, it would never have been removed with such a media fanfare. She convinced herself that she could almost be considered a joint author of the work, and certainly never doubted that her creative abilities were equal to those of the ghostly 'Anonymous'.

Jessica was happy. She had achieved what she always wanted. She was a successful contemporary artist, driving the boundaries of modern thought and shaping the discipline that she loved. In fact, she was so wrapped up in her own publicity that she didn't notice her work was becoming more derivative with each passing show.

After the 'Anonymous' scandal, Jessica began to produce work using other artists' throwaway materials. Her new-found celebrity gave her access to the studios of London's artistic elite, where she asked for souvenirs or supplies that they were not likely to use. Once she had enough material she went to work. Her first solo show contained portraits of famous contemporary artists, made out of the very materials they had donated to her cause. A prominent north London painter she rendered out of his discarded canvas, stretched over clay to show a white-relief face. A female sculptor who enjoyed fame for her woodcarvings was modelled in off-cuts and shavings, fastened together to form a rough gluey bust. These and other works Jessica displayed as a visual observation on society's obsession with celebrity and artistic genius. Everyone got the joke, though there was some debate as to whether it was a good one or not.

'What is talent?' said Jessica at the opening night of the show. 'Who has talent and who does not? How do we know talent when we see it? Do talented people look different? Do they look special? Can you see talent in their form and their features?'

She turned sideways so the audience could examine her profile.

'This show is a homage to talent,' she said. 'Because it takes one who has it to see it.'

In her second solo show Jessica's artistic appropriations went further. She approached the Lightschool, her old stomping ground, and offered the final year students a deal. She would display their work for them, but they could not have their names, or the names of their work, in the gallery. They would only be given credit for what they had done in the catalogue. None of them minded. The chance to expose their work to the artistic press was too good to pass up. Besides, once Jessica had explained what she was up to, most of them liked the idea enough to go along with it.

Working away in her studio, Jessica took a piece from each student and added some mark of her own. She amended the backdrops of paintings. She added new features to sculpture. With installations, she found some way to adapt the construction so it appeared marginally different than before. When finished, Jessica displayed these artworks in the gallery as if they were her own, placing a small metal plaque at the base of each one.

'*This work exhibited by the artist in question*', the plaque always read.

Critics quite liked the idea of stolen originality, or subversive labelling, or commissionable art, or whatever it was that Jessica was trying to say. They also liked the fact that the tabloids were outraged by the whole thing, screaming 'MONEY FOR NOTHING!' and giving them an opportunity to be pompous when discussing the show on TV.

'It has been said that only you would have dared to put on this show,' one interviewer told her. 'What do you think about that?'

'Well, it makes sense,' Jessica said with a twinkle. 'Only someone who is completely at ease with their own talent would be happy to exhibit everyone else's.'

With these two solo exhibitions, Jessica kept herself near the top of the modern art agenda for over a year. Though her work seemed to concentrate on only one theme, she was sufficiently outrageous to be hated by the media, and sufficiently arrogant and confident to be loved by the art establishment. Of course, she was also deemed to be worth keeping an eye on because of her infamous alter ego. She hadn't really done anything worthy of the name 'Anonymous' in the time since *Untitled: Attempts to deconstruct the system fall short*

(1), but everyone assumed that it was just a matter of time before such genius surfaced again.

It was half in the hope that 'Anonymous' would make an appearance that Jessica had been invited to contribute to a new show. This show was going to contain only work by the most renowned modern artists in Britain. It was to be curated by the most outrageous curators, exhibited in the most subversive and anti-establishment gallery, and attended by the most post-modern celebrities. The show was to be called 'Art Schmart'.

'I am honoured to be part of "Art Schmart",' Jessica announced to the world at her press conference. 'A great exhibition deserves a great artist.'

For 'Art Schmart' Jessica produced her most acerbic installation to date. She constructed a slideshow in a darkened room, with space for up to forty seats before an enormous screen. The slides she planned to show were all of famous works of art. Jessica had flown round Europe and America and snapped all the most recognizable work she could find. A good one hundred Masters were represented in the slideshow, but she had also put in some surprises. There were pieces of modern art, and even some architectural landmarks. There was also one slide that showed the Guinness logo, and another of the Sex Pistols' album, *Never Mind the Bollocks*.

None of the images showed these works in their entirety. Instead, her slides were restricted to the locus of ownership – the stamp of the creator. When photographing paintings, Jessica had selected only the area where the artist's name was signed. For shots of buildings, she had focused on plaques that celebrated the architect responsible. When dealing with logos and stand-alone objects, she had restricted the camera's view to details of manufacture. This was one thing all the slides had in common. They were all studies of authorship. Records of provenance. They were all centred on a name.

Back in her studio, Jessica took the images and fed them into her computer. Then, using the delicate web of software for a purpose never intended, she removed the names on the slides and replaced them with her own. Gaudi's *Sagrada Familia* was now Jessica's. *The Mona Lisa* was hers as well. Scowling at the little screen before her, Jessica appropriated the names of the greats. Munch was Jessica. Warhol was Jessica. Jessica was both Gilbert and George. Jessica had designed the Coke can and Jessica was the editor of *The Times*. Jessica was responsible for Mannerism, Romanticism, Neo-Classicism and the High Renaissance. Without a hint of apology, Jessica even claimed the rocks at Stonehenge. Her slideshow, once complete, contained almost two hundred slides displayed at five-second intervals. Every single one of them was resplendent with Jessica's name.

Jessica called her slideshow '*Untitled: The presence of God*'. She knew it would excite stark opinions when unveiled to the public.

Firstly, by restricting the focus of her slides, Jessica

had made it hard to determine which artistic works they depicted. Photos of paintings were clipped to the bottom left-hand corner of the canvas. Photos of buildings showed only ten stones at the base. The slides were an artistic quiz. A game of spot-the-genius. They forced viewers to extrapolate the rest of each work, and thus made a whole gallery appear in the mind. This in itself was unusual, and Jessica knew it would cause some debate.

Secondly, by signing her own name in the place of the creators, Jessica had continued her assault on the notion of ownership. Could anything really be 'owned'? Did she have a right to associate herself with these works just because she was an artist? Jessica's sub-conscious, still unsure of its rights in the case of Dave's installation, both illuminated and hobbled her work. The slideshow was a piece only she could've con-structed. It was a piece only she would have chosen to make.

No one was allowed to see *Untitled: The presence of God* before 'Art Schmart' opened. The work stood silent in Jessica's studio, waiting for the show's private view. She was very proud of it, and looked forward to the day of its release.

There were three other contributors to 'Art Schmart', all of whom were familiar to Jessica, not only as young gods of the London art scene, but also as acquaintances preceding her days of fame. The other contributors were Dave's former flatmates Stan and Carlos, and her classmate from the Lightschool, Nedrina Burchill.

214

*

The legal system had been relatively kind to Stan and Carlos in the end. Though the prosecution was pushing for manslaughter, the defence argued that the two students had not meant their abseiler to fall to his death. It had, after all, rather disrupted the message of their work. Manslaughter was clearly too ambitious a charge. However, the prosecution pointed out that Stan and Carlos had certainly been breaking the law when they coerced their bus driver to leap from the bridge, and as such they carried some responsibility for his accidental death. They could not escape punishment altogether.

In the end, Stan and Carlos got eighteen months, the entirety of which they were not expected to serve if good behaviour was observed.

'We are going to prison?' asked Carlos, who had been confused by the court legalese.

'Yes, but not for long,' said Stan. 'And I believe they will let us play golf.'

Carlos shrugged. 'It is only fair,' he said. 'We did cause that poor man to die.'

'Quite right,' said Stan. 'We must be upstanding artists with backbone.'

In the year or so since their conviction, Stan and Carlos had been through some ups and downs. Originally they were sent to an easygoing correctional facility, but it shut down because of a financial scandal and they were transferred to a slate-grey jail hidden between two satellite towns in the Home Counties.

Suddenly they were surrounded by rapists and murderers.

'These men are criminals,' said Carlos.

'So are we,' said Stan.

'But these are *proper* criminals.'

'They do seem insensitive.'

'Uncouth.'

'We must avoid them,' said Stan. 'They do not look like they will enjoy playing golf.'

'No, indeed not,' said Carlos. 'Their thumbs are much too large.'

'Anyway, the subtleties of the game will be beyond them.'

'They will not understand the use of different clubs.'

'Actually,' said Stan, 'I think they might under-stand the use of different clubs all too well. We really must avoid them.'

And so, to get away from the communal areas of the jail, Stan and Carlos began practising art again. Each day they secreted themselves in the old prison workshop, which their fellow prisoners were unlikely to visit, and passed the time with their creations. In more ways than one, these tactics were to liberate them. What started as escapism had become critically acclaimed work.

Their first pieces were modelled snippets of the prison – little caged lightbulbs, peepholes, window bars – which Stan and Carlos moulded and replicated with metal and plastic and stone. They painted and coloured and sprayed and varnished these models with such care that although disjointed from their natural environment, they were almost indistinguishable from the real thing. Then they asked permission to send them outside. After checking that the objects were not repositories for contraband, the prison authorities granted them this privilege.

Stan and Carlos wrote to the major London art exhibitors, explaining their idea. Soon enough, they received a letter from a prominent exhibitor based in Shoreditch, who said he'd like to see a few pieces. This astute individual recognized them from the wake of publicity that had followed the 'Anonymous' affair. He was aware that they had accidentally provided the subject matter for *Untitled: Attempts to deconstruct the system fall short (1)*, and he knew that their names were close enough to the piece to be anointed with some of the hype it had generated.

Along with their work, Stan and Carlos sent him detailed instructions on how to display their little sculptures. They supplied a blueprint of their prison environment, and marked out where the objects should go. In effect, they were recreating their capture externally, showing their jail to the world. The walls were missing, as were the guards and the inmates, but Stan and Carlos knew that people would fill in the gaps. They were sending out cues of imprisonment. They were unfolding a map of despair.

'Prisons of the mind!' shouted Carlos. 'We shall make prisons in people's minds!'

'Let them see how they like it,' said Stan. 'Let them see how they like it on the outside.'

When the exhibitor set out their artwork in his small but streetwise gallery, the space took on a potent and horrible tone. The origin of the sculptures, and the form of their layout, conjured the ghost of a prison from the floor. Even without walls, observers were all too aware of the dimensions of the imaginary cells and the tiny little windows above them. The exhibitor asked Stan and Carlos to keep the stuff coming, and put an aerial photograph of the prison site up in the lobby. The show, which he called 'Bird', thus grew every week, and as it grew, word of it grew. People heard about the idea, and told others, and soon the show was so big that Stan and Carlos couldn't keep the models coming fast enough to satisfy their repeat attendees. Having noticed that the prison guards were now very trusting about their packages, and giggling to each other at the joke, Stan and Carlos began to prise off real pieces of the prison and send these out instead.

'Art is life,' said Stan.

'And life is art,' chuckled Carlos.

At first no one noticed the real objects amongst the fake ones. Then a drunken stockbroker pulled a doorhandle out of its setting and discovered he was holding the real thing rather than a model. The secret was out, and the show's attendance levels doubled in one week. Speculation was rife. Were Stan and Carlos attempting an inverse escape? Were they smuggling out the prison rather than themselves? And when released, would they start sending it back in again? The show now seemed a brilliant observation on man's frustrated quest for his freedom. 'Bird' was a critical hit.

The prison management, who eventually noticed that bits of their building were disappearing, put a stop to Stan and Carlos' packages and extended their sentence to twenty-four months as punishment for such disobedience. Stan and Carlos didn't care. They were back on the artistic map.

When they were asked to contribute to 'Art Schmart', Stan and Carlos embarked on a more disturbing and subversive work than their forged prison equipment. They cut a deal with their exhibitor to sell the contents of 'Bird' (which, needless to say, went for a high price), and then used the money to bribe the guards into letting them have a video camera. After painstaking negotiations with each of their fellow inmates (and the use of a large proportion of their profits) they managed to convince them to be filmed in a variety of prison locations.

'We realize you are scary men,' Carlos announced to the convicts, 'but we will make you *famous* scary men.'

'To help us, please look inside yourselves,' Stan urged them. 'We need to feel your pain.'

When they had finished with the prisoners, Stan and Carlos sent the resulting tapes out to their exhibitor. They asked him to make the footage into a series of video installations for 'Art Schmart'. Their title was *Scenes from your neighbourhood prison*.

The first of the three grainy installations showed

five convicts taking a shower. Each of them was obviously aware of the camera. They soaped themselves nervously, and tried to pretend everything was normal, but with genitals hidden by shy paws and shaven heads bowed in embarrassment, the convicts looked dehumanized and afraid, like laboratory rats awaiting their fate. The installation was uncomfortable to watch, and the viewer was forced to take some responsibility for the incarceration of the threadbare men before them.

The other two installations were similarly disturbing. One showed a huge and angry prisoner staring out from behind the bars of his cell, his tattoos twitching in the shadows. Nothing happened for five minutes or so, and in that time the observer went from fear of the convict to pity for his impotency of action. The last film showed a gang of four men intimidating a smaller man in a storeroom. It was obviously a group of convicts administering a reprimand to a disobedient lackey. The observer expected a rape as part of the punishment, or at least a beating. Their image of prisons demanded it. When the man got off with verbal abuse, the observer was left questioning their own morality.

Having submitted their work, Stan and Carlos patrolled the art columns of the national press, awaiting the opening of 'Art Schmart' with great enthusiasm. Surprisingly, so did many of the prison inmates, who wanted to see if their efforts would be appreciated by the outside world.

*

Nedrina Burchill, the final contributor to 'Art Schmart', had achieved national fame after her graduation from the Lightschool. In her first solo show, Nedrina continued her study of evil by exhibiting a spent reactor rod from the core of a nuclear power station, which was encased in eight feet of treated glass to contain the radiation. She followed this up with a transcript of the orders to bomb Hiroshima, displayed in a small candlelit shrine and surrounded by pots of fresh sushi. The sushi soon cooked in the candlelight, and had to be replaced twice a day.

Nobody could decide whether Nedrina's art was any good or not, but it was generally agreed to be profoundly affecting when one saw it, and therefore always worth showing. Nedrina had crept up the list of must-sees to a point where no show attempting to define British modern art was complete without her. She was still working on her piece for 'Art Schmart' a month before the show was due to open, and although no one had seen it, it was reputed to be her most troubling work yet.

The artists who were contributing to 'Art Schmart' had received so many column inches between them that the organisers decided to promote the show using only the faces of their young stars. After all, Stan, Carlos, Jessica and Nedrina were now highly recognizable brands in their own right. There was no need to invest them with further notoriety.

Standing in Trafalgar Square at two in the morning, surrounded by the drunk and the mad of London, Dave tried not to look at the faces leering at him from the side of the night bus. He didn't recognize Nedrina, and he was pleased for Stan and Carlos, but he could not bear to look at Jessica's enormous grin. Most of all he could not bear to look at her eyes. The look in her eyes was so familiar. The last time he had seen that look, it had convinced him to surrender his installation into her care. The last time he had seen that look, he had thought it might be genuine. The last time he had seen that look, she had been about to kiss him.

Dave passed under Jessica's eyes and paid his fare.

Chapter Eighteen

Let them wear trainers

When he got to work on Monday morning, Dave was still reeling from the shock of Friday night. He had spent the whole weekend stewing about Jessica, and his eyes were thick with the insomnia this torment had spawned. Cursing the world, he dragged himself through Laurent Création's shiny glass lobby and stumbled upstairs to the creative department.

Once through the glass doors, Dave headed immediately for the kettle, but Marcy was too quick. He was intercepted by the water cooler.

'Take this to all creative teams,' Marcy said, holding out a large stack of photocopies. 'Do it now. Deadline is Wednesday.'

'In a minute,' said Dave, who was still thinking about Jessica.

'What did you say?' asked Marcy.

'Can't I do it in a minute?'

'You have something more pressing to do?' Marcy asked him pointedly. She crossed her arms. They were the size of Dave's legs.

'I just need a minute,' said Dave. 'Sorry, I don't

mean to be rude, but I didn't sleep too well. I need a cup of tea.'

Marcy tightened her arms. They made a cracking noise. 'Your cup of tea is more important than this brief?'

Dave's survival instincts began to kick in. 'Er, well, I suppose it could wait,' he said.

Marcy stood and stared at him, inhaling noisily. 'I'm sure it could,' she said, with monstrous emphasis.

'I can have a cup of tea later,' said Dave.

'Right then,' said Marcy.

Dave took the stack of photocopies, tucked them under his arm, and trotted off through the office.

Thankfully, the task Marcy had given Dave was so mundane that it could be completed on autopilot, leaving him free to entertain himself with dreams of Jessica's downfall. He had spent his weekend constructing such fairytales, and they looped happily round his head as he ferried his paper cargo between ports. Dave's fantasies were varied and colourful, containing a range of unpleasant comeuppances for his evil nemesis. However, they all had one thing in common. They all had the same ending. In this grand finale, Jessica was always unmasked as a fraud, and he was always identified as 'Anonymous' in her place.

Dave had been desperately trying to forget about Jessica for the last sixteen months. When she had taken the credit for his installation, his feelings had been too painful to confront. He had been so shocked by the strength of his anguish that he'd buried all recollections of the incident in a far-flung corner of his memory. He had also sworn off modern art completely, not wanting to revisit the emotional maelstrom that Jessica had set in motion. During the months that followed, he had attended no modern art shows, read no newspaper coverage of them, and watched no television debates about the issues that they raised. For over a year Dave had been trying to forget about the whole thing. For over a year he had hidden from his anger.

Now that Jessica had been thrust rudely back into Dave's consciousness, he realized that by avoiding her rise to fame he had only let his emotions ferment. Now he hated her even more. He hated her for the career she had achieved on the back of his efforts. He hated her for the way she smiled on the posters for 'Art Schmart'. He hated her stolen happiness. He hated her success.

More than anything else in the world, Dave wanted to take back what Jessica had stolen.

Even in his most optimistic moments, he was wise enough to appreciate this as impossible fantasy. There was no way of proving Jessica's theft of his work. He had no evidence of her crime, and even if he did, it would be too late for him to use it. From the springboard of his installation, Jessica had established herself as a successful artist in her own right. Now more than ever, any fuss Dave made would look like sour grapes.

'Bitch, bitch, bitch, bitch, bitch,' he muttered, jogging from one desk to another.

He was so preoccupied with his vengeful thoughts that he entirely failed to notice the impact his deliveries were having. Most creative teams normally found some minor but painful task that needed doing when they encountered him, like mocking up a colour board or typing out a memo. Today they seemed to forget he was there as soon as they read the header on the brief. Some of them even went a little pale, and most disappeared in a great hurry, leaving cups of tea and coffee smoking on the sideboards.

It wasn't until he got to Bill Bones' desk that Dave realized what he'd been passing out.

'Bloody hell,' said Bill when Dave passed him the brief. 'Bloody, bloody hell.'

Dave peered over Bill's shoulder at the brief he had just delivered.

'Ranna Corporation – The Challenge Ahead,' he read out loud. 'Is that Ranna who make trainers and things?'

'Ranna who probably make more sportswear than anyone else in the world,' said Bill. 'Bloody hell.'

Dave scanned the rest of the front page. A number at the bottom caught his eye. 'Blimey,' he said. 'Is that the budget?'

Bill looked at the number Dave was pointing to. It was very long.

'Looks about right,' he said with a small whistle. 'About right for one of the biggest brands in the world that is.' He glanced back at Dave. 'Look, I'm not one for self-deprecation, but why exactly have they given this to me? Philippe should be doing it. It's too important for anyone else.'

'Um, everyone is getting it,' said Dave. 'I think they want everyone to have a go.'

'I see,' said Bill. 'Well, Philippe can fuck off if he thinks I'm going to write his international pitch ads for him.' He crumpled up the brief and tossed it over his shoulder. 'I have a press campaign for osteopathic mattresses to be getting on with.'

'You really don't want to have a go at it?' asked Dave. As someone who was never asked to write advertisements, he couldn't understand why Bill would pass up the chance to do so.

'Fuck no,' said Bill. 'What do I know about sportswear? Anyway, Philippe will hate whatever I come up with. He's just too lazy to do it himself.'

'But I was told to hand it out to everyone,' said Dave.

'Well, not to me,' said Bill. 'You can have a go if you want, but I don't want anything to do with it. Tell Philippe to piss off.'

'OK,' said Dave, picking up the crumpled brief and leaving Bill to his Monday morning mood.

If Bill had bothered to read the appendix pinned to the back of the brief, he would have discovered that the Ranna brand was in fact the third largest in the world, having recently been promoted from fourth position when a large soft drinks manufacturer accidentally bottled one of its workers. He would also have been assured that the Ranna Corporation were indeed the largest sellers of sports equipment and apparel in the world, and that this was true whether they were ranked by volume sales, market capitalization or overall brand value.

It was brand value, the last of these measures, that the Ranna Corporation actually considered important. The board of the Ranna Corporation had recently employed a massive number of very clever people to value its brand, and had been told that the brand itself would generate revenue of more than twenty-five times the company's fixed assets if they sold it tomorrow. There was great relief when this fact was reported, for the Ranna board members were an extremely paranoid group of people. Having cuckolded Nike, Adidas and all the other sportswear brands in the space of a few years, they were permanently on guard for a reciprocal reversal in fortune.

In the first year of the new millennium, Ranna, which was then a medium-sized Japanese clothing label, had decided to move into sportswear. Researching the market to establish a point of entry, Ranna executives found themselves faced with a nightmarish frenzy of overnight trends. The data spoke of white sports shoes and hooded nylon jackets, which though popular only a few years before, had turned up their toes overnight. Brown ankle boots and cycling jerseys had been similarly short-lived crazes, and were now nowhere to be found. The sportswear market was a bloodbath. Fortunes within it could change at the drop of a sweatband. Its combatants were at a permanent disadvantage to fashion.

The Ranna board therefore decided that if they were to enter the sportswear arena, they would need to be more adept at meeting consumers' fickle demands than their erstwhile competitors. In order to achieve this objective, they avoided the acquisition of manufacturing interests and simply outsourced all their goods. This way, when the preference changed from shoes to sandals they could simply dump their shoe manufacturer and appoint a sandal manufacturer instead. They just sewed the Ranna brand logo onto whatever consumers wanted. They never had to waste time retraining workers, and the only people who suffered at the fickle hands of fashion were the manufacturers.

This strategy was the key to Ranna's success. Unencumbered by the albatross of production, they could concentrate all their efforts on honing a successful young brand. Within a few years, they had overtaken the long-standing leaders of the market, who were unable to keep pace with their movements. The Europeans and Americans were still *making* sportswear, and that, in the end, was their downfall. They spent too much time trying to *drive* fashion, and not enough time hanging onto its tailbar. Ranna, by soaking the airwaves with their advertising and sponsoring all the greatest athletes, soon edged them out of contention.

Of course, Ranna's lack of production capacity meant they did not actually own much, and their brand was therefore the only thing that mattered to them. Without the Ranna brand to rely on, consumers might realize that they were buying hastily-manufactured attire that was basically inferior to that of competitive companies. This simply would not do. Ranna's brand advertising had to be the best in the world. After all, they were charging premiums that were the highest in the world, so they had to have the best brand in the world to justify them.

The brief that Dave held in his hands was for a new advertising campaign for the Ranna brand.

The Ranna brief had been written by some of the most senior account planners within Laurent Création. Account planners had the job of balancing the ludicrous wants of the client with the whimsical desires of consumers. In liaising between these two armies, they garnered enough information to write a coherent creative brief, and it was this brief that the creative teams then used to write the advertising. At one time, agencies had tried including creative teams from the outset, but this had not worked very well at all. On the whole, creatives didn't like consumers, and had no desire to interact with them on a regular basis. As for clients, their enormous capacity to confuse everybody, including themselves, meant that creatives either fell asleep whilst talking to them, or reached such a level of perplexity that any subsequent advertising they wrote was completely unconnected with the matter at hand. After many failures it had therefore become accepted that creatives couldn't do anything but create, and agencies decided it was a bad idea to expose them to the rigours of the real world. From that point on they were kept in ignorance of all but a few vital facts, and mothered like infantile geniuses. For obvious reasons, the creative fraternity were quite happy with this way of doing things. They awaited the briefs from the planners, and avoided pretty much everyone else.

Dave had to admit that Laurent Création's planners had done a good job of simplifying the Ranna brief. It was clear. It was lucid. Though he didn't have any experience of actually writing advertisements, even he thought he understood what was required.

Sitting on the toilet after completing Marcy's errand, Dave read and reread Bill's copy of the brief. As he smoothed out the crumples his friend had inflicted, strange reactions began to occur in his brain. His anger with Jessica mixed with the desire for Philippe's approval, and these emotions spat and discoloured as they fused together, coalescing into a ball of artistic urgency. Frustrated creative energy suddenly felt like it was leaking from every pore. The purity of the brief broke through the dam that held back Dave's feelings. Its simple challenge inspired him to fight back. To prove everybody wrong.

'I'll show them,' he said to the cubicle walls. 'I'll show them a creative assistant.'

Dave made a decision. He had denied his ambitions for well over a year. He had bowed his head for too long. He would use the brief to escape the jail in which he was locked. He would write some ads for the Ranna campaign to prove his artistic worth. In fact, he would write the best ads that anybody had ever seen. Then Philippe would finally approve of him. Then, as a creative individual in his own right, he could face Jessica proudly, condemning her as the petty thief he knew her to be.

Chapter Nineteen

There's a hole in my bucket, dear Liza, dear Liza

Though the Ranna brand was now the pre-eminent sporting label in the world, it was constantly and nervously aware of smaller sportswear brands, who might repeat its antics of a few years previously and become Davids to its Goliath. With their streetwise typography and hip little logos, these baby brands found it easier to be 'cool', which was a word that filled the mouths of the Ranna board members with terrified bile.

It had happened in aerospace, it had happened in jeans. It had happened too many times to count in cosmetics and toiletries. It had happened in finance. It had even happened in government. The larger, dominant brand in the marketplace, happily outlaying budgets to maintain its place at the top, suddenly found that a smaller adversary had become much cooler than it was. At first the larger brand scoffed at the threat posed by such a rodent-sized rival, but soon they began to notice sales falling off, margins dropping, and stockists avoiding calls. A loss of standing in the cool stakes was a wound to the stomach, slow but inevitably fatal. Market-leading brands which allowed themselves to become uncool ended up twitching on the stockmarket floor.

The Laurent Création planners, when they went to see the board of the Ranna Corporation, found a market-leading brand which wanted to secure its position at the top. The Ranna board members showed them brand wheels, brand pyramids, brand hexagons and brand character maps. They showed them pictures of the ideal Ranna customer. They showed them financial reports and predicted sales curves. They even showed them confidential new sponsorship contracts and future business plans.

Through the mist of information they were given, the planners saw only one thing; a brand that was the biggest of its kind in the world, and thus vulnerable to attack from smaller, cooler, competitors. People didn't buy the Ranna brand because it was attached to the best-looking sportswear. And they didn't buy the Ranna brand because it was the most expensive. They bought it because it was the coolest. If a nimbler brand took that mantle from Ranna, then their empire would crumble overnight.

The creative brief that the planners wrote, the brief that Dave had delivered to the agency teams, was therefore very simple.

Why are we advertising? the brief asked.

'Because if we didn't, people would stop buying Ranna sportswear and start buying another brand that *was* advertising,' wrote the planners.

Who are we talking to? the brief continued.

'Sportswear purchasers, who are typically young and male.'

What should we say to them? the brief prompted.

'The Ranna brand is the coolest in the world,' wrote the planners. Then they underlined this statement and put it in bold.

Where should we say it? the brief demanded.

'In a few sixty-second TV films, for starters.'

Anything else?

'The Ranna logo and strapline ('Game won') should appear at the end of all ads,' the planners concluded.

It was the shortest brief that had ever been produced within Laurent Création. The budget for the campaign was the largest the agency had ever seen. Admittedly, there were three pages of appendices pinned to the back of the brief, detailing the brand personality that was to be preserved and other mandatories of the campaign, but despite this attending information, the meat of the brief came down to just one sentence:

'The Ranna brand is the coolest in the world.'

Nobody receiving the brief had any doubt what they had to convey.

Dave spent Monday afternoon thinking about things that were cool while he mounted magazine cuttings onto whiteboards. This job had been given to him by an account executive, who had asked for three 'mood boards', reflecting three different life stages. Specifically, he wanted one to represent twenty-something couples, one to show an average family and one to depict the affluent retired enjoying themselves in their dotage. To complete this task, Dave had been given a large stack of magazines from which to source images, a pair of scissors, and a can of spraymount to stick his clippings down.

'Three different life stages?' he'd asked the account executive. 'What d'you need them for?'

'Not that it's any of your business,' said the executive, 'but they're part of an attempt to convince a client that he should be making advertisements for the younger consumers, rather than the older ones.'

'Oh, right,' said Dave. 'I'll do my best.'

'You better had,' said the account executive. 'I've heard about you.'

'Oh,' said Dave.

'Just stick to the obvious and try not to get clever,' said the executive. 'Don't try to interpret things for yourself. Try to produce the standard stereotypes.'

'I'll try,' said Dave.

'Don't try,' said the executive. 'Do it.'

'Right,' said Dave. 'I'll try. I mean, I'll try to do it.'

Three hours into the afternoon, surrounded by magazine shrapnel and slightly intoxicated by spraymount fumes, Dave had an idea. Whilst struggling to envisage the most appropriate pet for a pre-family couple, it occurred to him that the best way to find out what made things cool was to compose a collage of things that already were. This, he felt, would provide amalgamated insight into the nature of cool, and form an excellent palette from which he could compose advertising for the Ranna brand.

Once he'd finished his stereotypical mood boards, Dave began ravaging the magazines for moments of cool. He started off with a fashion shoot that was set in an exclusive wine bar. It was all dark fur, shades of neon and sexual motion, but he changed his mind about using it because it was probably hip and funky rather than cool. Then he came across a brilliantly shot series of images from a Swedish house made of white plastic. The photos were sleek and modern and minimalist. The house looked like the home of a god. But Dave changed his mind about using these photos. Perhaps they were cool in part, but they were mainly sleek and modern and minimalist.

Shots from advertisements were similarly con-founding. A hundred footfalls scattered across a basketball court in west-coast USA. Cool yes, but also urban and generic and derivative of too many other things. Not mainly cool. Mainly American really. And a new kind of bottle for a brand of perfume; a trans-lucent bottle in two halves, both rimmed with a collar of magnets so that one floated permanently above the other. A bottle that was quite cool, but mainly stylish and contemporary. Not mainly cool.

An interview with the star of *Two Ways to Die* and *Two Ways to Live* was not mainly cool either. It was personable and urbane and witty and a host of other things that could be associated with the word cool, or that certain people might find cool, but it didn't sum up cool. Not even the quotes that the magazine had chosen to enlarge were cool.

'They made me drink before each hangover

scene,' one quote said. 'I promise you, I'm not that good an actor, those hangovers are real.'

This was modest, and a little disarming, but not really cool.

'In the final fight scene I felt kinda sexy,' said another. 'You know, all that blood and stuff.'

This could perhaps have been described as flirtatious, but cool? Definitely not.

Towards the end of the day, Dave began to wonder if this was what Julius felt like. Like he was chasing an infinitely small mouse round an impossibly large kitchen. He hadn't unearthed one image or quotation that illustrated what it was to be cool. Nothing could be described as cool without being lots of other things as well. To be cool, it seemed, was not as easy as it looked.

Eventually, Dave decided that looking for cool things in magazines was not going to work. He delivered his mood boards to the account executive and went to see Bill Bones.

'Hi Bill,' said Dave. 'Can I ask your advice about something?'

Bill grunted. He was bent over his worktop, drawing a picture of a carriage clock.

'I need to know what makes things cool,' said Dave.

'The eighties were quite cool,' said Bill.

'The eighties,' said Dave. 'Anything else?'

'Not really,' said Bill. He thought about it for a moment, scratching his hair with a pencil. 'Discos?'

he said eventually. 'Discos are quite cool, aren't they?'

'Um, thanks Bill,' said Dave.

Julius was no more helpful.

'Just use kittens,' said the research director, smiling sadly.

'But kittens aren't cool, Julius,' said Dave. 'I need to know what makes things cool.'

'If you use kittens, you won't need to be cool,' said Julius. 'Here, I'll show you.' He turned to his computer and brought up a large spreadsheet of numbers. 'See?' he said. 'Kittens.'

'That's great, Julius,' said Dave. 'But can you think of anything else?'

'No, not really,' said Julius, who was lost in a mine of depression. 'I only know things about kittens. I'm not much good with anything else.'

'OK. Kittens,' said Dave. 'Thanks, Julius.'

At the end of the day, with the folded Ranna brief still crackling in his back pocket, Dave realized he had been asking the wrong people. Philippe had issued the brief, and Philippe was going to judge the responses, so how would Philippe define cool? With a sinking feeling, Dave realized that the only way to find out was to ask him.

Though Dave desperately wanted to impress Philippe Laurent by cracking the Ranna brief, he had no intention of revealing this to his employer up front. He knew that Philippe would not want him working on the Ranna campaign. The creative director's opinion of him was far too low. Thinking about his options, Dave realized there was only one way he could obtain Philippe's assistance. He would have to pretend he was asking questions on behalf of one of the creative teams. Then Philippe might give him the answers he was looking for.

Steeling himself to carry out such an enquiry, Dave made his way towards Philippe's office.

Before Dave could request an audience with Philippe, he had to get rid of Marcy. Philippe's terrifying PA defended her boss's privacy with an almost biblical enthusiasm, and she was unlikely to consider his request important enough to warrant admittance. Dave, however, had been surviving in an office with Marcy for some time, and knew how to guarantee her brief absence.

'Can I get you a coffee Marcy?' he asked politely.

Marcy frowned at him. 'All right,' she said. 'Strong with lots of milk and three sugars.'

'Milk and three sugars,' Dave confirmed.

'Milk, three sugars and strong.'

'Right,' said Dave. 'Strong and lots of milk with two sugars.'

'*Three* sugars,' said Marcy, glaring at him.

'Right. Three sugars and milk.'

'*Lots* of milk.'

'Lots of milk,' repeated Dave moronically. 'How many sugars again?'

'Oh for fuck's sake, I'll do it myself,' said Marcy, stomping off to the coffee room and leaving the path to Philippe's doorway unguarded.

Once Marcy had gone, Dave took a deep breath. This was his big chance. His chance to gain access to the creative circle of advertising. He ran through his list of questions and the story that allowed him to ask them. If Philippe gave him the answers he was looking for, he'd know how to tackle the Ranna brief. Who knew what he would come up with? Who knew what scripts he could write? Dave was excited by the potential of his plan. It was his opportunity to prove he had talent. It was his first step on the road to success.

Steadying himself on the doorframe, Dave gave a faltering knock.

'Yes?' said an irritable voice within.

Swallowing hard, Dave opened the door and stepped through.

Philippe was sitting behind his glass desk with his hands clasped in his lap. Facing Philippe, with her back to Dave, was a horribly familiar figure. She was also sitting, and also had her hands in her lap.

'Yes?' said Philippe.

'Um,' said Dave, staring at the back of Jessica's head.

'Yes?' said Philippe again.

Dave could see an 'Art Schmart' brochure on Philippe's desk. The figure that was so obviously Jessica had not turned around. She was waiting for Philippe to finish his exchange.

'*Yes?*' said Philippe.

'Oh. The Ranna briefs have all been delivered,' said Dave. 'Deadline of Wednesday.'

Philippe raised his eyebrows at the obviousness of such a report, but before he could issue a reply, and before Jessica could turn round to see whose voice she'd recognized, Dave had shut the door.

Chapter Twenty

The shock of the nearly new

Dave sat on the tube going home. It had not been a good day.

The tube was full of powerful commuter odours, wet with sweat and designer fragrance. Dave had to stand up all the way home, which was not unusual. The man standing in front of him was trying to read a copy of the *Financial Times*, which clashed horribly with the red pinstripes of his shirt. To avoid the embrace of the companies and markets section, which hovered dangerously close, Dave leaned sideways and read the advertisements pinned to the walls of the carriage.

Jessica stared back at him from an 'Art Schmart' poster.

'Bitch, bitch, bitch,' he muttered to himself.

The *Financial Times* reader hurriedly withdrew the offending sections of his publication from Dave's proximity.

'Cow, cow, cow,' said Dave.

With a cautious glance in Dave's direction, the man raised the city listings pages to ward off a potential attack.

When he thought about it, Dave was not surprised that he had chanced upon Jessica in his boss's office. He knew that Philippe was involved in the modern art market, so it did not seem unlikely the two should know one another. Dave assumed that Jessica had been seeking sponsorship of some kind for 'Art Schmart', or perhaps even for the show after that. Given Philippe's interest in Jessica's profession, an alliance between them was an obvious possibility.

'Wouldn't be chatting to her if he knew what she was like,' muttered Dave. 'Manipulative slag.'

The city listings section quivered in anticipation of random violence.

Dave's home in London was as uninspiring as his job at Laurent Création. He lived on a disused trawler, converted to near-habitability by an enterprising fisherman. At the end of his maritime career, this bluff old sea-trout had found himself pining for the east-end gutters of his youth. Crossing the North Sea for the last time, he therefore flogged his vessel up the Thames and left it to rot in one of the many creeks that wound their way inland.

Stumping ashore, the fisherman located a pub that was open and started to drink himself to death. However, he had not accounted for the horrors of inflation (having kept his life savings in a metal tin aboard his boat) and discovered that he was short of the funds required. With nautical shrewdness, he therefore applied for a docking permit and began to advertise his trawler as 'Bargain real estate in a prime waterfront location'. Most of his early applicants were put off by the sinister location, lack of heating and pervasive smell of mackerel, but this didn't bother the fisherman in the slightest. He knew that someone more desperate would eventually turn up.

Dave didn't like living on a gradually-sinking trawler in the arse-end of London, but it was cheap, and that was all that counted. Anyway, he had habituated to the smell, and there were coping strategies in place for the recurrent blackouts and septic leaks. Over time, he had even become used to the terrible gurgles that arose from the water after dark.

Leaving the station, Dave padded carefully through the alleyways to his home. The trawler was docked behind a crusher's yard, and his path was walled with stacks of creaking metal. The ghosts of machinery groaned at Dave as he hurried past them.

The gangplank to Dave's trawler was guarded by a dog, thoughtfully installed by the fisherman to prevent uninvited guests from boarding. However, this well-intentioned strategy had gone somewhat awry. Briefed to provide a savage guard dog, the local pound had seen an opportunity to offload their most notorious inmate – a slobbering demon distilled from a hundred breeds of killer. This poor animal, whose lineage had driven it quite insane, was called Ringo, and it attacked anything it saw, including the tenants it was supposed to protect.

Every night, Dave and Ringo danced the same little dance.

'Hey, Ringo,' said Dave, approaching the furry menace with caution.

Ringo's lips spasmed backwards.

'Easy, Ringo,' said Dave.

Ringo bared his teeth, and ropes of drool belayed down from his mandibles.

'Good boy, Ringo,' said Dave, taking a few steps towards the terrible animal.

Ringo tensed his legs. They were full of lumps and muscle.

'Come on then, Ringo,' Dave whispered temptingly. 'Come and get me.'

Ringo rolled his eyes and lunged forward. Dave waited until the dog was nearly upon him, and then took three short steps backwards. Ringo's chain caught him round the throat just as he was about to make contact with Dave's legs, and he was snapped tautly in place. He clopped his teeth together and growled at Dave's knees.

Very carefully, Dave began to walk sideways, being careful not to stray into range. Ringo moved with him, his circumference still set by the chain. The two of them crabbed their way leftwards, towards an old metal post in the dirt, and as they moved past it, Ringo's chain wound around its base.

His safety ensured, Dave walked past Ringo and then turned in behind him towards the gangplank. Ringo was unable to work out that he had to go back around the post if he wanted to eat Dave for dinner, and he strained at his bindings desperately, covering the ground with his spittle.

Once inside the boat, Dave made his way to the galley for a well-deserved cup of tea. There he found Vartak, who was looking at the pictures in yesterday's paper.

Vartak had appeared at Dave's front hatch some months earlier, completely unsolicited and largely unwashed. After Dave left Newcastle, Vartak had received an invitation to a dinner celebrating 'the diversity of our city's ethnic background'. The title of this event had thrown him into a panic, and convinced it was part of an elaborate plot to remove him from the country, he had started searching for escape routes. Dave had left a forwarding address in London in case there was any post, so Vartak packed a dustbin liner and got on a bus.

Dave had actually grown quite used to having the old man around, and no longer resented his presence on the trawler. It was nice to have some company, however cantankerous it might be, and in the nasal cacophony of their living quarters, Vartak's personal hygiene could go unremarked upon. While Dave was at work, the Polish pensioner normally stayed at home and watched an old black-and-white TV that sporadically produced a visible picture. He lived on bananas and tinned ravioli, which Dave was occasionally sent out to acquire.

' 'Ello,' growled Vartak as Dave clambered into the galley.

'Hi, Vartak,' said Dave. 'How was your day?'

'Bad,' said Vartak. He selected a venerable looking banana from the fruit bowl. Its skin was black and mottled.

'Really?' said Dave. 'Why's that?'

'Rats,' stated Vartak. He was in the midst of a war with the trawler's rodents, who occupied a significant portion of the vessel.

'Are you winning yet?' asked Dave.

'No. Heavy losses. They've taken the hold.'

'Oh dear. Still, I'm sure you put up a good fight, didn't you?'

'Did,' said Vartak. 'Cost 'em dear.' He bit off the stalk of his banana.

'And tomorrow?' asked Dave. 'What are you up to tomorrow?'

'Battle of the afterdeck,' said Vartak. 'Bite the beast in its lair.'

'Isn't that where they nest?' asked Dave. He had avoided visiting the deck for some time. It was the rats' stronghold.

' 'Tis,' said Vartak bluntly. He reached beneath the table and produced a hosepipe attached to a gas cylinder. 'They won't expect me up there. Won't expect me at all.'

'Blimey, Vartak, be careful,' said Dave, eyeing the handmade flame-thrower nervously.

'Don't worry,' said Vartak. 'Never see me coming.' He stroked the hosepipe like a snake.

'Actually,' said Dave, 'that wasn't what I meant. I meant *you* be careful. Be careful you don't hurt yourself.'

'Soldier's duty,' Vartak grunted, slightly embarrassed by Dave's show of concern. 'Element of surprise.'

'Nonetheless Vartak, do be careful.'

'Will,' said Vartak. He avoided Dave's gaze.

'Well,' Dave coughed. 'I'm sure you know what you're doing.' He suddenly wanted to change the conversation, and was about to tell Vartak how bad his day had been too, when it chose to get worse.

In the centre spread of Vartak's newspaper was a huge photo of Jessica. The caption read 'ART GETS SCHMART page 16'.

'Can I have a look at that please, Vartak?' Dave asked.

'Can,' said Vartak, handing over the pages.

With trembling fingers, Dave took the paper and flipped to page sixteen. It was an article about the artists who were contributing to 'Art Schmart'. The reporter lavished praiseworthy adjectives on their past creations, and spoke of even higher hopes for those to come. Jessica received the most column inches, and included in the homage was a quote from Philippe Laurent. His comments stood out from the text in arrogant italics.

'*She is the best of her generation. She examines talent with talent. She makes art about art. She is the brightest star we have produced since Hockney.*'

Rage bubbled in Dave's stomach as he read Philippe's praise for his adversary.

Then he had an idea.

*

On Tuesday morning Dave called in sick. Nobody ever seemed to mind when he called in sick. Marcy took the message with her usual aggressive solemnity, and assured him that Philippe had no further use for him until Wednesday afternoon, when the responses to the Ranna brief were due for collection. Dave refused to be depressed by this further endorsement of his uselessness. He was eager to put his idea into practice.

Dave's idea was simple. Philippe, he knew, liked modern art. Therefore, he reasoned, Philippe thought modern art was cool. Ergo, if he wrote advertising for Ranna that was as cool as the modern art Philippe liked, it could only be received by his temperamental employer with the greatest admiration and respect. Admiration and respect were the two things that Dave most wanted from Philippe Laurent. Especially since Jessica had them already.

Faced with the challenge of competing with Jessica for Philippe's affections, Dave now regretted his long artistic hibernation. Leaving the trawler early, he carried a pen and some notepaper. He was going to bring himself up-to-date.

Dave packed a great deal into his day off. He not only went to all the modern art shows he could find, but also bought several books on the subject, which he read in the contemplative spaces that galleries set aside for the passage of aesthetic reverie. Overall, he enjoyed himself immensely, though he was careful not to read anything that concentrated on Jessica's back catalogue, and he avoided her exhibited work with great care.

Dave saw the 'Bird' show, which he liked very much, and not just because he was pleased that Stan and Carlos had finally gained some recognition. He also saw some of Nedrina Burchill's work, which he liked less and found more disturbing. In particular he was affected by a piece Nedrina had done on paedophiles. The piece was a field of miniature gravestones, about the right size for children. On each gravestone, in place of the conventional name, date and quotation, was an entry from the national paedophile register. The names of the paedophiles were chiselled into the stonework with great care, and their addresses and the details of their illegal activities were also listed. The offences ranged from looking up child pornography on the internet to abducting and murdering an eight-year-old girl. The piece had been acclaimed by critics as 'A powerful format in which to examine both the implications and the morality of a national paedophile register.' The popular press had merely called it 'sick' and had claimed it was 'making monsters famous.' It was work like this that had established Nedrina as a name to watch, along with her incarcerated reactor rod and transcript of Japanese death.

As he was going into another gallery, Dave was handed a photo of Marilyn Monroe, dead and naked on the coroner's table. Everyone going into the gallery was handed one of these sacrilegious but beautiful images. Marilyn's gorgeous form was flawless under the bleached lights of the operating theatre. Her face was serene, and her hair was perfect. Her legs were slightly open. The artist handing out the photos said she was trying to challenge people's perceptions of beauty. The Marilyn in the photo was an actress, but she didn't look like one. She looked just like the real thing.

Dave also went to a show by an artist who was inspired by his atheism. The major exhibit in this show was a life-size Catholic confessional, inside which had been installed a ticker tape dispenser. Once the observer had climbed in and shut the door, the ticker tape dispenser whirred into life and spat out a random extract from the Bible. Beneath this quote were the words 'You are forgiven'. The confessional was popular and Dave had to queue to get in.

Dave wandered from the south bank to the northern suburbs, and from the West End to the east. He drank coffee in the gallery cafes and eavesdropped on frothy critical debates. He couldn't really afford coffee, or indeed the books and gallery tickets he had bought, but he was rich with new art and didn't want to feel like he couldn't afford things. In one gallery, they served drinks that had been whipped up with milk like cappuccinos, but which were actually other drinks in disguise. Dave liked this idea, and he tried a percolated pineapple juice, but the milk had curdled and it was revolting.

There weren't many beautiful things in the galleries Dave went to, and he only came across one artist who rendered the world in a heavenly form. This artist painted light bulbs that were switched on. They were fantastically attractive paintings. It was almost as though the artist had spilt light on the canvas. Dave didn't like them as much as the horrible things that he saw.

Some of the art Dave saw struck him as very funny indeed, though he was not always sure if this was the intended effect. One piece was a huge and intricate picture of a society wedding, rendered in oils on a gigantic wall-length canvas. Everyone in the painting was looking at the best man, who had stood up to make a speech. He looked small and panicky. His hair was slightly wispy and his buttonhole was askew. The painting was entitled *Forgotten speech*, though nobody knew whether this was referring to the best man's predicament or the forgetability of his words.

Another exhibit Dave liked was a series of stone busts. They were all wearing outrageous wigs, and some had false moustaches glued to their lips. The piece was called *The fall of western civilization*, and after a while Dave realized that the busts beneath the ridiculous wigs and moustaches were all of prominent politicians. Nobody seemed to find the busts funny except Dave.

Dave made notes throughout his day, trying to identify exactly what he was seeing. He hoped to isolate the contemporary themes. He thought that if he could distil the favourite flavours of modern art, he could surely write a very cool set of advertisements for Philippe.

*

At the end of the day, in a particularly over-the-top gallery café featuring tape-recorders on the tables so you could take a copy of your conversation home with you, Dave sat down and went through his notes.

Shocks are in, shocks are cool, he had written. *And subversion. Subversion is cool.*

On a second piece of paper he had changed his mind: *Shocks are definitely cool, but subversion is only sometimes cool as well. Perhaps shocks are only cool if they are subversive. Or subversion is only cool if it is shocking.*

Or perhaps not, he had written on a third piece of paper.

Beauty and abstraction and minimalism are definitely not cool, he had written elsewhere. *Nobody likes them unless they are shocking and subversive. Which they aren't any more.*

On a new piece of paper he had written something else. *Jokes are funny, and sometimes cool. They are cooler when they are joking about themselves than when they are joking about something else. They are not cool when they are too funny, but they are very cool when they are quite funny.*

A good idea is cool, he had written on the last piece of paper. *But only if nobody has ever thought of it before. Or if everybody has already thought of it but they don't dare tell anyone about it. That's cool too.*

Dave had also noticed, though he didn't actually write it down, that most serious artists did things in either ones or in threes. Three, apparently, was a good creative number. If there was more than one piece of art, there were normally three of them.

Dave doubted that one advertisement would be enough for the Ranna brand campaign, so he decided he should write three. He looked through his notes to find three ways of writing them that would be cool.

Pulling out a clean sheet of paper, he wrote:

1.   *A shocking advertisement (that is slightly subversive).*
2.   *A subversive advertisement (that is slightly shocking).*
3.   *A funny advertisement that is full of witty self-reference (but not too funny).*

Then he threw all the other pieces of paper away so they wouldn't confuse him in the morning.

'Right,' he said. 'Sorted.' And he went back to the trawler to get some sleep.

He dreamt about Jessica, Philippe, and advertising.

Chapter Twenty-one

Mendel's allotment

Before his days in advertising, when he was a student in Paris, Philippe Laurent acquired an elderly mentor called Monsieur Galvoche.

Philippe had been an unusual student, even by Parisian standards, and ended up reading a combination of philosophy, visual arts and business studies. His university offered no such amalgamation of disciplines, but Philippe crafted his own curriculum, adeptly hopping between the departmental highways as his fancy took him. There was some faculty muttering at his fickle academic allegiance, but he was a good student, and his father paid his fees promptly, so his habit of serial re-enrolment was generally overlooked. Philippe did his first year at university three times; as a philosophy student, then as a visual arts student, and finally as a business studies student. He never got beyond his initial year, and left the university incomplete and ungraduated.

For one reason or another, Monsieur Galvoche was almost entirely responsible for Philippe's tenuous hold on academic life.

*

Monsieur Galvoche was an artist who lived in a singularly unromantic government building just down the
road from Philippe's fashionable and romantic
student flat. The two first met at a party Philippe was
holding for some friends on the philosophy course.
Some weeks before the party, Philippe's left-wing
philosophy professor had referred to him as 'typical of
the nineteen-eighties bourgeoisie', and smarting from
this insult, Philippe decided he would hold a
bohemian rambunction in refutation of the slur. He
arranged a date with his friends and then installed a
short notice in the lobby of the government building
down the road. It invited all residents to attend, and
promised free wine.

On the night of the party, Monsieur Galvoche
arrived, somewhat dishevelled and covered in paint.
His hair was sticking up like Einstein's, and there was
a diagonal tilt to his sneer.

'I was told wine?'

Philippe poured him a glass. 'Hello,' he said. 'I'm
Philippe.'

'Monsieur Galvoche,' said Monsieur Galvoche.
'This is your soirée?'

'It is,' said Philippe.

'A promising soirée,' said Monsieur Galvoche.
'You are a student?'

'Yes,' said Philippe. 'Philosophy.'

'Ah. Philosophy is stupid.'

'It is?'

'Very stupid,' said Monsieur Galvoche. 'I can't

think why you chose it.' He slurped his wine and eyed up Philippe's apartment.

'And what do you do?' asked Philippe. 'Are you . . . I mean, do you work?'

'I work harder than most philosophers,' said Monsieur Galvoche. 'Who is this?'

He was referring to the offending philosophy professor – the one who'd questioned Philippe's left-wing credentials. The man was approaching them, glass in hand.

'This is my philosophy professor,' said Philippe. 'Professor? This is Monsieur Galvoche. He lives in the building down the road.'

'Monsieur,' said the professor, dipping his head with politeness.

Monsieur Galvoche raised a hand in return.

'Monsieur Galvoche lives in a *government* building, Professor,' Philippe explained proudly. 'Perhaps you should ask him what he is doing at the party of such a *bourgeois* young man?'

The professor did not bat an eyelid. 'This actor will not fool me,' he said dismissively. 'You have clearly dressed him for the occasion. I realize, Philippe, that you took my slur to heart the other day, but this is no way to deal with your insecurities.'

Monsieur Galvoche raised an eyebrow at this exchange.

'You wish to say something?' the professor asked him rudely.

'I would simply ask that you leave us,' said Monsieur Galvoche. 'Bourgeois though he may be, this young man's company is infinitely preferable to your own.'

'Monsieur?' said the professor, taken aback.

'Anyway, bourgeois students are a rare breed, to be cherished,' Monsieur Galvoche went on. 'They are the only ones with decent wine. I went to a party held by communists last night. The wine was dreadful.'

And, saying this, Monsieur Galvoche took Philippe's arm and steered him off in search of another bottle.

As the evening wore on, Monsieur Galvoche worked his way through Philippe's modest cellar, becoming ever more luxurious with his opinions and gathering a small crowd of onlookers around his mad hair. The latter stages of the party were marked with his performance on the piano, and he was largely responsible for the continuation of frolics till dawn.

'I shall paint you a picture,' he said to Philippe upon his departure. 'In return for your hospitality tonight.'

'Thank you, Monsieur,' said Philippe gravely. 'Will you need any materials for your work?'

'Some of your silverware, and that mademoiselle,' said Monsieur Galvoche, pointing to the best-looking woman in attendance.

He left soon after, with a final bottle of wine tucked under one arm and several pieces of antique silverware under the other. The muse he had selected followed him out, tittering at her little adventure.

*

Of the prizes Monsieur Galvoche took with him, Philippe saw only the girl again. Several weeks after his party he came across her weeping inconsolably on a kissing bench by the Seine. The bench was designed for two, and looked painfully lopsided with only one of its arms full.

'Chérie?' said Philippe, approaching the girl with caution. 'What is wrong?'

The girl choked out a few seeds of verbal hatred, and then lapsed back into her desperate sobs.

'Monsieur Galvoche?' said Philippe, who had caught the name somewhere in her phlegmy outburst. 'The old man at my party? He has not hurt you, has he?'

'He does not love meeeeee!' wailed the unfortunate beauty.

Remembering the puffy beard of the old artist, his uncontainable hair and his paint-stained clothes, Philippe wondered what other heavenly characteristics Monsieur Galvoche was in possession of to have captured the heart of the goddess before him. He resolved that he would go and find out for himself.

Monsieur Galvoche was actually quite a successful painter, a leading light of French political art since the late nineteen-seventies. He was renowned amongst the creative fraternity because of his appetite for the mademoiselles, and was thought to be rather bitter because Yves Klein had thought of making art out of naked women before him. His work focused on the surrealist expression of political ideals and structures, though he didn't really think of himself as a surrealist, often claiming that their work was only suitable for lining the bedroom walls of anxious teenagers.

When he heard the knock on his door, Monsieur Galvoche was just putting the finishing touches to a huge and twisted cityscape featuring a variety of national emblems and monuments. Cursing the interruption to his work, he threw the door wide and found Philippe standing in front of him.

'I have sold your silverware and drunk your bottle of wine,' said Monsieur Galvoche, so as to clear up any confusion.

There was a pause while Philippe wondered what to say.

'It was good wine,' said Monsieur Galvoche. 'You may come in.'

As he walked into the two-room apartment, which was bare except for a dirty mattress and a series of half-bitten candles, Philippe was confronted by Monsieur Galvoche's near-complete painting. From a distance the elements of the painting seemed perfect, but up close Philippe could see that the buildings, which each signified a different nationality, were all suffering from degrees of decay and disrepair. The Eiffel Tower was missing some of the struts from its lower arches, making it look like it was crippled, or pulling up its skirts. The Kremlin was bloated, and the hammer and sickle emblazoned on the flag flying above it were twisted round so they could look into each other's eyes. Each structure, each component, was slightly wrong in some way. The buildings were set against one another in a pattern that added further complexity and subtlety to the image. It was a painting both pleasing and worrying at the same time.

'What do you think of my painting?' asked Monsieur Galvoche.

'It's wonderful,' said Philippe, who really meant it. He was finding it difficult to tear his eyes away from the image. 'What's it called?'

'It's called *The philosopher's new clothes*,' said Monsieur Galvoche. 'I'm glad you like it. It's a shame when you paint things for people and they don't like them.'

'It's for me?' said Philippe in amazement.

'Of course,' said Monsieur Galvoche. 'I promised you a painting. I assumed you were here to collect it.'

'No,' said Philippe. 'I don't know why I'm here actually.'

'Never admit you don't know something,' said Monsieur Galvoche. 'If you're going to study art, you must always be certain of everything.'

'But I don't study art,' said Philippe. 'I'm doing philosophy.'

'We'll see about that,' said Monsieur Galvoche.

After this encounter, Monsieur Galvoche and Philippe spent almost every day together for the next year and a half. The old man, who disapproved of philosophy on the grounds that it encouraged introspection and led to a lack of confidence around women, was instrumental in persuading Philippe to repeat his first year and take visual arts. He also took Philippe to his first private view and oversaw his first artistic efforts.

'What do you think?' asked Philippe, displaying his initial attempts at the canvas.

'Don't ask me what I think,' said Monsieur Galvoche. 'Tell me how brilliant your work is.'

'But I'm not sure whether it's brilliant or not,' said Philippe. 'What do you think?'

'If you ask me that, you ask for a battle,' said Monsieur Galvoche. 'If you ask for the opinion of others, then the most confident opinion will win.'

Despite Monsieur Galvoche's repeated admonitions, Philippe remained a hesitant artist. His work showed promise, but it was inconsistent. It advanced in headlong rushes, followed by periods of personal doubt and confusion. His style was undecided and nervous. His commentary polite and unthreatening. This internal criticism had a simple set of roots; Philippe was awed by his mentor's talents, and he never quite believed that his own efforts were worthy of the life Monsieur Galvoche breathed into them.

'Should I use oils for this piece or watercolours?' he would ask the old artist.

'I would use oils, but you should do what is best for yourself.'

'But you would use oils?'

Philippe's self-doubt continued to develop throughout his time as an art student proper. As he and Monsieur Galvoche toured the artistic map of Paris, Philippe gradually came to believe in genius, the divine allocation of artistic talent. He often saw art that he quite liked, or art that amused him, or art in which he recognized craftsmanship, but only occasionally did he come across something that was so good he felt alive in its presence. Something that made him pray for the ability to have been able to produce it. Most of Monsieur Galvoche's work, needless to say, fell into this category. Philippe could not bring himself to believe that such inspired productions were merely the sedimentary layering of experience and artistic maturity. He believed that they were inherently *different* to other work. Inherently *special.* He never felt this way about his own efforts.

'I am proud of my recent work,' he said to Monsieur Galvoche, 'but I'm worried I won't be able to do better.'

'Why would you need to do better?' asked Monsieur Galvoche.

'Well, to compete with real artists. Proper artists.'

'Philippe,' said Monsieur Galvoche resignedly, 'haven't you been listening? Real artists are sure of themselves.'

By the time he was halfway through his second year at university, and therefore his first year as a visual artist, Philippe had become competent in many media. He was making progress, his tutors informed him. They were starting to see real glimmers of depth to his work. His concepts were becoming more sophisticated, his style more individual. He needn't worry about producing the one piece he would be remembered for all his life, they said. For the time being, he should just forget about other people's work and concentrate on enjoying his own.

Philippe, putting his doubts to the back of his mind, tried to do as they said. Then Monsieur Galvoche died.

He died in front of a canvas, in the studio rented for him by one of his wealthy female friends. She considered the charges on the building a small price to pay for the pleasures of Monsieur Galvoche's nightly attentions, and had happily overseen his removal from the unromantic government building to a site where she could keep a closer eye on him. It had been she who had found his body, still sitting on his stool, head bowed in front of a freshly painted canvas. The canvas was entirely white, which was odd, because she was convinced he'd been halfway through a painting when she had visited him two nights before.

Other visitors also testified that Monsieur Galvoche had been some way towards completion of a momentous work. They swore in outraged Parisian that they had witnessed his happiness with the way the piece was going. He had said it would be his best. He had specifically mentioned his pleasure in capturing the mood of his study, saying that he had stolen it exactly from his mind. He had, they concurred, been delighted with the painting. He would not have wanted it destroyed, even if it were to be forever incomplete.

With so many voices in agreement, the obvious conclusion was quickly reached: someone had erased the great man's final efforts.

There was a small media outcry at this injustice, and a demand in artistic quarters for an investigation. But, said the gendarmes, the painting was not sold, there was no owner to steal it from. Though they pursued the matter for a few days out of courtesy, they eventually dropped it altogether. Technically, there was no crime to investigate.

It was Philippe, of course, who had erased his friend's work. He had stumbled into the studio some nights before, clutching a good bottle of Chablis with which to celebrate Monsieur Galvoche's brilliance, and had been greeted by the solemn meditation of his old mentor's corpse. The painting was only half-finished, and its meaning and gravity were mocked by the empty spaces on the canvas. The loss of finality in the brushstrokes damning it, in Philippe's opinion, to mediocrity. He had cried silently in front of it for half an hour, kneeling beside his hero's quiet form.

The thought of the critics getting their hands on the unfinished painting had been unbearable to Philippe. He could hear the derision that the sight of an imperfect work from the great Monsieur Galvoche would cause. Philippe believed that his friend was a genius. A man with a God-given gift only a few possessed. He decided that he could not stand back and permit the shadow of failure to fall on such a man. He would protect his friend's perfection. He would delete this half-complete hint of fallibility. He painted the canvas white.

'Philippe?' said the gendarmes when they

interviewed him. 'Do you know anything about your friend's final work?'

'I know it would have been brilliant,' said Philippe.

'But do you know anything about the vandalism? Do you know anything about the white paint?'

'I only know what Monsieur Galvoche would have said about it.'

'And what is that?'

'He would have said at least the vandal was sure of himself.'

Philippe gave up his own art almost as soon as Monsieur Galvoche had been added to the world's foundations. He had decided to stop looking for genius in himself, and from now on be happy with finding it in others. He re-enrolled on a business course almost immediately as a sign of this new pragmatism, and when he was offered work by a French advertising agency at the end of his first year, he felt no need to return to his studies.

Of course, the fact that Philippe had been the only one to see Monsieur Galvoche's last painting in its most complete form meant that, in a sense, he owned the image. Only he could plunder his memory and steal another glance. Only he could judge it against the artist's public works. He liked this feeling, and in his private remembrances of the unfinished painting, a seed for the appropriation of genius was planted. In later years it grew into a tree, nourished by the fertile soil of his business success. Philippe did not become an art collector simply because Saatchi had been one before him. He had his own subconscious reasons for pursuing modern art.

Philippe's belief in creative genius also remained a part of him. He was never convinced that creativity could be nurtured to fruition, but continued to believe that it was present from birth, a gift from God, or perhaps the devil. He thought he saw this gift in the artists he bought and borrowed from, which is why he bought and borrowed from them. He thought he saw it in Jessica; if not in all her recent work, then certainly in the piece she'd completed under the name 'Anonymous'.

Philippe thought Jessica was that rarest of things – a true creative soul. That was why he'd invited her to his agency. He wanted her help on the Ranna pitch.

The Ranna pitch was still worrying Philippe. He was horribly aware that the target audience for the campaign were amongst the most advertising literate people in the world, and would therefore struggle to find advertising cool in any way whatsoever. To them, it was just more advertising. They had seen it all before. Philippe was also afraid that his creative teams would be unable to break out of the box of industry convention. They were used to writing polished and professional advertising, which was exactly what the target audience would expect. He needed to surprise the target audience, not conform to their expect-ations. He needed advertising that was as creative as modern art.

So Philippe had offered Jessica a guaranteed

purchase price for her next three pieces of work if she could compose three advertisements for the Ranna brief. He had been explaining this proposal to her when Dave had barged in.

Dave, in researching the messages and tones of modern art in order to write better advertising for his boss, was somewhat missing the point. Philippe did not necessarily like modern art for itself. When Philippe shopped for modern art, he was shopping for genius. In Jessica, he believed he had found it.

Chapter Twenty-two

Looking for the win win

On Tuesday, while Dave was researching modern art in the avant-garde spaces of London, Jessica stayed at home and watched the tape Philippe had given her.

Jessica's flat was in Soho, above a slowly decaying coffee bar and a strip-club with unusual opening hours. The former residents of Jessica's flat had been two elderly ladies, resident since the Blitz, who had used it as an unofficial headquarters for the surviving members of the women's auxiliary corps. Prior to Jessica's arrival these ladies had been in continuous conflict with the owner of the strip-club beneath, who traded under the name of Monty's Midnight Moments. The old ladies felt that the fleshy noises Monty's girls emitted in pursuit of their infamous Moments were a most unsuitable background to their evening games of bridge. This distinctive soundtrack was all too easily distinguishable through their kitchen floorboards, and in the event of particularly successful Moments, could even intrude on them in the dining area itself.

Citing numerous after-dinner embarrassments, the old ladies therefore took their case to court, where they successfully argued that they'd been playing bridge long before Monty and his momentous colleagues took up residence. The judge, who was a friend of theirs, informed Monty that in future he would have to schedule the culmination of all Moments before the hour of seven in the evening, and fined him several thousand pounds. Monty, who was a resourceful man, promptly re-branded his enterprise as Monty's Tea-time Treats and created a new market in pre-dinner pornography. The old ladies were now subjected to the aural consequences of Monty's enter-prize over their afternoon scones, and they soon abandoned hope and sold the property. Jessica bought it because it was in the creative heart of the city, and because its proximity to the hyper-real Monty's Tea-time Treats tended to impress her Bohemian artistic set. She was normally out when Monty's Treats were being purchased, so the noises never bothered her.

On Tuesday afternoon however, Jessica became aware of the goings-on beneath her floorboards. She turned up the TV to block off these emanations and studied Philippe's cassette. As far as she was con-cerned, a degree of orgiastic pollution was a fair price to pay for the cachet that her abode commanded in artistic circles.

The tape that Philippe had given Jessica was a comprehensive reel of sportswear advertising, cover-ing several continents and all the biggest campaigns of the last fifteen years. He wanted to show her how things had been done in the past, thinking that she would need to understand the conventions of the discipline in order to break them.

'I'm sure I don't need to tell you,' Philippe had said, 'that I'm not looking for regular adverts.'

Jessica smiled across the table.

'Well, I'm sure I don't need to tell *you*,' she replied, 'that I'm not a regular artist.'

Jessica had not had to think for very long before she accepted Philippe's offer. She was no fool. She knew that no artist, even one currently riding the voguish wave, could refuse such patronage. Philippe was becoming more and more important in the world of modern art. These days only Branson, Saatchi and the estate of Hanrik Teeson were collecting more prolifically. Anyway, he was offering her a very good deal. All she had to do was produce a trio of reasonable advertisements for him and she could relax in the knowledge that her next three pieces of art would find a reasonable price. It never occurred to Jessica that she might not be able to write the advertisements. She was a successful modern artist who worked in many different media. By comparison, she reasoned, how hard could advertising be?

Philippe's reel of sportswear advertising was a marathon of clichés. Tanned limbs boiled in the camera's eye. Logos jumped into existence. The action was played out like a ballet dance, balls floating into delicate nets, trundling over green boundaries and sailing through quiet blue sky. As she watched the tape, Jessica became mesmerized by the habits of the sporting advertisement. Teatime approached and she didn't even hear Monty's customers begging for their treats. She was absorbed in a world of cotton, canvas and leather.

As always, Jessica's inspiration flowered from stems already in place. Slowly, her mind began to make new shapes of the stuff it saw before it, reworking things for her own benefit. She wasn't plagiarizing consciously; she was just building, as she always did, on the foundations that others had laid.

The first facet of sportswear advertising that Jessica chose to focus on was the concept of a sporting hero. The ads she watched were littered with such Goliaths, and her artistic mind, trained over many years to parody and reference entrenched convention, soon went to work on them.

Using one of the blank script layouts that Philippe had given her, Jessica started to write her first ever advertisement.

'The hero'

Ranna Corporation — 60 seconds
Laurent Création

ACTION	WORDS
We open on a school football pitch. It is clearly some years ago. The haircuts and outfits look several decades old. Boys of ten are playing. The weather is bad, the pitch muddy. The coaches are watching from the sidelines. They shout instructions to the boys.	
We focus in on one particular boy. The camera tracks his movements. He is clearly not as good as the other players. He is tackled several times. He passes badly, and seems slow. The other boys shout insults at him and shake their heads.	Adult male voiceover: 'When I play, I am a god.'
A penalty is given. The coach points to the boy we have been focusing on and shouts something. The boy steps up to take the	

penalty. His teammates
watch him walk towards the
spot in silence. He looks
determined.

V/o:
'In my mind, I
never miss.'

The boy bends down to
tighten his bootlaces. We
see that he is wearing
Ranna boots. Then he stands
up and runs at the ball. He
strikes the ball badly and
it trundles to the keeper's
feet. The rest of his team
roll their eyes and shout
insults at him as he walks
away.

We fade out on the coach.

Coach:
'Hard luck
son.'

Fade in on a vast stadium
filled with screaming fans.
From the appearance of the
players it is obviously the
present day. The two teams
are well-known, their
colours mirrored by huge
fields of spectators in the
stands. The managers are
hopping around in their
dugouts and signalling to
their players. The
atmosphere is electric.

The camera focuses in on a
very famous player. He is
well known to anyone who

follows football for his
stylish play and frequent
goals. We see him spin and
turn a defender. We see him
pass with pinpoint
accuracy. We see the fans
cheer him on. He seems
unstoppable.

V/o:
'When I play, I
am a god.'

A penalty is given. The
manager points at the
famous player we have been
focusing on. He walks to
the spot. His teammates
watch him. The fans watch
him. The referee watches
him. He looks determined.

He bends down and tightens
his bootlaces. Once again
we see that he is wearing
Ranna boots. Then he stands
up and faces the ball. We
cut to the fans, who are
gripped by the moment. We
cut to the manager's face,
looking tense but
expectant. Then we cut back
to the player.

V/o:
'In my mind, I
never miss.'

He runs at the ball and
strikes it badly. In slow
motion, we see it roll
straight to the keeper's
feet.

```
Fade out on the              Manager:
manager.                     'Hard luck son.'

End frame: Ranna logo.
Game won
```

Jessica liked her fallible hero. He was so much more human than the normal ones. She also liked the undertone of favouritism that ran through the script, the implication that the right sportswear could take you to a higher level than your talent deserved. The ad was pleasantly disobedient. She would be able to stand by it when the artistic fraternity rounded on her and accused her of selling out. Her contribution to consumerist society gently mocked itself even as it conformed.

Jessica was on a roll. She wandered into the kitchen to make a cup of tea, completely failing to notice the slap of flesh arising from beneath the linoleum. Her mental engines were now mulling over another trend they had witnessed; the corporate pre-occupation with sporting involvement at the 'grass roots' level. The reel she had watched was awash with attractively down-to-earth footballers, shrugging off a heavy night with a game in the park. Fuzzy handshakes jiggled in the foreground and model communities sparkled in the back. The sponsor was '*Your greatest supporter*', or '*Just another one of the boys*'. Orange quarters and healthy-looking kids in sports jerseys were everywhere.

Jessica's artistic mechanisms decided that they could have some fun with this corporate obsession.

The obsession with being liked. Forgetting the tea she had just made, she wandered back to the front room, sat down in front of the still-playing video, and began to write.

'The friendly'

Ranna Corporation — 60 seconds
Laurent Création

ACTION

WORDS

We open on a golf course.
Three friends are at the
first tee. There is a haze
in the air, and the sun
looks like it might come
out. The three friends
laugh and joke as they
select clubs and take practice swings.

A figure appears on the
path from the clubhouse. We
cannot make out his face.
He walks towards the three
friends, who have stopped
what they are doing and are
staring at the newcomer.
The newcomer reaches the
three friends. We suddenly
get a good view of him, and
we see that he is a very
famous golfer. A winner of

major international
trophies.

The three friends look
slightly awed, but pull
themselves together and
gesture that he should join
them.

Famous Golfer:
'Do you mind if
I make up a
four?'

Friend:
'Not at all.
Please . . .'

We cut to a beach, where a
group of twenty-something
men and women are playing
touch rugby. There is
evidence of a picnic, and
some spectators are watching. They laugh and shout
encouragement to the
players.

Another group wanders into
view along the beach. Again
we see little of them as
they approach, but the
twenty-somethings stop
their activity and watch
the new group approach in
silence.

When the new group reach
the twenty-somethings we
suddenly focus in on them
and see that they are all
international rugby play-
ers. Together they are a
rugby 'dream team'.

Particularly
famous rugby
international:
'Fancy a game?'

The twenty-somethings
glance at one another in
shock, and then seem to
come to an agreement. One
of them nods.

We cut to a basketball
court, where two young men
are shooting hoops. They
are bantering as friends
do, and pushing each other
around in a familiar way.

Two tall figures walk onto
the court. We cannot see
their faces as they walk
towards the two friends.

When they are revealed, the
newcomers turn out to be
two of the best basketball
players in the world. They
grin at the two friends.

Basketball
superstar:
'Two on two?'

The two friends glance at
one another in surprise,
and then both shrug and
nod, eyebrows raised in
amazement.

We cut back to the golfers.
The famous golfer is on the
tee. He levels up to the
ball. He alters his grip.
The three friends are
watching him silently. The

281

camera passes over his
Ranna sponsored clothing.
His eyebrows flinch with
concentration. He pulls
back to take the shot.

One of the three friends
coughs loudly.

The famous golfer mistimes
his swing completely. The
ball shoots off to the
left, straight into a sand
trap. He looks round in
disapproval at the three
friends. They are all trying to look as innocent as
possible, studying the sky
or their shoes.

We cut back to the rugby
players. They are ready to
kick off, facing each other
in the sand. The twenty-
somethings eye the Ranna
shirts that the rugby
internationals are wearing.

One of the twenty-
somethings hoists the ball
into the air. It is caught
by a rugby international,
who starts to run with it.
He appears to be getting
through the twenty-
something's defence easily,

but then one of them sticks
a leg out and trips him up.
Then, whilst he's on the
floor, another kicks him
discreetly between the
legs.

We cut to the basketball
players. They are facing
off in front of the basket.
One of the superstars has
the ball. The two young men
eye the expensive Ranna
trainers that their famous
opponents are wearing.

The superstar who has the
ball looks at his teammate
and seems to signal some-
thing. Then, just as he is
about to make his move, the
two friends run forward and
pull him to the ground.

End frame: Ranna logo
Game won

Jessica read her second script. It seemed a lot funnier than the attempts at corporate altruism she saw on the screen before her. She liked it.

Tea cooled in the kitchen as Jessica's cylinders fired on the next basis for reinterpretation. Special effects from the ads she had watched blossomed in her memory. The lighting showed the muscles of a runner standing out like ropes. The arms of a baseball pitcher flew back and forth in an iridescent haze, suggesting godlike strength. The camera lied and lied.

Jessica picked up her pen again.

'The real world'

Ranna Corporation — 60 seconds
Laurent Création

ACTION   WORDS

We open on a running field.
A few metres away we can
see a lone athlete limbering up. The camera zooms in
on him. He smiles and
waves. We can see his face,
and this identifies him as
a very successful Olympic
sprinter. He is dressed in
Ranna sportswear.

We hear the cameraman shout
something to the sprinter,
who nods. He gets into the

blocks and flicks his heels
in anticipation of the off.
The cameraman steps out in
front of the camera and
snaps a shutter board. It
reads Ranna ad — take 1.

The cameraman steps back
behind the camera and we
hear him shout a countdown
to the sprinter in the
blocks.

Cameraman:
'Three, two,
one, GO!'

The sprinter flies off the
blocks and disappears out
of the range of the shot.
We hear an exclamation, and
the camera pans across to
follow him. There is still
no sign of the sprinter.
The camera pans faster.

Eventually the camera
catches up with the
sprinter. He looks like he
has finished. His breath is
freezing in big clouds as
he stands with his hands on
his hips.

Sprinter:
'Did you get
it?'

Cut to a tennis court. The
camera is focused on a very
famous player, showing his
profile. He is about to
serve. Once again we hear

the cameraman shout
something.

Cameraman:
'Ready!'

The tennis player pulls
back and swings the ball
into the air, his racquet
arm flying round to make
contact. There is a mighty
'Crack!' and the ball
shoots out of view. The
camera quickly pans left to
track the ball in flight,
but only encounters the
player's opponent, who is
looking round behind him-
self to find out where the
ball went.

Tennis player:
'Was that OK
for you?'

The tennis player turns to
the camera.

We cut to an American football field. There are a
number of players facing
each other in a snap,
apparently waiting for some
kind of signal. Then we
hear the cameraman shout
from behind the camera
through which we are
viewing.

Cameraman:
'Go!'

The ball is passed to the
quarterback, who throws it
to one of his teammates.
The player with the ball

then begins to run towards
the camera. Other players
are blocking each other
with grunts and thuds.

Just when it looks like the
player with the ball has a
clear run towards the
camera (and presumably the
end zone), one of the
players on the opposing
team breaks away and
hurtles after him. They are
both headed directly at the
camera, which is tracking
the action beautifully. As
they near us, we can see
they are both very famous
players. The action slows
and heroic music starts up
in the background.

Then, when the player with
the ball is only a few
metres from the camera, the
pursuing player leaps
magnificently through the
air and crashes into him.
They both tumble to the
ground and suddenly our
view is turned upside down,
showing sky, then grass,
then sky.

There is silence for a few
seconds. The camera contin-

ues to show sky. Then we
hear one of the two play-
ers speak to the
cameraman:

American football
player:
'Are you all right,
bud?'

End frame: Ranna logo
Game won

Jessica giggled at the refreshing humanity of her
cameraman. She threw her pen down, read all three
scripts again, and felt a gratifying rush of satisfaction
as she surveyed her work. She would ask Philippe to
send a bike for it immediately.

Downstairs, one of Monty's customers gurgled
with pleasure at the Teatime Treat he had received.
Unable to register his satisfaction over her own, Jessica
switched off the looping video and went to her bedroom to get a cigarette.

Chapter Twenty-three

Outside the box

On Wednesday morning, Dave awoke at five o'clock. The bite of sleep in the corners of his eyes made him scratch at himself, but his mind was on fire. He was stoked with artistic energy, desperately eager to get started on his advertisements. Momentarily, he had even forgotten about Jessica and Philippe. He was just excited about the prospect of creating something again.

Early in the morning, central London was like a dead spaceship. Dave clicked through a landscape of brick casing and tarmac wires. He encountered only the city's mechanics, sweeping clean its parts and hosing down its bodywork. The engine was quiet.

He approached Laurent Création in the half-light.

The security guard at Laurent Création was an old Jamaican called Amos. Cursed from birth with the disease of insomnia, Amos worked twenty-four hours a day, five days a week. His firm, Amos and Amos, only had one employee, and that was Amos. Every Monday morning Amos would come into work as Amos the day worker, take up his position in the security office, and surround himself with the grainy faces of his security monitors. There he would spend the day quietly officiating over the safety of Laurent Création. Amos could observe any corner of the building from where he sat.

At six o'clock on Monday evening, Amos would slip quietly out to the Gents lavatory, and re-emerge wearing a false moustache, ready to start the night shift as Amos the night worker. Then at six o'clock the next morning, before anybody had arrived, Amos would remove his moustache and Amos the day worker would magically reappear. This alternation went on all week.

With his continual vigil at the monitors, Amos made lucrative use of his disability. His normal sleep patterns, which consisted of thirty-second segments of darkness randomly interspersed throughout the day, went unnoticed in the security office, and through his bisected existence he was able to collect double the benefits of a working week. The use of dual bank accounts allowed him to pick up two pay packets, and he had the company pay into two different pension schemes. He also claimed two sets of travel expenses, although he never actually left the building.

Not only did the employees of Laurent Création fail to notice the uncanny physical similarities between Amos and Amos, but they genuinely believed the two men to have drastically different lives and person- alities. They said hello in the morning to Amos the day worker, and goodbye in the evening to Amos the night worker. Amos the day worker always asked the receptionists to make his tea without sugar, whereas Amos the night worker had two spoonfuls. Amos the day worker also tended to leave his top button undone, and his tie a little loose, whereas Amos the night worker was a stickler for appearances, and would not suffer such untidiness gladly.

There were differences in the approachability of the two men as well. Amos the night worker was a little brusque, it was pointed out, whilst Amos the day worker was always convivial. Amos the night worker hardly even grunted hello, but Amos the day worker would be delighted to hear tales of weekend exploits or romantic entanglements. The two men could not have been more different.

Actually, apart from the minor adjustments their creator put in place, Amos the day worker and Amos the night worker were identical, both in terms of appearance and behaviour (Amos was a terrible actor and did not lend his two characters any credibility whatsoever). The perceived differences between the two men were primarily a function of workers' changing moods throughout the day. After a pitch meeting or a day of managerial friction, employees did not want to banter with Amos the night worker, so they regarded him as an unfriendly type. The evening was not the right time to talk to the security guard. Amos the day worker, on the other hand, got them fresh from their breakfast of choice, so they remembered him fondly.

*

Appearing at Laurent Création early in the morning, Dave took Amos by surprise.

Not used to company at such an hour, Amos had decided to author his transformation at the front desk so he could watch the sunrise through the glass walls. His partially removed moustache fluttered on his face as Dave burst through the revolving front doors, and the vital feature became glued to his chin instead of his upper lip. Amos naturally assumed that the game was up, and with miserable resolve he turned to face his nemesis.

Dave's attention, however, was elsewhere. He did not notice the kaleidoscopic composition of Amos' facial hair.

'Hi, Amos!' Dave shouted as he smacked across the glass lobby.

'Mornin',' said Amos, watching Dave pelt by with a puzzled frown.

'Can't stop, Amos! I've got something to do!'

'Hope it goes well,' said Amos.

'Thanks!' shouted Dave. 'Have a good day!'

Amos exhaled his relief and refocused on his diurnal persona.

When Dave got upstairs to the creative department, he ripped a set of scripting templates from a glass cupboard and threw himself into the nearest glass seat. Placing the fruits of his research in front of him, he selected a pen from the desk-tidy.

A shocking advertisement (that is slightly subversive), advised his piece of paper.

'Shocking, shocking,' said Dave to himself. His heart was racing.

He began to write.

'Inspiration'

Ranna Corporation — 60 seconds
Laurent Création

ACTION   WORDS

We open on a locker room.
Two Adonis-like sprinters
are changing. They are
semi-naked. Their frighten-
ingly developed bodies
glisten in the half-light,
and they eye each other   Adult male
from beneath heavy eyes.   voiceover:
One has silver hair, while   'Excellence
the other has hair as black   inspires
as coal.   hatred.'

We close up on the
sharpened eyes of the
black-haired sprinter. Then
we cut to him alone, in a
public lavatory. He has a
tourniquet tightened round
his arm. He is injecting   V/o:
himself with a drug. His   'Hatred
eyes are dead and   inspires
determined.   competition . . .'

Now we are back in the locker room. We see the two sprinters pull on Ranna running tops. With a final glance at one another, they turn and walk out the door.

V/o: '. . . and competition inspires excellence.'

We cut to a slow motion shot of the race. The two sprinters are charging down the track. They are both ahead of the pack, but the silver-haired sprinter is marginally ahead of the black-haired sprinter who we saw injecting himself. The drug-taker's eyes are fixed on the man in front of him. His face screams murder.

V/o: 'Excellence inspires hatred.'

With terrible deliberate-ness, the black-haired sprinter takes an espe-cially long stride and catches the heel of his silver-haired adversary. A horrified expression on his face, the silver-haired sprinter loses his balance and tilts towards the rush-ing shale.

V/o: 'Hatred inspires competition . . .'

We cut to a montage of images. The black-haired sprinter receiving his

winner's medal. The flashing of cameras. And then a
close-up of a stretcher.
The silver-haired sprinter
is laid out on it. He is
screaming in pain. There
are flashes to his body,
which is raw with flesh.
There are white moments of
bone.

We close up on the edge of
the stretcher. Blood is
pooling, and eventually a
drop of it spills over and
floats down to the floor.
We cut to a close-up of the
splash of blood, and we can
see that it has a Ranna
logo on it.

V/o:
'. . . and
competition
inspires
excellence.'

End frame: Ranna Logo
Game won

When he had finished the script, Dave hardly paused.
This felt so good to him, so natural. He felt alive again.
Like he was doing what he was meant to do. He
grabbed a fresh template, underlined the word
subversive on his notepaper, and flew into the next
idea.

'Dreams'

Ranna Corporation — 60 seconds
Laurent Création

ACTION

WORDS

We open on a dusty football
pitch. The grass is
sporadic. The ground is
uneven, particularly in
front of goal. There is no
one on the pitch. It is
quiet and empty. We cannot
see the surrounding scenery
because of the way the
pitch is shot from above.
Only the pitch exists for
us.

Adult male
voiceover (far-
eastern
accent):
'My son has
wanted to be a
footballer for
as long as I
can remember.'

We see a group of foot-
ballers come running out
onto the pitch. They are
young, in their early
teens. We see them warming
up and kicking the ball
around on the patchy turf.
Close-ups reveal that they
are all of far-eastern
ethnicity.

V/o:
'It is good for
a boy to have
dreams.'

The kids start to play an
impromptu game. The camera
tracks them as they laugh
and tackle and dive past

one another. They are not players of a high standard, but they appear to be having a lot of fun.

V/o:
'He makes me so proud when I watch him play.'

We see that some men are standing on the sidelines, shouting instructions to the boys. We focus in on one man, who is gesturing and grinning and hollering instructions to one particular boy. The boy is wearing a dirty Ranna top, and glances over at his father constantly, seeking approval.

V/o:
'Perhaps one day he will be famous.'

The son is tackled, and looks upset, but he gathers himself together and runs after the player who has taken the ball from him.

V/o:
'Perhaps one day he will make us all rich.'

We hear a klaxon, and the camera pans upwards away from the pitch. A huge factory comes into view. We realize that this pitch is for the use of the factory workers — there is a huge Ranna logo on the side of it. The father turns away from the game and walks towards the factory. It is

V/o:
'Perhaps one day I will be making boots with my son's name on them.'

```
time for him to start his
shift.
```

```
As the man walks towards      V/o:
the gates of the factory,     'It is good for
he looks over his shoulder    a man to have
and waves to his son. His     dreams.'
son, smiling, waves back.
```

```
End frame: Ranna logo
Game won
```

By the time Dave had finished the second script, he could see fits of light through the glass walls of the Laurent Création building. The city's circuits were twitching into life. Despite this, Dave was confident that he had plenty of time. Agency creatives were notoriously unproductive in the morning, and most of them biased their hours of attendance towards the back end of the day. He doubted that he would be disturbed for a while.

A funny advertisement that is full of witty self reference (but not too funny), his notes reminded him.

'Funny,' said Dave.

His leg stopped jiggling and he began to write.

'The taking part'

Ranna Corporation — 60 seconds
Laurent Création

ACTION	WORDS
We open on a quiet warehouse of Ranna goods. The size of the place is godlike. Racks of clothing and boxes of footwear stretch out to infinity.	Adult male voiceover: 'Last year we sold more sportswear than anyone else in the world.'
Cut to a montage of new designs and products. Special effects make them look even more cutting-edge than they are. They spin and blink on the screen. Pie charts and graphs with steeply ascending lines are interspersed throughout the footage.	V/o: 'This year we plan to sell even more.'
We cut to a parade of world champion athletes, representing every sporting discipline. They stand shoulder to shoulder. Each one of them is wearing Ranna sportswear. They look like a team of superheroes.	V/o: 'Last year our sportswear was worn by more champions than any other brand.'

Cut to a series of
beautifully-shot victories.
We see the raising of
mighty arms. The snapping
of finishing tape. The bil-
low of a football net and
fans screaming behind it.
In each of these shots we
see parts of the victors,
but we cannot make out
their faces.

V/o:
'This year even
more will wear
it.'

We cut to footage of slowly
revolving trophies. They
seem to be some kind of
industry award. This
footage is spliced with
images of clapping hands
and people stood before a
stage in ovation.

V/o:
'Last year our
advertising
campaign won
more awards
than any
other.'

Cut to a trophy cabinet,
which contains an empty
space with this year's date
beneath it. This sight is
mixed with footage of a
judging panel in deep
conversation. They are
nodding, and appear to come
to an agreement.

V/o:
'This one is
even better.'

There is a palpable pause
in the speed of the film.
The screen goes blank for a
few seconds.

V/o:
'Come on
guys . . .'

```
Suddenly we are confronted
with a series of images
that epitomize losing. We
see a swimmer's hand touch
the wall a second too late.
A boxer's prone form on the
canvas. A golfer slicing      V/o:
his ball into a copse of      'It's no fun
trees. A runner giving up     when you're
the pace as he sees the       this far
leader accelerating away.     behind.'

End frame: Ranna logo
Game won
```

Dave finished his last script with an hour to spare, and by the time the office blood began flowing again, he had typed his work up on Bill Bones' computer.

At the end of the day, when Dave had collected all the responses to the Ranna brief, he put his own efforts at the bottom of the pile. They did not look out of place amongst those of the creative department, and he felt proud and excited. He could not wait to see what Philippe thought of them. He had signed the scripts in his own name. He wanted his boss to know that he had written them.

At five-thirty, he knocked on Philippe's office door.

'Come in,' boomed the voice beyond.

Dave sidled in with his shipment of creative effort. 'Here they are,' he said. 'The finished Ranna scripts.'

'Hm,' said Philippe.

'Everyone's been working very hard on them,' said Dave, pleased to be able to think of himself in that sentence.

'Hm,' said Philippe, who had not yet looked up from his papers.

'I'm sure there are some crackers,' said Dave enthusiastically. 'I'm sure we'll win the pitch.'

Philippe glanced up at him. 'I think I'll trust my own judgement on that.'

'Yes, of course,' said Dave. 'Sorry.' He had let his emotions carry him away. He had forgotten what his boss was like.

'Put them there,' ordered Philippe, gesturing to a spot on his transparent work surface.

Dave did as he was told. He was so preoccupied with the potential of his own scripts that he completely failed to notice Jessica's, which were already sitting in the spot Philippe had indicated.

He put the pile of paper down on top of them. 'Good night then,' he said.

'Hm,' said Philippe, ignoring his departure completely.

Chapter Twenty-four

The eye of the beholder

On Thursday morning, Philippe sat at his desk and read the scripts that his creative department had submitted in response to the Ranna brief.

After surviving so many years in the advertising industry and appropriating so much brilliance in the world of modern art, Philippe was very confident in his creative opinions. He seldom changed his mind about a script that he liked or disliked, and he was never prepared to debate his decisions. Philippe saw no reason to doubt his eye for genius. He had been running Laurent Création for over a decade, and his agency continued to produce some of the most original advertising in London.

Philippe did not, however, see much that was original in the scripts before him. Most were just variations on the tired old themes of the sporting advertisement. Sportsmen in Lycra completing feats of endurance and determination. Jagged brows and blocky jawlines. They were faint and pathetic shadows of ads that already existed. One creative team had suggested the use of disabled athletes, but Philippe knew it had already been done. Another team had the idea of filming combatants in a gigantic theatre, sprinters racing past the orchestra pit and footballers chipping balls into the circle. Philippe knew this had already been done as well.

There were recommendations to use the newest filming techniques. Cameras that could be attached to golf balls. Computer manipulation that could impose the action from three different sports on top of one another. Someone had even suggested the use of IMAX cinema technology. This had all been done before as well. Philippe read the scripts with increasing frustration, each one making him angrier than the last.

One set of scripts poked fun at the abilities of athletes by likening them to animals. Philippe sadly concluded that it was the best of the efforts he had seen so far. The first of these ads described a group of Olympic sprinters sitting on a quiet lawn in suburbia. They appeared to be waiting for something. Then a car drove past and they all ran after it, barking like a pack of dogs. The second script described a couple of hikers stumbling across an enormous rugby player in the woods. They stood still, staring at him in fear, and he stared back.

'Do you think it can climb trees?' one of the hikers was scripted to say.

It was no good. None of the scripts were cool enough. None of them were truly original. Underneath, they were all the same as any other sports-wear campaign. Skill and ability. Gods and miracles. Camera trickery. Visual puns. Old hat.

Philippe tore through the scripts with despondent anger, bewildered that an entire creative department felt so compelled to follow the conventions of a genre. He was furious with his employees, who could not see that they were being led by the nose.

This meant that when he came to the bottom of the pile, and to Dave and Jessica's executions, he was in the mood for a little irreverence.

Whilst Philippe was swearing in French at the shortcomings of his creative department, Dave was helping Bill Bones bind some documents. The binding machine, with strangely anthropomorphic taste, appeared reluctant to bite down on Bill's review of impotency cures. It spat out the document every time they inserted it, and kept trying to turn itself off.

'Why don't you call the technician?' asked Dave.

'Would do,' said Bill, who was now lying underneath the machine like a car mechanic, 'but the technician is twenty-three and probably wasn't even born when this old girl was made. She and I go way back. She needs the attention of an old friend.'

He fiddled with something and the binding machine menstruated ink onto his forehead.

'*Bitch!*' roared Bill.

Dave stifled a giggle. He was in a good mood. Any moment, Philippe would be reading his advertisements. He could barely keep himself from telling Bill what he had done.

'I guess Philippe will be choosing the Ranna scripts today,' he said.

'I guess,' said Bill, his voice at foot level.

'Do you think there'll be any good ones?'

'It won't make much difference whether they're good or not,' said Bill. 'Philippe will choose what he likes. That's his job.'

'And what does Philippe like?'

'Philippe likes what Philippe likes,' said Bill. 'Don't ask me to figure him out. He chooses something quickly, and he never changes his mind.'

'Well, I guess that's what he's good at,' said Dave.

'In a way,' said Bill from under the binding machine. 'What he's actually good at is being confident. I don't believe anyone can be right all the time.'

'Right,' said Dave. He wasn't really thinking about Bill's comments. He was fantasizing about the certainty with which Philippe would pronounce his scripts the winners.

'Did you see Philippe in the office this morning?' he asked Bill's legs.

'Hmm?' said Bill, eliciting shrieks of metal protest from the binding machine. 'Oh, yes. I did see him this morning actually.'

'Was he in his office?' asked Dave.

Bill reappeared from below, clutching an oily piece of the binding machine's entrails. 'Of course,' he said. 'Where else would he be?' He looked at Dave enquiringly.

'Of course,' said Dave, who realized he was sounding a little strange. He gestured to the oily lump in Bill's hand. 'Have you found the problem?'

Bill peered at the metal organ he was holding. 'Maybe,' he said. 'I'm pretty sure I put this in last time she wasn't working. Figured I could try taking it out again and see if that helps.'

In the corner, the binding machine gave a small hiccup. Then it hummed into life.

'Good girl,' said Bill.

When Marcy found them, Dave and Bill were quietly reapproaching the binding machine, trying to take it by surprise. Dave heard an aggressive cough, and looking behind him, he saw Marcy's enormous frame filling the doorway.

'Philippe wants to see you,' she said. 'Now.'

Bill raised his eyebrows at Dave and gave him a worried smile. 'You best be going then,' he said. 'I'll finish off here.'

Dave followed the gigantic secretary back through the creative department, chewing his tongue in excitement. Philippe wanted to see him! He tried to hold back a flood of images. Philippe shaking his hand, a mixture of surprise and admiration on his face. Philippe introducing him to the Laurent Création board. Philippe sitting with him in the agency canteen at lunchtime . . .

'You're looking good today, Marcy,' Dave said cheerfully.

Marcy glanced at him with hatred. 'You being cheeky?'

'No really, you look very nice.' Dave grinned up at Marcy's dour face, but she just scowled back at him.

'Hurry up,' she said, unable to figure out his motives. 'Philippe asked for you right away.'

They passed the glass alcoves of Philippe's creative teams, and Dave wondered happily which one he would be given, and whether Philippe would try to find him a talented partner to work with. Perhaps he would break with convention and allow Dave to work on his own.

'You're simply too good to be hampered by collaboration,' said the imaginary Philippe in Dave's head. 'Although if you ever wanted to work with me, you'd only have to ask.'

The best of Dave's imaginings was the replay of his discovery of Jessica's meeting with Philippe. This time he watched as Philippe rose from his chair and excused himself from the conversation. Could she, Philippe asked, give him a few minutes to spend with one of his most talented creatives? Had she heard of him? Did she by chance know of his work? Perhaps he should attend the opening of her next show so he could offer his creative opinion?

Dave grinned like an idiot and added a heraldic soundtrack to his mental utopia. He didn't even notice he was standing in Philippe's office until he heard the creative director speak.

'What the fuck is this?' said Philippe, his voice cold and expressionless.

Dave looked up, and saw that Philippe was holding one of his scripts. His pink and fuzzy future evaporated.

'What the fuck is this?' said Philippe again.

The script was the one where Dave had attempted to shock in the same way that modern art did. The one where he had flayed bare the elements of competition.

'Drugs? And cheating and lying? In a sportswear advertisement?' said Philippe. 'Are you really that fucking stupid?'

Dave tried to say something.

Philippe threw down Dave's first attempt and picked up his second. The script in which he had subverted the usual conventions of the sporting advertisement, showing how the Ranna Corporation manipulated people's lives and ambitions.

'This?' said Philippe, his voice now cracking with anger. 'What do you think would happen if the board of Ranna ever saw this? Do you think they'd think it was ironic and amusing? Or do you think they'd just sue us for libel?'

Dave looked at his shoes.

'*Well?*' shouted Philippe.

Dave tried not to cry.

Philippe grabbed Dave's third attempt. The one that satirized corporate intentions and the mantras of the advertising world. With a shaking fist, he held it aloft.

'And *this* is just a personal fucking insult,' he said. 'How *dare you*? How dare you, a graphic fucking design student, insult my agency and my career? I was writing advertisements when you were still in nappies. You should feel fucking *dwarfed* in this place. Dwarfed by the enormity of what you will *never* be able to achieve.'

Philippe was purple now, and flecks of spittle were stuck to the transparent surface of his desk.

'Sorry,' said Dave wetly.

'Get out,' said Philippe.

Dave turned and stumbled towards the door.

Chapter Twenty-five

The decision-making unit

Eddie Radacker, global marketing director of the Ranna Corporation, was not sure whether he should spend the remaining hours of his transatlantic flight being massaged or exfoliated. It was a very difficult decision, and in the end he insisted on receiving both services at once.

The area of the plane in which Eddie was seated did not appear in brochures. It was impossible to upgrade to, and it boasted a staff to customer ratio of five to one. The staff of the airline spoke of this area in hushed tones, referring to it only as 'Class Zero'.

Enjoying his kneaded and porous flesh, Eddie glanced around at the seven other passengers with whom he was sharing Class Zero. He recognized a couple of CEOs from gargantuan multinationals, a brace of dotcom billionaires, and a film star or two. There were no other marketing directors, but then there were never any marketing directors in Class Zero. They were forced to dwell in the comparative poverty of first class, sharing elbow space with the rest of the executive proletariat.

'Miss?' said Eddie to the hostess. 'Miss? Could you fetch me some French fries?'

'Of course, sir,' said the hostess. 'Would you like anything with them?'

'Some Coke, please,' said Eddie. 'And a lobster.'

Eddie's access to Class Zero was symptomatic of his importance to the Ranna Corporation. Since the company relied purely on its brand to drive sales, Eddie had to do most of the work. The other Ranna board members all kept quiet about this disparity in workload. Hailing from more conventional sportswear companies, they were quite delighted with the way Ranna was run.

Ranna's international research director, for example, was a huge fan of the company's image-based structure. Given Ranna's ability to switch manufacturers in an instant, it was impossible for him to report bad news. If he went to the board with a survey that said tracksuits were coming back in, then the board said fine, let's make more tracksuits. In his previous job at a European rival, such a survey would have been greeted with howls of disbelief because the company had just acquired a large factory in Romania that was scheduled to produce nothing but fleeces for the next five years.

The director of new product development was also a fan of Ranna's ethos. When doing his job in America, he'd been forced to *create* fashions, but now he just had to follow them. He no longer needed to design a new tracksuit that would ensure the garment's ascendancy. He just waited until the board realized that tracksuits were the sensible thing to make, and then selected the ones that would go best with the Ranna logo.

The financial director was equally overjoyed with his job spec. Unlike most financial directors, he did not have to consult a thousand different balance sheets for a thousand different factories. He just checked that the company was still in profit, fired any manufacturers who could not supply the goods that Ranna needed, and then went to lunch.

The managing director was also delighted with the tree he sat atop. His company was lauded in the financial press for its great foresight in moving away from a production-based business, profits were easy to maintain, and he was man of the decade in trading halls around the world.

There was only one job at Ranna that was difficult, and that was the job of marketing. The Ranna brand was quite literally the lifeblood of the company, and its guardianship was of unthinkable importance. In recognition of this fact, the board had employed the best brand marketeer in the business. They had employed Eddie Radacker.

Eddie Radacker's career in sportswear marketing had been long and illustrious. At the tender age of nineteen, he cut his teeth as a salesman of baseball caps in New York City, where he decided that peddling sporting endeavour was the easiest way in the world to make money. With this in mind he moved to Chicago, where he got a job as an assistant brand manager at an odd little hockey label. A few years of corporate machination followed, and when the long knives were sheathed, Eddie was the most senior member of the brand team left standing. His path cleared, Eddie set about reinventing the brand as he saw fit, and transformed it from a niche streetwise logo into an international player in the world of sporting goods. After that he was hot property, and spent the next decade skipping from one sportswear giant to another, occupying ever more senior roles.

In his various jobs and positions, Eddie had been responsible for driving most of the innovation in sportswear marketing over the last decade. He had pioneered the technique of brand/game integration, arranging for the very fabric of sports to be altered so they could better carry his message. An early triumph in this area had been new bunkers on the largest international golf courses, cut in the shape of Eddie's company logo. He followed this up with branded sand granules to put in them, and branded swathes of rough lying to the left and right. At the Commonwealth Games, he arranged for a thin sheen of residue to sit on top of the swimming pool. Prior to races, it reflected the light to show off Eddie's message, but when broken by swimmers it dissolved into nothingness, allowing the athletes to literally immerse themselves in his brand.

Eddie had also instigated the trend of branding whole sports teams, rather than just players or placards or shirts. Securing several football sides and stadiums at knockdown rates, Eddie had renamed them according to his corporate objectives and sent them flying up their respective leagues. Now there were branded clubs in almost every country that played football, vying for contention with those that retained their true provenance.

The fashion of using religious themes in sportswear advertising was also Eddie's doing. He started this movement when he dramatized the Jews' flight from Egypt for an ad about trainers. Now they were all at it, with biblical tales and Hindu parables battling it out on the airwaves. And he had been the first to sponsor an unborn child, securing a deal with two Olympic gold medallists who had recently announced their conception. These days, there was hardly a DNA line left to be sponsored.

Eddie had seen it all. Done it all. He was the father of modern sportswear advertising.

When he arrived at the Ranna Corporation, Eddie recognized the same fundamental truth as the Laurent Création planners; namely that it is very hard to be the biggest and the coolest at the same time. He called a re-pitch of Ranna's advertising account because he wanted to change the style of the campaign to address this problem, and he included London agencies on the roster because they had a reputation for creative rule-breaking, and he needed to side-step the pervasive repetition of the market. Besides, he got to fly to Britain in Class Zero, so it was hardly a chore to make the trip.

'Goodbye, sir,' said the hostess as Eddie disembarked. 'I hope your stay is successful.'

'I hope it is too,' said Eddie, and he set off for the advertising agencies of London, looking for something he had not seen before.

The efforts of the first three agencies depressed Eddie. He was proudly shown into rooms draped with the Ranna logo, and then presented with familiar scripts of bravery and heroics. Style triumphed over content. Deserts of thought were hidden by executional mirages. Smiling and nodding, Eddie began to feel a horrible sense of déjà vu.

'Nice work,' he said falsely to the first creative director.

'Like what you've done here,' he lied to the second.

'You guys may really have something,' he misled the third.

Eddie clasped the hands of the agency cheeses and promised to be in touch. Then he excused himself and made mental notes never to work with those agencies again.

On the way to Laurent Création, the last agency on his list, Eddie asked the cab driver to find him a decent cup of coffee. The driver stopped at an American style coffee bar, complete with Canadian muffins and a New York bagel machine.

'Howya doin' today?' asked the serving girl in an Essex accent.

'Pretty good, thanks,' said Eddie automatically.

'Can I get a large latte?'

'Sure thing!' piped the serving girl. She doled out his beverage and clapped a lid on the cup. 'Have a nice day!'

'Miss?' said Eddie, paying for his fare. 'Can I ask you something?'

'Yes?' said the serving girl.

'Don't you ever want to break the mould?'

'What?' said the serving girl.

' "Have a nice day" is an American phrase. Don't you ever want to say something British to your customers?'

'British?'

'Yes,' said Eddie. 'Like "cheers" or "toodle-pip" or "ta very much"?'

'Er, we're not allowed,' said the serving girl. She bit her lip nervously.

Now it was Eddie's turn to be confused. 'You're not allowed?'

'No, they teach us how to talk American on our first day.'

'They teach you to say things like "Have a nice day"?'

'Yup,' said the serving girl. 'It's all part of the brand experience.'

'I see,' said Eddie. 'Well, thanks for the coffee.'

In this frame of mind, sick of sportswear advertising and the triumph of global conformity, Eddie made his way to Laurent Création to see Jessica's scripts.

Philippe had always been likely to choose Jessica's

scripts as the ones he would present to Eddie Radacker. Not only was he predisposed to like her work because she was a famous modern artist, but he was in the perfect frame of mind to read her scripts when he picked them up, straight after ejecting Dave from his office. Jessica had provided the perfect antidote to Dave's blunt dissection of the Ranna world. Where his parodies were cruel and satirical, hers were gentle and ironic. Where he had used subversion as a weapon, she had used it as a sales device. Remembering the predictability of his creative department, Philippe had chuckled at Jessica's cleverness as he read her scripts. She was laughing at the sportswear advertisement, and the sportswear consumer, a veteran of the same war, would laugh with her. He left a message of congratulations on her answerphone, and set a team of illustrators to work on her ideas.

The meeting between Philippe Laurent and Eddie Radacker was a short one.

'I gotta warn you,' said Eddie as they shook hands in the lobby, 'if you show me another famous soccer star playing keep-it-up, or play me another "undiscovered" dance track, I'm gonna scream.'

Philippe laughed. 'You've had a bad day?'

'Terrible,' Eddie admitted. 'Does no one value individuality any more?'

Philippe laughed again. 'In fairness, Mr Radacker, you can hardly complain if they don't. You've made a lot of money encouraging them to conform.'

'Fair point,' said Eddie, 'but that street's a bit too

busy these days. I'm tired of agencies who don't realize that the world has moved on. I'm tired of being shown the same things I ran ten years ago. I'm tired of ads that are predictable.'

Philippe gestured Eddie towards the boardroom. 'I'll try not to disappoint you,' he said.

Once inside, he unveiled Jessica's scripts.

'Cool,' said Eddie.

Jessica's scripts poked fun at all of Eddie's past work, but in his current frame of mind that was just what he was looking for. He wanted the opposite of a normal sportswear campaign, and Jessica's scripts were exactly that.

Fifteen minutes later, Laurent Création was appointed as the new agency of the Ranna Corporation, and Jessica's scripts were approved for rush production. Airtime was booked for the following month, and Eddie wanted to astonish the world.

Third Half

Chapter Twenty-six

The problem with good intentions

Dave leaned forward and drove the pads of his feet into the pedals. The freezing rain made his forehead feel like cold metal. With one eye on the oily tarmac, and the other closed to the cruelties of the world, he forced the wheels of his bike through the streets of Soho.

Trying to ignore the ache of dead blood in his fingers, Dave made his way past a column of beetle-black cabs. The cabbies watched him pass, unresponsive as lions. He spied his destination through the curtain of drizzle and mounted the kerb, his feet hitting wet pavement outside the offices of a cutting-edge production agency called Citrus. The doors of Citrus were dressed in sheets of bald aluminium, and were so cold that when Dave pushed them open, he left a fingerprint of skin on the handle.

The front desk of Citrus was sentried by two young men in tightly fitting black shirts. They were wearing black nametags, on which their names were printed in a slightly different shade of black. At Citrus, it seemed, black was very much the new black.

'I'm here to collect a package,' said Dave.

Neither of the two men answered. They were both staring downwards at their monitors, which stared back from black mahogany casing.

'Laurent Création,' said Dave. He waved his plastic-coated ID in their direction.

'Rear,' said one of the men without looking up from the screen in front of him. The monitor was alive with pixels, and he appeared to be playing some kind of game. His fingers jabbed at the keyboard and faint artificial gunfire arose from beneath the desk.

'Sorry?' said Dave.

'Rear entrance,' said the man in black. He punched a key with great finality and a lonely death cry sounded to Dave's right. It was apparent that both men were playing the same game, and the one who was speaking to Dave had just shot his colleague. Dave could see a pair of upturned boots and a smoking corpse on the other man's monitor.

'Oh,' said Dave. 'I see.' He glanced round at the icy world beyond the aluminium frames. 'Can I go through the building to the rear entrance?' he asked. 'It's a bit chilly outside.'

The second man in black spoke. 'Have to go back to Dean Street,' he said. 'No way we can let a courier through the building.' He flicked a key and a triumphant note sounded from below. His eyes slid back to his electronic soldier, who had been miraculously reincarnated and who was now charging through the corridors of an imaginary fortress.

'I realize you aren't really allowed to,' said Dave,

'but isn't there some way you could make an exception? I'll have to go all the way round the block, and it really is very cold outside.'

'No,' said the first man, his fingers pattering on the keyboard.

'No couriers in the building,' said the second, his eyes facing down.

Dave gave up and went back out into the slicing rain. As he left he heard the two men in black muttering to one another.

'Gonna kill you,' said one.

'Gonna gut you like a fish,' said the other.

When Dave got to the rear entrance of Citrus, he was given two videotapes. Then he called Amos for further instructions.

'Take one of 'em to Schilling Associates in the city,' said Amos. 'Drop it for the attention of a Mr Tyson.' His warm Brixton-Jamaican accent was sympathetic. 'Then bring the other one back here and I'll fix you a nice mug of hot chocolate.'

'Where's Schilling Associates?' shouted Dave into the radio.

'Chancery Lane,' crackled Amos. 'You want marshmallows or cream?'

'Cream please,' said Dave through the weather. 'I'll see you in half an hour, OK?'

Dave had been working as a courier for the last four weeks, during which time he had come to love Amos. The security guard was the very thin silver lining around the enormous cloud that had descended since Philippe Laurent read his Ranna scripts.

After reading Dave's scripts, Philippe had decided it was time to fire him, but his director of human resources had disagreed. The PR fallout could be harmful, he explained. The boy was only young, and they had been paying him significantly less than the minimum wage for the entirety of his employment. Useless though they might have thought him, the last thing Laurent Création wanted Dave to become was a poster child for the abuses of their industry.

'It would be best to give him another job within the agency,' said the director of human resources. 'Somewhere unimportant but necessary. Somewhere where we can say we are giving him another chance but where he cannot do any harm.'

'Fine,' said Philippe. 'Just get him away from my creative department. I don't want him polluting it any longer.'

So they had given Dave a job as a courier. He had received a small increase in pay and a little tag in a plastic sheath, and they'd sent him downstairs to report to Amos, who soon had him equipped with a heavy but serviceable mountain bike and a two-way radio. He'd spent the last four weeks traversing the slopes of London, accompanied by his trusty *A to Z*.

On the surface, Dave accepted this new abuse with resignation, but as he patrolled the alleys and byways of the capital he grew pregnant with a strange new feeling. He had no basis for comparison, so it was hard for him to identify this emotional offspring, but he wondered if it might not be rebellion.

All his life, Dave had followed the advice of others. He'd done what Mr Cliffguard had asked of him, he'd done what the Dean had asked of him, and he'd done what Philippe had asked of him. This diligence had not improved his fortunes. His most creative moments seemed to fall out of something other than graft and application. They arose from frustration, ambition, and adoration; feelings over which he had little control. Dave was proud of two things in his life, *Untitled: Attempts to deconstruct the system fall short (1)* and his three Ranna advertisements. He wanted more moments like that. More moments when he could step back from his work and feel lightheaded with happiness.

So Philippe hadn't liked his ads. So what? He had liked them, and surely that was what mattered. He was tired of listening to the opinions of others. He was tired of putting himself down. He was tired of being sensible and attentive. He was finally beginning to see how Jessica had achieved so much whilst he had achieved so little. The next time the opportunity presented itself, Dave resolved that he would not hold back from doing what he wanted. He would follow his artistic heart.

Dave left Citrus, remounted his bike, and leaned into the London winter once more. He made his miserable way through the back of Covent Garden and Holborn, avoiding the migrating herds of shoppers. The way to

Chancery Lane was soaked in sheets of carbon, which he ruefully inhaled. His journey to the city was dark and clogged with affluence.

Dave tried not to think as he pedalled. He tried not to think about Jessica, and how she had ruined his life. He tried not to think about Philippe, who considered him worthless. He tried not to think about Bill and Julius, and the pity he could see on their faces. He tried not to think because there was no point. His tears would only be lost in the rain.

The offices of Schilling Associates were a shrine to commerce. The lobby was a sea of marble. An archipelago of Doric columns. The receptionist, who was elderly and immaculate, looked rich.

'For Mr Tyson?' he said. 'What is it?'

'I'm not sure that's any of your business,' said Dave, whose mood had followed him into the building.

'Young man, you'd better tell me what it is, or I shall have it opened right here.'

'It's a new advertisement,' Dave said. 'I think Mr Tyson wants to show it to the board.'

'I see,' said the receptionist, relaxing slightly. 'Well, why didn't you say so?'

'I assumed you'd know,' said Dave. 'Look, can you sign? I've got to ride back to Embankment, and the weather is about to get worse.'

The receptionist primly scratched his name onto Dave's wet delivery sheet. 'Goodbye then,' he said stiffly.

'Goodbye,' said Dave, too grumpy to apologize for his attitude.

Outside Schilling Associates, Dave heaved himself back onto his bike. Thinking wistfully of the hot chocolate Amos had promised, he pulled up his collar and steeled himself for the ride back to the agency.

Wheeling out into the street he was knocked off his bike by a Porsche. The man behind the wheel, a little plumper than Dave remembered him, was Vincent.

Dave sat in the gutter and watched the Porsche drive off. The numberplate read 1 4 ROAD.

Chapter Twenty-seven

Shareholder confidence

A week before 'Art Schmart' was due to open, a whispering campaign began against Jessica in the provinces of the art world. This campaign was the consequence of a poorly contrived seating plan, and was thus entirely the fault of a Mr George Frederick.

George Frederick was the owner of a small gallery out near Tottenham, which had been in the family for generations, along with a vague but unsophisticated interest in modern art. The Frederick Gallery was a battleground for determinedly first division artists, all of whom hoped they would one day be promoted to the premiership, thus leaving George Frederick and his gallery behind for ever. They clustered around him in the hope of being signed up by better-known patrons, and if they were, he never heard from them again.

George, a significant noise in supermarket management north of Finchley, was cheerfully unaware of the way his artists treated him. Indeed, he was cheerfully unaware of almost all the political sensitivities within his chosen field of interest. Twice a year he would host a dinner and private view, to which he would invite all manner of critics, artists, curators and dealers, assuming that with such overlapping interests they would all get along quite famously. It was because of this blind optimism that he caused enormous damage to Jessica's reputation with his seating plan.

A more politically alert gallery owner would have foreseen the potential disaster on table three and taken drastic action. Table three was divided amongst a variety of guests, but it was two names in particular that would have caused the more enlightened host unease. The two names were Fulmonella Matthews and Robin Haddock, and they were seated opposite one another. Worse, they were seated at the very end of the table, so they would find it almost impossible to talk to anyone else.

Fulmonella Matthews and Robin Haddock were both part of Rorschach, a new conceptual entity that had emerged within the modern art scene over the last six months. Rorschach was a collective of critics, acting independently but answering to the same name. This meant that Rorschach could cover any private view in the city, even if several were scheduled concurrently.

Membership of Rorschach carried with it strict rules. Firstly, component critics had to give up all hope of their names appearing in print, because any comments they made would be attributed to the Rorschach entity as a whole. This was part of Rorschach's charm, as it would say conflicting things

from one day to the next, and sometimes even disagree with itself within the space of a single
publication or article. Secondly, in order to maintain
these post-modern disagreements, members of
Rorschach were required to maintain a decent
distance from one another at private views and events,
and if they *did* happen to find themselves in proximity,
they were forbidden to say whether they liked or disliked what they'd seen. Too much conversation, it was
feared, might lead members towards an agreed and
single viewpoint.

So when George Frederick positioned Fulmonella
Matthews and Robin Haddock opposite one another
on table three, he created the likelihood of more than
just a stilted after-dinner conversation.

'Are you glad you came?' asked Fulmonella over
dessert.

'Are you?' asked Robin.

'Well, I'm glad I *came*,' said Fulmonella. 'But I'm
not saying I liked what I saw.'

'Of course not,' said Robin. 'I'm also glad I came,
though I'm also not saying whether I liked or disliked
what I saw.'

'Quite,' said Fulmonella.

There was a brief silence.

'Were there any particular pieces that you were
glad to have seen?' asked Robin.

'I'm glad I saw some of the sculpture. Particularly
the piece by that Sayers woman. A striking use of the
fingers to give depth to the clay.'

'Striking?' asked Robin.

'Yes. Striking can mean either good or bad,' said Fulmonella.

'Ah,' said Robin.

There was a pause while they waited for the cigars to arrive.

'And were there any pieces that *you* were particularly glad to have seen?' asked Fulmonella.

'I'm glad I saw the collectable bogeymen,' said Robin, rolling the remainder of his wine round in circles.

'The bogeymen?'

'Yes, you know. Bogeymen. The little rows of them.'

'Ah, you mean the piece about test-tube children,' said Fulmonella.

'Test-tube children?'

'Yes,' said Fulmonella. 'There were little bands on their wrists. I assumed . . .'

'We shouldn't be talking about this,' said Robin abruptly.

'No, you're right,' said Fulmonella. 'Sorry.'

'That's all right. We'd better talk about something else.'

'Yes,' said Fulmonella.

There was a long pause.

'Are you going to "Art Schmart" next week?' asked Robin finally.

'Yes. I think they're going to let a few of us attend. It's such a big show they want a wide range of comments. They're going to let us walk round at five minute intervals.'

'Oh really? I hadn't heard that.'

'Yes.'

'I suppose I'll be going as well then.'

'Yes.'

Another pause.

'Do you think there'll be something new from "Anonymous"?' asked Fulmonella.

'Not sure,' said Robin. 'I heard she was working on a commercial project at the moment.'

'Philippe Laurent?' said Fulmonella. 'Yes, I'd heard the same thing.'

'Are we allowed to talk about *this*?' asked Robin.

'I don't see why not,' said Fulmonella. 'If it's a person rather than a piece of art, then the rules can't apply.'

'That's a relief,' said Robin. 'So, you've heard the rumours too?'

'Oh yes,' said Fulmonella. 'What do you make of them?'

Robin took a deep breath. 'Let's get some more wine,' he said.

A few days after George Frederick's party, Jessica became aware of the tug of gossip. The members of Rorschach were prevented from agreeing on much, but having heard the same rumours, they did agree that a major British artist writing advertisements for a well-known advertising agency was a very bad thing indeed. Such an apprenticeship was considered demeaning by those who still valued their integrity, and the inferred sponsorship of Jessica's efforts by

Philippe Laurent was deemed to underline the notion that art was too often subservient to the commercial world.

The Rorschach quotes that appeared over the next few days sent tremors through the body of critical thought. To her horror, Jessica found that opinions of her back catalogue were suddenly being revised. Columnists who once cited her work as the best of its genre were finding replacement idols. When praise did appear, it was muted and grey. Several voices, eager to pour water into the chip-pan of controversy, even dared suggest that there was some doubt over her claim to the title of 'Anonymous', citing the fact that the tone of her current output was very different to that of her supposed alter-ego. Nobody really took this claim seriously, but it had been made, and it was remembered. Staring out of her Soho windows at the artistic world, Jessica grew very worried about what she saw.

'Of course, I take no notice of reviews,' she told a reporter nervously. 'I have sufficient confidence in my work to survive without them.'

'You haven't grown used to the praise?' the reporter asked her. 'You haven't become accustomed to the attention?'

'As if!' Jessica squeaked, her voice slipping into the hysterical. 'I live for my art, not the limelight. If the critics want to concentrate on someone else for a while, let them. They'll be begging for an exclusive when my next piece is unveiled.'

'Ah yes,' said the reporter. 'The piece for "Art

Schmart". Can you tell us anything about it?'

'Unfortunately, I'm not allowed to describe it,' said Jessica coyly. 'You'll have to wait for the private view.'

'Has Philippe Laurent seen it?'

'Certainly not!' said Jessica. 'What makes you think he would have?'

'And how would you compare it to the work of "Anonymous"?' asked the reporter, scenting distress. 'Would you say it's as good?'

'This interview is over,' said Jessica firmly. 'Thank you so much for your time.'

As the darling of the gossip mill, Jessica was hugely sensitive to changes in its machinery. To her, there was no worse punishment than becoming unfashionable. She would rather stop producing art altogether. Standing atop the house of cards she had built, she cursed herself for rocking the foundations. She should have foreseen the ramifications of agreeing to work for Philippe. She should have realized that his touch would call her artistic integrity into question. Jessica wished she could turn back the clock and undo her work on the Ranna project. She wished she could erase her advertisements from existence.

This, however, was impossible. It was too late to stop the advertising process. Filming was already finished, and post-production was nearing completion. The final cuts were due back within days. Jessica knew she could not prevent the Ranna ads from running, all she could do was try to downplay her part in their creation.

To compound her gathering panic about the Ranna advertisements, Jessica was also becoming doubtful of the quality of her piece for 'Art Schmart'. *Untitled: The presence of God* had seemed ironic and knowing when she was controversial and introspective. Now, with attitudes towards her art infected by cynicism and doubt, she was worried that her slide show of other people's work would be misinterpreted as plagiarism.

With only a few days to go until the opening of 'Art Schmart', Jessica knew that something had to be done. She was not the type to let events unfold around her. She was too used to driving her own success to quietly observe matters from afar. She resolved to reverse the direction of her fortunes. She decided to go and see Philippe.

Chapter Twenty-eight

The bathtub

Vincent never realized that he'd knocked over an old friend with his Porsche, because when he drove past Dave, he'd been drunk.

Graduating with a Thora Hird in furniture design and upholstery, which he was somewhat surprised to find was the degree he had been studying for, Vincent had caught a train to London just as Dave was taking up the position of creative assistant at Philippe Laurent's agency. Charming when sober, and more capable than most young men when drunk, Vincent soon got himself a job as a junior bond trader at a small firm in the city. His interview had been conducted in the local pub, and by the time the subject of his qualifications came up, the interviewer was so drunk that Vincent probably could have told the truth and still been employed.

'Which collegsh did you shay you went to?' the interviewer slurred.

'College?' said Vincent, finishing his tenth pint. 'What do you mean?'

'Which collegsh?' said the man. 'You know, in Ogsfoot?'

'I didn't go to Oxford,' said Vincent. 'I went to Newcastle Institute of Arts and Media.'

'Schplendid,' said the interviewer with a small hiccup. 'I knew you were an Ogsfoot man.'

Vincent's unique ability to drink endless amounts of alcohol and still maintain a coherent conversation were much valued by his new employer. A great deal of the bond trading business was reliant on gleaning unknown information from indiscreet sources, and Vincent demonstrated an uncanny ability to perform this function when he attended a garden party held by a large Norwegian shipping firm. Having single-handedly drunk all forty of his hosts under the table, Vincent then encouraged them to spill the beans on their strategy for an imminent take-over bid, which they promptly did, laughing and wetting themselves all the while. The Norwegians could not remember a thing the next day, but Vincent had written several pages of notes before he himself passed out, and over the coming months his firm made a small fortune speculating on the back of the harvest he'd brought in.

After this incident, Vincent was given ongoing responsibility for 'entertainment' at the firm, meaning that he was provided with an enormous expense account with which to cajole secrets from his sources. He was very good at what he did, and was soon able to negotiate a profit-related pay scheme that brought him enough wealth to pay for a new Porsche, as well as the most expensive programme of liver treatments that private healthcare could offer. He was dating a lap dancer, lived in a penthouse, and someone else paid for his booze. All in all, Vincent's life was complete.

Of course, Dave didn't know any of this, but he could see that another of his peers had made it to the big time, which just brought his own failings into even sharper relief. The implications of Vincent's Porsche had crystallized Dave's anger. Jessica had succeeded where he had not, thanks to nepotistic stepladders, a stolen identity and a gullible art world. Now Vincent had also succeeded, no doubt for some equally unfair reason.

'You've got to take what you want in this life,' he muttered to himself as he pedalled back to the agency. 'You've got to take what you fucking well want.'

Back at Laurent Création, Dave sat in front of the myriad of security monitors, drank his hot chocolate, and dwelt on the mess that his life had become. He watched the larvae of the agency scurry from screen to screen with their whiteboards and ideas. He could see practically everything from where he sat; the Brownian motion of commercial enterprise was laid bare. Artistic creations were given life twelve inches from his nose, several times a minute. He was captivated by the sight of all those people, doing things that he desperately wanted to do himself, and he was angrier than he had ever been in his life.

The blood crawled back through his fingers with

hot and malevolent purpose. Dave shivered and clenched his mug tightly.

On one of the monitors, he could see Philippe talking to Marcy. The camera was obviously positioned in the top left-hand corner of Philippe's office, because Dave was looking down on Marcy, who was standing next to Philippe's desk. He could make out Philippe's frown, which was creasing the top of his head. Leaning close to the screen, Dave addressed Philippe's Lilliputian form.

'Should feel fucking dwarfed, should I?' he asked the miniature Philippe. 'Should feel fucking dwarfed by what I cannot fucking achieve?'

Amos, who was enjoying three minutes of sleep in a chair to Dave's right, opened his eyes and turned to face him. 'All right?' he asked kindly.

'Fine,' said Dave grumpily, not taking his eyes off the screen. 'Isn't it about time you changed personalities?'

Dave had discovered Amos' dual life after two weeks as a courier. Until that point he had been completely unaware of the security guard's ruse.

On the night in question, defeated by the complex anatomy of the Mayfair one-way system, Dave had arrived back at the agency a lot later than planned. Walking into the deserted building, he'd come across a lady called Clementine in deep and proximal conversation with Amos the night worker. He was justifiably horrified by this discovery, because Clementine was Amos the day worker's wife.

Clementine, a cleaner by trade, was required to make daily deliveries to her husband to ensure he did not starve as he pursued his endless vigil at the security monitors. Once she discovered that Dave had a penchant for coconut macaroons, she started bringing these in as well, and under the influence of her home-cooked offerings, Dave became as fond of Clementine as he was of his daylight supervisor. Consequently, he was shocked and hurt when he discovered that she was betraying his friend's trust, and with none other than her husband's nocturnal colleague. He was sure of her guilt in the matter, because when he stumbled across her in conflagration with Amos the night worker, she sprang out of the embrace as though she had been stung.

Dave spent sleepless hours wondering whether he should tell Amos the day worker that he had been upstaged by his nightly counterpart. Like the rest of the agency, Dave had never liked Amos the night worker much, finding him unsolicitous and aloof, but he cared about both Amos the day worker and Clementine, and he wanted to do what was best for their marriage. Though he was terrified of making things worse, he decided that he couldn't keep such dreadful knowledge to himself. He had to do something.

The following evening, Dave cornered Amos the night worker and demanded that he cease his clandestine appointments with Clementine. He said he knew everything, and that he would go to Amos the day worker and spill the beans if their sordid arrangement continued.

Amos, deeply touched by Dave's concern for the wellbeing of his alter ego, peeled off his fake moustache like a badly-trained magician and revealed his secret identity.

Since this discovery, and as the only person within Laurent Création who knew about Amos' double life, Dave had grown closer to the old man than ever. Sipping the hot chocolate that his friend had made him, he regretted his waspish comment.

'Sorry, Amos,' he said, turning away from the security monitors. 'I'm having a rough time of things at the moment.'

Amos smiled. 'More hot chocolate?' he asked.

'No, you're all right,' said Dave, who was beginning to wonder if his lifetime allocation of hot chocolate was being consumed too rapidly. 'You'd better go and change. Do you want me to watch the screens for you?'

Amos climbed out of his chair and retrieved his neatly folded moustache from a desk drawer. ''S'all right,' he said. 'All on digital tape. Perfectly safe. Last month of each camera.'

And he left Dave alone with his black-and-white world.

Dave slurped the last of his hot chocolate and returned his attention to the puppet-like Philippe on the monitor before him. Philippe was now sat in his office reading a newspaper. He looked like a little tin-foil king. Dave fought back another wave of bile and closed his eyes. He was bloated with emotion. Anger, frustration and resentment boiled in his head like lava. He needed to get his feelings out. He needed to do something with them.

Opening his eyes once more, Dave randomly selected another screen to look at. Its view encompassed the area to the left of Marcy's desk, and he could see her sorting documents for Philippe's approval. Again he let his eyes wander across the fractured agency, but again he found evidence of Philippe, this time in the bustle of minions, headed towards the creative director's office with a platter of scones. Dave felt like a general who had surrounded his enemy, but who could not launch an attack.

As he stared at Philippe's grainy kingdom, an idea germinated in the wet soil of Dave's misery.

'A month,' he said. 'On tape.'

Chapter Twenty-nine

Free lunches

Dave awoke on the floor of the security office. The tiles were stubbley and smelled of olive oil. He peeled himself off them and sat up.

'Chocolate,' said Amos, handing him a steaming mug. The moustache was gone, so Dave assumed it had to be morning.

'What time is it?' he asked.

'Eight forty-five,' said Amos. 'Relax, you got time for a little brush up.'

Dave glanced around at his night's work; three digibeta videotapes stacked up by the security monitors. No labels, no markings, but it didn't matter. Dave knew what was recorded on them. He'd spent hours working with the security system to get what he was after, and he'd done it. The feelings in his stomach were gone. His anger had partially abated. He had explored the places that were hurting so much, and for now at least, they were quiet. He could think of Philippe without hatred. He could think of himself as an artist once again. He was proud of the three tapes. They were real. They had come from within.

Dave stood up slowly, his body reminding him of the punishment it had received the previous night, hours twisted over his work in the production room. He rubbed his skin, which was sticky with effort.

'I think I'll go and wash,' he said to Amos, and shuffled out into the lobby.

Given that he had not spoken to her since she visited his house in Newcastle and appropriated his installation, it was a shame that it was in such a condition that Dave happened to bump into Jessica. She was clicking her way through the lobby, focused on the lift ahead, and he neatly bisected her path as he scurried mouse-like towards the toilets.

'Dave?' she said, staring at him in astonishment.

'Oh,' said Dave. He glanced at the face of his enemy and fingered his courier's uniform. It was thick with the strata of multiple wear. He wasn't ready for this. There was no way he could come out of this conversation a victor. He looked tired and ragged, deserving of her pity but not her respect. He had not wanted to meet her again until he was established as a creative soul. A peer, rather than a peasant.

'How are you?' asked Jessica. 'How have you been since . . . well, how have you been?'

Dave could not help noticing that Jessica asked the question with something like exhaustion. She seemed a bit distracted. She was emitting tiredness and worry.

'I'm fine, thank you for asking,' said Dave. He was determined not to assume the familiar position of inferiority. Not this time. Not after what she had done to him.

'That's good,' said Jessica. She hadn't really listened to the tone of his reply.

There was a pause.

'I didn't realize you worked for Laurent Création,' Jessica prompted.

'Yes. Have done for almost eighteen months,' said Dave stiffly. He was going to present his employment by Laurent Création as a positive achievement. After all, Jessica probably assumed he had just gone off to draw roadsigns somewhere.

Jessica nodded wisely. 'And what do you do here?' she asked, peering at the writing on his courier tag. 'Oh, I see,' she said.

Dave was suddenly aware of how downtrodden he looked in his courier's uniform. How it marked him out as a creative failure. The catharsis that his night's work had provided was gone. He suddenly found it difficult to hold up his chin.

'Oh, I do odds and sods,' he muttered, looking at the floor. 'You know, this and that.'

Faced with Dave's life, Jessica was filled with a mixture of pity and contact embarrassment. It did not occur to her to feel any responsibility for Dave's condition. He was his own man, she believed, and he could not blame her for the way he had ended up. It didn't surprise her that he'd fallen on hard times. It was probably proof that his creative talent had just been a fleeting moment. He had been lucky to know her really, or his work wouldn't have gained any respect at all.

'Well, I hope they make use of your skills here,'

she said, looking to flattery to ease the tension.

'Of course they don't,' said Dave. 'And don't patronize me. I won't be listening to your compliments this time.'

Jessica laughed awkwardly. Dave's anger was embarrassing. His life had clearly been a failure since Newcastle, and she didn't want to be infected by it.

'Are you still practising?' she asked.

'Practising?' said Dave.

'You know,' said Jessica. 'Do you still practise art? Have you produced anything since, well, you know . . .'

Dave's indignation doubled. His chin rose a little higher. 'I finished a new piece last night,' he said. 'But I'll keep this one to myself, if you don't mind.'

Jessica laughed again, this time wholeheartedly. He actually believed she had taken his installation for her own benefit! She marvelled at his ingratitude.

'Yes, that was funny wasn't it?' she said with a chuckle. 'I didn't want to take the credit, but you know how journalists are. They always think they know the answer to everything.'

'Well, I'm sure you did everything you could to convince them they were wrong,' said Dave, not smiling.

'Actually,' said Jessica, 'it's a bit of a pain being "Anonymous". Nobody thinks my stuff is as good as his. I'm struggling to live up to his standard.'

'I'm sure it's very hard for you,' said Dave sarcastically.

'I'll survive,' said Jessica with a smile. She could see a possible end to this conversation, and rushed towards it gladly.

'Listen,' she said, 'I must be off, but you should keep at it. I'm sure you could get your work shown somewhere. One of the smaller galleries perhaps?'

'Perhaps,' said Dave. He stared at Jessica in hatred. It was no good. The conversation was going to end without an opportunity to exact some revenge.

'I'm sure I could help you get it displayed,' Jessica gushed. She was on the home stretch now. 'You should give me a call and I'll try to help.'

She fished around in her bag and came out with a brochure for 'Art Schmart'. Clicking open a pen, she scribbled her mobile number on the back.

'Here's my number,' she said. 'And this is my new show. You should go and see it. It might give you some ideas.' She handed over the brochure, feeling that this gesture proved her munificence.

'Maybe,' said Dave, scowling at the pamphlet.

'Well sweets, it's been lovely to see you again, but I must be going,' Jessica said once more. The ordeal was nearly over, and she was desperate to extricate herself so she could start the process of forgetting about it. She seriously doubted that Dave was practising art in any real form, and she thought it was unlikely that she would ever hear from him again. All in all, she felt very pleased with herself. The phone number on the back of the brochure was a nice way of reiterating the fact that she had carved a career alone, and that 'Anonymous' had actually been more of a hindrance than a help to her. She didn't want Dave thinking she owed him anything.

'Bye then,' said Dave in a dead voice. His anger lay inside him like lead. The 'Art Schmart' brochure was printed on heavy gloss paper and looked expensive. It wasn't fair. His most recent artistic effort would never leave Amos' security office. Hers would be seen by thousands of people.

Jessica gave him a little wave as she ran towards the lift. Failing to return her gesture, he trudged towards the toilet to get cleaned up. It was not until he was standing in front of the mirror that he realized he hadn't even asked her why she was visiting the agency.

Jessica's conversation with Philippe was a lot less successful than her encounter with Dave. She was hoping to convince him to postpone airing the Ranna advertisements until after the 'Art Schmart' private view, which was scheduled for the following evening.

'I'm afraid that's impossible,' said Philippe. 'The final cuts are coming in tomorrow morning, and we're going to get them polished for a five o'clock playout. They'll be running tomorrow night as we stand in the gallery and observe your latest work.'

'There's no way you can delay things a teeny bit?' asked Jessica, putting on her best little girl's voice.

'Absolutely not,' said Philippe. 'They're booked for the middle of the football match. The spots cost a fortune.'

'But Philippe,' said Jessica. 'They think I've sold out. It will affect opinions at the private view.'

Philippe waved a hand in the air. 'Everyone is accused of selling out eventually,' he said. 'For you it has just come earlier than most. Anyway, you've nothing to worry about. I promised you a respectable price for your next three pieces if you delivered on the Ranna scripts, and that is exactly what you have done.'

'But critical opinion . . .' Jessica began again.

'Critical opinion is irrelevant,' said Philippe. 'When I buy your work tomorrow, you will be worthy of debate. Whether they think you are any good or not is unimportant.'

He raised his cup of coffee in a toast. 'See you tomorrow night then.'

Jessica left Philippe's office with her eyes on the floor. She could feel the end of her popularity advancing like cancer.

Chapter Thirty

The camel's back

The day after his disastrous reckoning with Jessica, Dave arrived at work to discover salt being rubbed into his wounds.

'First delivery,' said Amos, handing him a soft package wrapped in white plastic film. The package was too large to fit in a courier knapsack, so Amos had thoughtfully made a shoulder strap out of masking tape.

'No hot chocolate this morning?' Dave asked miserably.

'You got a busy day today,' said Amos, looking most unfamiliar with the concept. His Jamaican ancestry had not prepared him for busy days.

He handed Dave his *A to Z*, which was already open. The pages were annotated in pencil.

'I drew the route,' he said. 'You need to come straight back after this one. We got a big job on something this afternoon.'

Dave looked down at the guts of London, laid out like a post-mortem on the little black and white pages. The location that Amos had highlighted was on the eastern end of the Thames. A white space was circled, and next to it, in Amos' shaky handwriting, were written three words. *Smart art xhibition.*

Dave nodded sadly and took the book from Amos. Through the translucent wrapping of the package he could see the ghost of a bow tie. It seemed that he was transporting Philippe's eveningwear to 'Art Schmart' so that his employer could change into it before the private view.

'Fine,' said Dave, clenching his fists. 'Fine.'

As he left the office, he saw his three tapes, still perched on the security desk like lost children. Avoiding their gaze, he went outside to unchain his bike.

An empty warehouse down by the river in Bermondsey had been selected as the most appropriate gallery space for 'Art Schmart'. The area in which the warehouse stood was rapidly becoming one of new London chic, with restaurants and theatres emerging from the old manufacturing plants on a monthly basis. Several developers had made a small fortune from the conversions, but the practice was not yet deemed to be part of the vulgar mainstream, distanced as it was from the opulence of the central south bank. It was a location of simultaneous sophistication and subversion. The perfect place for the 'Art Schmart' exhibition to be housed.

Behind the new conversions, away from the silt of the Thames, less glamorous structures remained. Although a virulent gentrification was infecting the area, islands of poverty still defended their borders with antibodies of unemployment and violence. This resulted in a strange patchwork of privilege and poverty. The roads that Dave cycled through on his way to the gallery were harlequins. Security gates and re-pointed brickwork gave way to dirty footballs and broken glass.

It was a crystal cold day, and Dave adjusted his grip on the metal handlebars constantly, seeking to avoid the sapping contact. He had chosen the leaner of his two hats that morning, and he now regretted his choice. The wind whittled his ears down to nothing.

The thought of his destination had drawn Dave deeper into his cavern of resentment. The fact that his only contribution to 'Art Schmart' was to be the maintenance of Philippe's trouser creases seemed yet another slap in the face. While Jessica leered at him from the height of her success, Philippe treated him like a manservant, which was even worse. Tears of anger, now quite familiar with their surroundings, welled up in his eyes.

'Fuck 'em,' he told the cold air. 'Cheating cow and cruel French bastard. They deserve each other.'

The entrance to the 'Art Schmart' warehouse, where the evening's guests would be received, featured a giant poster of Jessica and her fellow artists in suitably accomplished poses. Stan and Carlos, Dave was happy to see, still had a sense of humour, and peered out from behind grey prison bars. Nedrina Burchill looked disturbed, and half her face was in shadow.

Dave could barely look at the giant Jessica, who was smiling down at him and flashing her duplicitous eyes.

The foyer in the gallery was full of responsibility and last minute preparation.

'Yes?' said the girl at the front desk.

'I've got a package,' said Dave. 'For tonight.'

'I can see that. What is it?'

'It's a dinner jacket,' said Dave. 'For Philippe Laurent.' He tried not to grimace as he pronounced the name.

'Ah, Mister Laurent's change of clothes,' said the girl. 'Yes, I was told this would be coming.' She beckoned a burly-looking man who was sweeping the floor. 'Ben? Could you put this in the collectors changing room please?'

The man came over and relieved Dave of his parcel.

'Can I have a signature?' Dave asked the girl.

'What?' said the girl. She had picked up the phone and was making a call.

'A signature,' said Dave.

'One second,' she told him, gesturing that the phone was about to connect. 'Yes, Marcus? Yes, it's Patricia. I'm just ringing to check that the artists' lounge is fully stocked. Yes. Oh, I don't know. The usual, I suppose. Champagne and brownies and whatever else you think they might like. Yes. OK. Thanks, Marcus.'

Dave listened to the arrangement of Jessica's luxuries with a heavy heart. By the time the girl had finished her conversation, he was lost once again in a pit of despair.

'What did you say you wanted?' she asked him.

'Hmm?' said Dave, thinking about Jessica's jet-set lifestyle.

'What else did you need?'

'Oh. A signature please,' said Dave.

He stood beneath the idolatry of Jessica's enormous façade for as long as it took to get confirmation of his delivery. Then he fled.

By the time Amos rang him to ask when he'd be back, Dave was in a pub just behind the gallery. The pub was called the Workman's Rest, and it was this name that had attracted Dave as he rode past. The inside of the Workman's Rest was spongy and red, and Dave had ordered a hot chocolate to burn away the cold and satisfy the dependency on the drink that Amos had fostered within him. The landlord of the pub, sensing a customer of unstable mood, was rather glad Dave had not asked for any alcohol.

'. . . Delivery,' crackled Amos over the two-way radio, 'Philippe has a delivery he needs. Quickly now.' He sounded most uncomfortable having to pressure his employee, and Dave felt a pang of guilt for letting the old man down.

He put his half-finished chocolate back on the bar and made to leave.

'Cheer up,' said the landlord. 'Might never happen.'

'No,' said Dave as he walked out into the unfriendly air. 'Might not.'

As it turned out, Dave hurried back to Laurent Création for no reason at all.

The final cuts of the Ranna advertisements had landed on Philippe's desk by mid-morning, and once piped across to Eddie Radacker's PC in Japan, they had been approved. However, one last detail needed ironing out before they could be broadcast to the masses that evening – the Ranna logo and strapline had to be added to the end of each film. Laurent Création did not have the most up-to-date version of the logo on their system, so Philippe planned to send the films to Citrus, where they could paste on the image required.

Ranna's advertising airtime had been booked some months previously within coverage of an international football match that was being played that night. Though the deadline was technically past, Philippe had used up several of his more valuable favours to ensure the TV stations would open their reels and allow the Ranna executions late entry. They had given him until five o'clock, and this deadline had been passed on to Citrus.

Laurent Création had also been instructed to beam the advertisements to agencies around the world so that Eddie could break the campaign globally. Again, Philippe had asked Citrus to take care of this for him.

With so much at stake, and so little time left, Philippe was therefore horrified when he went down to brief Amos on the transportation of his tapes and discovered that Dave would be responsible for the job. Dave, with his track record of incompetence, was the last person Philippe wanted carrying the priceless Ranna executions across London.

'No, it's much too important for him,' said Philippe. 'Isn't there anyone else?'

'We used to have temporary couriers,' said Amos, 'but now we've got Dave, we don't really need them.'

'Well, he's not touching these tapes,' said Philippe. 'He's fucked up too many things round here already.'

'But sir,' said Amos, becoming slightly panicky. 'Getting another courier will take time. What can we do?'

'Find me a knapsack and bag these up,' Philippe said to Amos. 'I'll call you a cab. You're taking them yourself.'

When Dave arrived back at Laurent Création, he was surprised to discover that the urgent delivery he had been recalled for was no longer necessary. He was even more surprised when he discovered three slips of paper on the security desk. It wasn't the existence of the slips that surprised him, or the fact that he had found them on the security desk. It was the contents of the slips that made him want to throw up.

The slips were records of production for three digibeta tapes. Their issue was standard practice within the industry, and allowed production houses to keep track of the jobs they had done. Each slip showed the name of the client, the title of the execution, the director of the execution, and the names of the creative team who had written it. The slips had been on top of the tapes that Philippe had handed to Amos, but in his haste, Amos had failed to put them in his envelope.

As he read Jessica's name next to the titles of the three Ranna advertisements, Dave felt something snap inside him. He suddenly realized why Jessica had been visiting the agency. Philippe had been paying her to work on the Ranna brief. That was why she'd been in Philippe's office when he'd barged in on them a month ago. That's why she had come in to visit the day before. Once again, Jessica had succeeded where he had utterly failed. Philippe had almost fired him for his Ranna advertisements, but hers had been turned into reality.

Dave's knees almost buckled with the strength of his hatred. He choked back an onrush of fury that threatened to engulf his senses. Playing back their meeting of twenty-four hours ago, he remembered Jessica's smiling face and condescending manner. He remembered her refusal to apologize for stealing *Untitled: Attempts to deconstruct the system fall short (1)*. He remembered her dismissal of his own work as only worthy of smaller galleries. And all along, her Ranna executions had been waiting for her upstairs. Not content with denigrating his artistic abilities, she was now encroaching on the other creative field he had tried to make his own. In advertising, as in modern art, Dave had been rejected, but Jessica had been welcomed with open arms.

'That bitch,' he said to the empty room. 'That fucking bitch.'

Dave decided that the most important thing in the world, more important than his own success, was ruining Jessica's career.

He was still standing by the security desk, holding the three slips of paper in his shaking hands, when Amos returned.

'I think we deserve hot chocolate,' said Amos, very pleased with himself for completing Philippe's important task.

Dave did not answer. He was working out a plan.

Chapter Thirty-one

A lifetime in seconds

Digging out the brochure she had given him, Dave rang Jessica's mobile. She agreed to his plan so fast that he began to think there might be something wrong with it.

Dave's plan rotated entirely around his most recent artistic endeavour. The tapes he had collated two nights previously were the basis for a three-screen video installation, and it was with this video installation that Dave planned to destroy Jessica's career.

When Amos informed him that a month of footage from each of the security cameras was kept in digital storage, a beam of inspiration had struck Dave full in the face. On that night, drunk with resentment and frustration, he had decided to revisit the scene of his humiliation, the house from which he had been banished. He was hungry to relive the moment when Philippe had expelled him from the creative department. That moment, when Philippe pushed him to earth, had squared the circle of suffering that Jessica began in Newcastle. That moment had been the most painful in his life. For the same reason that passers-by peer into the souls of car accidents, Dave wanted to see himself standing in Philippe's office, receiving his punishment.

When the glow of life left the glass village above him, Dave went to work. It was easy enough to search through the old footage on the security monitors, but it took longer to record the signal onto an external device. In the end, he had to liberate certain pieces of equipment from the production studio to complete his task. The wiring was difficult, but he had some experience of such toys from his days as a creative lackey, and he figured it out eventually.

Dave selected his footage with great care. He found twelve different camera sources that could each show a part of the action, and then pasted them onto three separate tapes. Each of the three films lasted just under a minute, and in total they showed Dave's creative banishment from start to finish, beginning with his march towards Philippe's office, and ending with his flight from the scene.

Dave's mind was in a gallery as he worked, observing his finished installation. He foresaw three separate screens placed next to one another, the public standing or sitting before them.

The first of Dave's three films showed his approach to the gallows, and used shots of the waiting executioner interspersed with the march of the condemned man. The cameras had captured Dave's excitement as he bounced along beside Marcy, and he looked like an expectant puppy, completely unaware of the terrible fate that awaited him. The images ended with Dave's arrival in Philippe's office, and as the creative director looked up, the viewer was given a premonition of the abuse that was to come.

The second film used footage from the camera inside Philippe's office, and overlapped with the end of the first. Height and proximity would confuse the viewer at first, but gradually they would come to realize that the men facing each other in the little office were the same as those in the initial film. The subtleties of exchange were difficult to interpret from this perspective, but the viewer would be able to observe the spastic twitches of Philippe's sitting body as he vented his anger, as well as Dave's form, which gradually pixelated in horror.

The final film in Dave's installation showed his exile from the creative department, beginning at the end of his boss's tirade and catching the impact of the last few injuries inflicted. Dave's grainy form turned and staggered from the office, as though blinded by embarrassment and rejection, and the cameras tracked his descent through the building. The shots showed Dave weeping as he ran, grey face sodden, shoulders down, and hopes abolished. At the end of the film, the viewpoint flipped back to Philippe's office, where the executioner was calmly sorting papers, his destruction of Dave's ambitions already forgotten.

Dave, compiling his work within the torture of inspiration, had created an installation that not only narrated the events of the moment, but also commented on the frustration and misery of office life. The films, which he planned to show simultaneously, would confuse the viewer at first, but gradually they would come to realize they were seeing a time-condensed montage of one person's professional death. There was no soundtrack to the footage, only a mild wet static that came from the belly of the recording equipment, and without the noises that were expected for such a dialogue, the physical movements of the protagonists' bodies would be etched more sharply on the screen. Despite the elevated viewpoints that Dave had provided, all nuances and undertones of the silent conversation would be painfully visible. By the time the films ended, the observer would feel uncomfortable, as if they had intruded on a private space – a little office deathcamp. The films had a sense of evil about them. They were someone's worst nightmare.

When he'd finished his installation, Dave was spent but happy. He had achieved both personal and artistic catharsis, and fell asleep on the security office floor, to dream of triumphant reviews.

But after the slights of the previous twenty-four hours, Dave had changed his mind about the three films. Though he was still proud of his installation, he now had a more malevolent purpose in mind for his work.

It was to be his agent of revenge.

When Jessica answered the phone, Dave put on a conciliatory voice.

'Hi there,' he said. 'It's me. Dave.'

'Hello,' said Jessica warily.

'I hope you don't mind me ringing,' said Dave, 'but you told me to call if I ever needed some help.'

'Of course,' said Jessica stiffly. 'Though the thing is Dave, I'm having a few problems of my own at the moment and . . .'

'Would you like to resurrect "Anonymous"?' Dave interrupted.

There was a brief silence on the line.

' "Anonymous"?' said Jessica.

'Yes,' said Dave. 'I wondered if you'd like to bring him back from the dead?'

'What exactly do you mean?' asked Jessica.

'Do you remember the offer you made?' said Dave. 'To help me exhibit my recent work?'

'Yes,' said Jessica cautiously. 'I remember.'

'Well,' said Dave. 'There's no way I can get it displayed on my own, and even with your help, it would only get into a very small gallery.'

'That's true,' said Jessica. 'Go on . . .'

'But I was thinking, if we were to display it under the name "Anonymous", then you might be able to get it into a larger show.' Dave coughed with fake embarrassment, trying to convince Jessica that he felt cheeky for asking this favour.

'You realize that if we did that, people would assume it was mine?' said Jessica. 'Yesterday you seemed very angry that your last installation was attributed to me.'

'Yes, I've been thinking about that,' said Dave

humbly. 'I think I was being a bit unfair. It was hardly your fault, and at least my art was seen by lots of people. I've got very little reason to complain.'

'Well, that's very mature of you, Dave,' said Jessica. 'That's a very mature attitude indeed.'

'It's only the truth,' Dave went on. 'My last installation would never have become so famous without your help, so you deserve most of the credit really. I was just hoping that you would be generous enough to lend your standing to this one as well.'

Dave was terrified that Jessica would not take the bait, but he was hoping that her plagiaristic tendencies had not diminished in the last year and a half. Surely she would recognize free credit when she saw it?

There was another long pause on the line.

'Of course I'll help, Dave,' said Jessica. 'It's the least I can do for an old friend.'

For the past twenty-four hours Jessica had been sitting in her flat in Soho, trying desperately to think of some way out of the downward spiral in which she was trapped. Her slide show *Untitled: The presence of God* had been installed in the 'Art Schmart' warehouse, and now that she saw it alongside the work of her peers, it just did not seem up to scratch. In addition to this, the press were getting worse. Her phone had not stopped ringing, and in its denigration of her talents, Rorschach was hardly disagreeing with itself at all. The artistic world was turning against her.

Worst of all, it was her own fault. It was her involvement with the Ranna ad campaign that had set this ball rolling, and now there was no way she could stop it. Jessica cursed herself for her failure to see the impact that Philippe's favouritism would have. She should have rebuffed him on day one.

When Dave rang with his request for help, Jessica saw a possible way out of her purgatory. If his new piece was good, if 'Anonymous' made a triumphant return, then she would be placed firmly back on her pedestal. Quieting a few flutters of guilt, Jessica told herself that she would not take all the credit. In the event of critical acclaim, she resolved that she would keep the press in suspense about the identity of the artist, just as she had done before.

'I'll tell you what, Dave,' she announced grandly. 'I'll not only get it displayed for you. I'll get it displayed at the biggest modern art show this year.'

'What do you mean?' said Dave, pretending he had no idea what she was talking about.

'I'll get it displayed at "Art Schmart".'

'Really?' said Dave, trying to sound as wide-eyed as possible. 'That big show? Would you really do that?'

'Of course,' said Jessica. 'I can get it in tonight. They'll make space for it once I mention the name.'

'That's brilliant,' said Dave. 'Thank you so much for this.'

'Think nothing of it,' said Jessica. Her worries were receding. She could see her career in ascent once again. 'Now,' she said. 'How are we going to transport it to the gallery without anyone seeing it?'

'Oh, that's easy,' said Dave. 'I'll bring it by later. I'm a courier. That's what I do.'

'Sounds good,' said Jessica. 'Will I need to arrange anything in the gallery space?'

'Yes. Set up three screens next to one another,' said Dave. 'Wire them to three digibeta projectors. The screens need to be big, and make sure the tapes can play exactly in unison. The spectators will sit in front of the screens, and the tapes will all play at once. I'll bring them to the gallery later on, and leave them on the front desk for your attention.'

'OK,' said Jessica, who was getting more and more excited by the potential rewards of Dave's plan. 'What's it called?'

'It's called *A lifetime in seconds*,' said Dave. 'It's about death.'

'Ooo,' said Jessica. 'Death's very fashionable this year. They'll like that.'

Dave struggled not to laugh. This was too easy. 'Well,' he said. 'Thanks again, and good luck. I'll leave it at the front desk like I said.'

'The winning team is back!' said Jessica.

'Yes,' said Dave. 'The winning team.'

After he had hung up, Dave had to sit down for a while. He couldn't quite believe his scheme was working.

He was planning to deliver the tapes late, long after the private view had started, so that Jessica would have no time to vet them before she showed them to the masses. He had caught a glimpse of the 'Art

Schmart' layout when he'd delivered Philippe's dinner jacket. Each of the artist's works was situated in an open space, and the whole area would be full of people from the moment the doors opened. Dave knew that the three-screen arrangement he had asked for could not be kept clear of spectators for any period of time. If he delivered the tapes after the private view had commenced, Jessica would have to put them on as the world watched.

The crux of Dave's plan was the appearance of Philippe in his videos. With so many members of the art world present, someone would be bound to recognize Philippe's head and his office, obtuse as the angles were. Some might think the film an act, but there would be enough speculation that it wasn't. Jessica would have displayed Philippe's cruelty to all the most powerful men and women in modern art. He would be unveiled as a monster, and she would come across as a snake. They would both be ruined.

Raising himself on wobbly legs, Dave went off to find his tapes, which Amos had apparently moved from the security desk.

Chapter Thirty-two

A room without a view

Within fifteen minutes of the phone conversation between Jessica and Dave ending, most of the artistic world knew that 'Anonymous' was about to reappear.

The sponsors of 'Art Schmart' went into collective palpitations when the curator rang them to relay Jessica's request for extra display space. Then, having given their immediate assent to her requirements, they called everyone they knew. These people then called everyone else. The guest list, previously running at a seventy per cent acceptance rate, shot up to full capacity during the course of the next hour.

Everyone who was anyone wanted to go, as did a great deal of people who were not anyone at all. Critics confirmed their attendance in droves, and every art dealer with serious financial intentions also pledged to be present. All the members of Rorschach confirmed they would be there, with one of their number even arranging for a live satellite link-up so he could comment on proceedings from New York.

Celebrities, who were a precious commodity at private views, also looked like they would be thick on the ground. In an unprecedented move, all five members of the most voguish young pop group in London accepted invitations to the event (they normally considered themselves too unpredictable to be seen in the same place at once). Perhaps even more surprising, hundreds of famous artists wanted tickets as well. Artists were seldom seen at private views, preferring to remain a fashionable minority within their own limelight, but a chance to witness the new work by 'Anonymous' proved too good for them to pass up. Their overwhelming response suggested that the 'Art Schmart' private view was going to be something very special indeed.

The other contributors to 'Art Schmart' were awestruck when told that they would be sharing display space with the great 'Anonymous'. Stan and Carlos were so excited that they started a food fight in the prison canteen at dinner, and Nedrina Burchill, who had not seen Jessica since their time at the Lightschool together, spent a small fortune on an outfit to prevent being upstaged.

Three hours after Dave had set his plan in motion, the crowds began to arrive. By seven o'clock, the gallery was a cocktail of humanity, the air in the warehouse sizzling with expectation. The enormous explosion in attendance figures had exacerbated the problem of insufficient drink, but this was a regular occurrence at private views, and many guests had come prepared. Silver hip flasks moved around the room, along with whispered conjecture and gossip. At private views, convention normally held that one kept one's opinions to oneself (after all, you never knew when the artist was standing behind you). At 'Art Schmart' however, the guests made outrageous comments on an almost continual basis. There were two reasons for this show of honesty. Firstly, they hoped to trick Jessica into revealing her secret identity as 'Anonymous', and secondly, they simply didn't think that what they had seen so far was very good.

Carlos and Stan's *Scenes from your neighbourhood prison*, the footage of their fellow inmates which they exhibited on giant video screens, was thought to be rather obvious. The three films, which invited barbaric interpretations of the events to come, were read as an indictment of the penal system and a way of forcing society to deal with the concept of punishment. Many commentators liked the style of the films and the way in which they demanded the involvement of the viewer, but the subject matter had already been dealt with elsewhere. Even less forgivably, Carlos and Stan's efforts appeared to tread on the toes of their own back catalogue. The artistic inmates did not seem to have a new idea, and they were shunned accordingly.

Nedrina Burchill's exhibit was a huge painting of a blue sky, dotted through with constellations of rain-cloud. The clouds formed many shapes, but in the centre there was one that looked like the Devil. He was arching over and clutching at his groin, leering at the ground laid out beneath him. The audience, whilst quite liking the way the piece referenced the modern world's flippant attitude towards evil, again thought this had been done before. They damned Nedrina with faint praise and moved on.

Jessica's piece, *Untitled: the presence of God*, in which she displayed slides of appropriated greats, was also derided by the artistic world. They now had the bit between their collective teeth, and decided that Jessica's use of other artists' work within her own was final proof of a slide towards sarcasm and conformity. It was also agreed that the piece was basically about the establishment's tendency to over-celebrate genius, and given the audience that were judging it, this message did not go down very well at all.

At half-past eight, the guests were served with post-modern refreshments, presented on remote control cars that were sent speeding through the gallery. This meant that the refreshments were very difficult to grab hold of, and kept spilling on the floor. The talk over refreshments, like the talk before them, was of nothing but 'Anonymous'. The rest of the show was ignored.

Then Jessica announced that the latest work by 'Anonymous' was ready for viewing.

Dave had delivered his tapes late, as planned, and Jessica had been going out of her mind with worry for the last hour. She had watched the mood in the gallery turn sour, the critics leading an aesthetic charge against the work within it. She had wandered the floor, listening to conversations, and every time she had spoken to someone they had asked her when *You know who* was going to make an appearance.

Jessica had avoided all these questions and merely smiled a mysterious smile, but she was growing near to panic when word finally arrived that a package had been left at reception.

As Dave had hoped, Jessica could not prevent a flood of spectators settling themselves within the area that had been set aside for his work. Three screens had been erected as per his instructions, and when Jessica walked up to the projectors with the three tapes in her arms, she found the most influential figures of the art world already seated on the floor before her. All the members of Rorschach were there, sitting as far away from one another as possible, and Philippe Laurent, along with his fellow collectors, was also placed within the high-profile crowd. Jessica avoided his eye, as she had been doing all night. She was acutely aware that she would further stoke the bonfire of speculation if she spent any time talking to the man who was now known to be her patron.

The tapes Dave had brought over were labelled with the numbers 1, 2 and 3. Jessica loaded them into the three projectors accordingly. Then she called for silence.

The enormous crowd stilled instantly. The lights were dimmed.

'This is a new piece by "Anonymous",' said Jessica. 'It is called *A lifetime in seconds*.'

And she hit the play button that was wired to all three projectors.

Chapter Thirty-three

The beginning of the end

After Dave had delivered his tapes to 'Art Schmart', he went to the pub. He felt a little flat.

Though he had directed endless versions of Jessica's downfall in his head, there was no substitute for actually being there to witness events, and Dave left the steps of the gallery with reluctant feet. He would not get to see his enemy defeated in person. He had no ticket to the private view, and even if he had managed to slip in, he would have been taking his life in his hands to do so. Once Jessica realized how he had duped her, she might not have been able to refrain from physical violence.

Cycling away from the scene of his crime, Dave passed the Workman's Rest for the second time that day. Pulling on his brakes, he stopped. For some reason, the idea of being nearby when his plan came to fruition was pleasing. If he wasn't going to be present for Jessica's crucifixion, at least he could be in close proximity. Idly wondering if he would be able to hear her shrieks of despair, Dave racked up his bike and stepped through the crooked door.

*

The landlord of the Workman's Rest, who was also the barman and the chef, was a shrewd judge of character. This trait had developed prior to the recent gentrification of the area, and had been invaluable for sensing imminent bodily harm, which the previous occupants of Bermondsey had inflicted on each other all too regularly. When Dave had walked in that morning and ordered a cup of hot chocolate, the landlord had felt a familiar sense of unease. That morning, Dave had looked like he might cause trouble, if not within the confines of the Workman's Rest, then somewhere thereabouts.

However, the landlord's danger molecules were unexcited when Dave appeared for the second time in one day. He sensed a customer far more at peace, and far less volatile. Thinking himself lucky that Dave had chosen an area other than the Workman's Rest to exorcise his aggression, the landlord smiled.

'What can I get you, laddie?' he asked.

Dave scanned the drinks. They gleamed like jewels. 'I think,' he said, 'that the most appropriate thing would be a gin and tonic.'

The landlord made a gin and tonic as badly as only a publican south of the river could. 'Sorted out your problems, have you?' he asked.

'I'm sorry?' said Dave.

'You came in this morning,' said the landlord. 'Had a face like a slapped arse. You seem a lot happier now.'

'Oh,' said Dave. 'Yes, that's right. I was having a bad day this morning.'

'But not now?'

'No, not now,' said Dave. 'Actually, it might turn out to be a very good day indeed.'

'I'm glad to hear that, son,' said the landlord. 'I told you, didn't I?'

'Told me what?'

'I told you it might never happen.'

'Yes. Yes you did.' Dave reached into his pocket and paid for his drink.

'Although another way of putting it,' he said to the landlord, 'is that it might happen to someone else instead.'

Taking his drink and leaving the bar, Dave wandered through the pub and found a red velvet armchair by the fire. There were some boys, not more than sixteen years old, huddled round the table nearest to him. They were cocky with youth and their lack of experience. One of them was holding a small games machine in his lap, and the others were peering down at it. Their pints of cider fizzed quietly in accompaniment to the pinprick tune that the little grey box was emitting.

In order to avoid their eyes, Dave turned his attention to the TV screen that was suspended above the bar. There was a football game on, and little men in primary colours were scattered across the baize. Dave had never cared for football as a sport, but he had always liked the artistry of the ball's movement, the wave and weft of its flight through the air. He contemplated these parabolas as his gin and tonic disappeared, and by the time he had fetched another one from the bar, it was half-time.

Returning to his armchair, Dave glanced up and saw himself on the screen. He dropped his gin and tonic in shock.

Back at 'Art Schmart', conversation was raging like a bush fire. The most recent work by 'Anonymous' – a triptych of hyper-realistic advertisements for a sportswear brand – had not been received very well at all. The three films were still playing, and there were some who had not yet managed to squeeze into the installation space to take a look, but the majority of those present had seen enough to issue their judgement.

There was overall agreement that the installation was not up to the standard set by the artist's previous work. Though the quality of production was found to be challenging and accomplished, the message of the piece was thought to be rather mundane. The false 'advertisements' had each been accompanied by a healthy soundtrack, and so playing them together had produced an incoherent cacophony of noise. By this, the artist was presumed to be referencing the pervasive and inescapable nature of the commercial world. The parodies of advertising convention that 'Anonymous' had produced were recognizable and amusing, but it was felt that the reliance on such convention undermined the piece, making it hard to set aside the message from the content.

Ultimately, when opinions settled like snow, it was

agreed that the installation had been too ambitious. The topic it set out to deal with was too ungainly to be rescued by slight novelties of delivery. Other artists had been examining the relationship between art and the commercial world for decades. There was already a huge body of work dedicated to the subject, and this piece was merely another in that line. It was not, as everyone had hoped it would be, the defining moment of the genre.

Once a negative consensus had been reached, critics began to trickle away from the show. They were eager to warm up their word processors and start assassinating their hosts. Robin Haddock and Fulmonella Matthews, making a simultaneous escape from the gallery, ran into one another on the steps of the building.

'Well,' said Robin. 'It looks like we were right. She's too deep in Philippe Laurent's pockets if all she can produce is sub-standard commentaries on the world of advertising.'

'We shouldn't really talk about it,' said Fulmonella primly, 'but I can't disagree with your views.'

Philippe Laurent experienced very different emotions to the critics when his Ranna advertisements came up on the installation screens before him. He assumed, quite naturally, that Jessica had deceived him – that she had been planning to use her scripts for this purpose all along. The end frame was missing from the films, so Philippe furiously concluded that Jessica must have obtained them from a friend at Citrus before the final stages of production were complete. He now understood why she had begged him to delay the appearance of the ads on TV. She obviously didn't want her unveiling of the films at 'Art Schmart' to be superseded by their appearance elsewhere.

'If you think I'm buying my own ads off you, then you have a very sick sense of humour indeed,' muttered Philippe as the films rolled before him.

As soon as the ads finished playing, Philippe rose from his seated position and moved quickly through the crowd in search of his mutinous protégé. When they saw the expression on his face, people got out of the way very quickly indeed. He covered most of the warehouse in his rage, but he never found Jessica. She was hiding in the female toilets, which is where she stayed until every last guest had left the building.

Jessica nearly suffered a heart attack when the Ranna advertisements blazed into life before her eyes. Realizing that Philippe would be furious about the appropriation of his property, she ran from the projectors before they had even finished playing. Whimpering in the toilet, she cursed Dave for double-crossing her. It was a cruel joke he had played, delivering her own work and telling her it was a new piece of art. Jessica squatted in her porcelain prison and sobbed quietly whilst the critics discussed the end of her career.

Philippe cursed Jessica, and Jessica cursed Dave, but they should both have been cursing Amos, who was entirely to blame for the events of the evening, having accidentally switched the Ranna tapes with Dave's masterpiece earlier in the day.

Amos was not really used to high-pressure environments, so when Philippe appeared in his office and demanded that he personally deliver the tapes to Citrus, he got in something of a tizz. Worrying his way over to the courier room, he put the tapes that Philippe had given him down on the floor and rummaged around for a large enough satchel. Having found one, he stood up and wondered where he had left Philippe's tapes. Dave's creation, sitting in three identical boxes next to the security monitors, never stood a chance.

Arriving at Citrus, Amos handed over the incorrect tapes with relief. 'Ranna commercials,' he said to the editorial director, who was taking charge of them personally. The team who had compiled the original cuts of the Ranna ads were out at a meeting, and the job was so important that the editorial director had decided he'd better do it himself.

'Good man,' said the editorial director, signing the proffered delivery slip with a flourish. He had never seen the original Ranna films, and the last chance to rectify Amos' mistake passed silently by.

Sitting in the Workman's Rest, Dave watched one third of his installation play over the airwaves with an empty hole in his stomach. Now he knew why he'd found his three tapes on the floor of the courier room instead of sitting on the security desk where he'd left them. He had given Jessica the wrong tapes. His plan had backfired horribly.

On the TV, Dave's grainy self wandered into Philippe's office, unaware of his forthcoming punishment. As Philippe looked up at him, the film concluded, and the Ranna logo and 'Game won' strapline appeared on the screen.

Dave went back to the bar. 'I think I'd better move onto something stronger,' he said.

The landlord, whose customer imbalance sensors were once again firing, poured him a whiskey. 'Problems not completely solved after all?'

'Not quite,' said Dave, staring blankly ahead. 'Not quite solved.'

The landlord looked at him nervously. 'Well, things have turned around once,' he said. 'Maybe it'll happen again?'

Dave shook his head. 'Not this time.'

The landlord handed over Dave's drink. It was very generously proportioned. 'Let's not have any trouble, eh laddie?'

'No trouble,' said Dave.

As he returned to his seat, Dave noticed that the next Ranna spot was showing. This time it was the view of Philippe's office from above. His tiny employer twitched and speckled in anger, and the little image of Dave hunched over in pain and confusion.

Dave shut his eyes and began to drink. He didn't even notice that the kids on the next table were talking excitedly and pointing at the screen.

Chapter Thirty-four

The end of the beginning

By lunchtime on the day after the 'Art Schmart' private view, the critics had decided that *A lifetime in seconds* was the best piece of modern art ever produced.

Robin Haddock was the first amongst the artistic fraternity to notice the Ranna ads on television. After the private view had finished, he went home to watch the football game that had been played out that evening. Robin was a loyal supporter of his national side, and had taped the whole programme so he could watch it later on.

Observing the silent ads, Robin felt a strange sense of déjà vu. When the Ranna logo appeared, he realized he had seen it elsewhere that evening. He had seen it on all the athletes featured in the installation at 'Art Schmart'.

Then he remembered that Jessica, alias 'Anonymous', the author of the installation, had been working on an advertising campaign for Laurent Création.

Laurent Création, he'd read somewhere, had recently won the Ranna advertising account.

Robin Haddock laughed out loud in his front room.

'Fulmonella?' he said as soon as she picked up the phone. 'It's Robin.'

'Robin? What on earth are you calling me for? It's not allowed!'

'She's done it again, Fulmonella! She's gone and done it again!'

'Done what?' said Fulmonella. 'What are you talking about?'

'Jessica,' said Robin excitedly. 'Jessica as "Anonymous". She was pulling the wool over our eyes. Just like she did the first time.'

'Slow down,' said Fulmonella. 'What are you saying?'

'The "Anonymous" installation we saw earlier was only half the finished work,' Robin explained. 'I've just been watching the game and it's full of ads for Ranna sportswear. The ads she wrote for Philippe. That's the rest of the piece. It's just like *Untitled: Attempts to deconstruct the system fall short (1)*. You need to see it all before you can judge it.'

'Good lord,' said Fulmonella. 'That clever girl.'

'Damn right!' said Robin. 'She's absolutely brilliant!'

'You'd better get off the phone,' said Fulmonella. 'This really isn't allowed. We'll both be kicked out if they discover we've been talking about it.'

'I know!' said Robin. 'But I just had to tell

someone! I just had to tell someone how brilliant she's been!'

The critical brain of London awoke the following morning to find it had dreamed a strange and wonderful dream. Neurones of communication had been open all night; faxes, emails, and phone calls straddling the city. Over breakfast, every corner of the artistic world was forced to reappraise the most recent work by 'Anonymous', and every corner of the artistic world came to the same conclusion. *A lifetime in seconds* was universally acclaimed.

There were many reasons to admire the work, which was already being cited as another superb example of interdisciplinarity in the tradition of *Untitled: Attempts to deconstruct the system fall short (1)*. The use of advertising itself within the fabric of the piece was regarded as unique, demonstrating the cultural power that this discipline commanded. It was now clear to everyone why the installation had failed to make this point; it was merely a prop for the real commentary, which was occurring within the very arena it examined. The combined work used an art gallery to broadcast advertisements and the TV airwaves to gain creative acclaim, thus revealing the true shape of the national media machine. It was a paradox adored by the artistic establishment.

The use of a powerhouse of world business as the forum for discussion was also regarded as a brilliant move. The Ranna Corporation embodied the control that leviathans of business exerted over social convention and thought. It was the perfect brand to use for such an introspective analysis. How the hell Jessica had got Ranna to agree to it, the critics did not know, but they were delighted with the subversion of commercial enterprise with which they had been presented.

The ads that were running on TV, Dave's black-and-white films, were interpreted as having several possible subtexts. The quality of production, in direct opposition to the installation films, was poor. Was this a comment on the style-over-substance preoccupation of the modern era? The fact that the ads were set in an office building, and focused on a dismissal, was interpreted as a comment on commercialism. Viewed alongside the three fake 'advertisements', the films showed the other side of the corporate face. The destroyer of dreams. The controller of lives. They were bleak and portentous. They shattered the illusion that companies like Ranna sought to create.

Like all great modern art, *A lifetime in seconds* drew response from every critical camp. For the first time since the entity's birth, the different cells of Rorschach were in unanimous agreement, and the responses of others were no less ecstatic. The installation spawned a hundred press articles and a hundred television reports, scheduled for present-ation to the public over the next few days. There was no doubt about it, 'Anonymous' had delivered once more.

As for the identity of 'Anonymous', there was now unanimous support for Jessica's claim to the title.

Everyone knew she had been working on an advertising campaign with Philippe (indeed, they had all been gossiping about it for days). Everybody had seen her introduce the installation at the 'Art Schmart' gallery. She had even disappeared straight afterwards, presumably preferring to collect her plaudits after the critics had seen the other half of her work. These were impossible coincidences. Jessica had to be 'Anonymous'. There was no other explanation of events.

Whilst Jessica basked in the adoration of the art world, she tried to work out what had happened. Recognizing Dave in his tortured TV vignettes, she guessed that he had been intending to deliver *those* films to the gallery all along. It was a short step from that understanding to the realization that he had been trying to poison her career. Jessica laughed at Dave's incompetence, and the irony of how his plot had turned out. Her house of cards was built again, and on firmer foundations than ever before. She was reinstated as 'Anonymous', and had a monumental new work to her name.

'Jessica?' shouted the press outside her Soho flat. 'Jessica? Can you comment on your new piece?'

Jessica leaned out of the window and surveyed the adoring crowd of journalists. 'I will give a comment,' she confirmed.

'Does this mean you are claiming credit for the piece?' they shrieked up at her. 'Does this mean you are finally admitting that you are "Anonymous"?'

Jessica paused until she had their full attention. She waited for a peak in the drama.

'Yes,' she announced into the silence. 'I am finally prepared to admit that I am indeed "Anonymous".'

There was only one person who knew that Jessica was not 'Anonymous'. One person who had recognized the scene within the Ranna advertisements and understood what it meant. Philippe spent an hour alone in his office after he saw the ads. Like Jessica, he recognized both himself and Dave in the erroneous broadcasts, but unlike her, he worked out what they meant. They were catharsis. A creative work in the real sense.

Philippe thought and thought, and eventually he deduced the truth. He realized that Jessica must have known Dave for years, appropriating his ideas and productions until their unholy marriage spawned the mythological 'Anonymous' as a cover for her crimes. He remembered that Dave had completed a graphic design degree in Newcastle, where the event that formed the basis for the first work by 'Anonymous' had taken place, and he kicked himself for not working things out sooner.

Philippe realized that he had backed the wrong horse. The real 'Anonymous' had been working for him all along.

'Merde,' he said mournfully, rubbing at his forehead in annoyance. 'Merde, merde, *merde*.'

To Philippe's enormous surprise, the Ranna Corporation did not sue Laurent Création when they found out that the wrong advertisements had been aired in seventeen different countries. In fact, Eddie Radacker seemed rather pleased.

'You clever limey,' he said when Philippe rang him to beg for forgiveness. 'You clever, clever limey.'

'I can explain, Eddie, please,' said Philippe desperately. In his mind's eye he watched his agency falling apart. A decade of work down the drain.

'I'll let you off this once,' said Eddie. 'But next time, let me know if you want to run something of your own, OK?'

Eddie's international marketing department had been thoroughly prepared for the launch of their new commercials. They had commissioned live market research in every country where the new campaign was breaking. Across the globe, as the commercials came on air, a thousand pens were poised over a thousand clipboards. Eddie wanted to know what the 'kids on the ground' thought of his new campaign as soon as possible.

A few hours after the films started running, the researchers reported in with unexpected news. 'Laurent Création are showing different ads,' they said.

'Huh?' said Eddie.

'They're showing different ads,' said the researchers again. They played him a tape of Dave's three films.

'Oh my God,' said Eddie. 'Those stupid Brits.' There was a shocked silence whilst he thought for a while. 'Well?' he said to his researchers. 'What do the kids think of them?'

'They think they're cool,' said the researchers.

Kids across the world did indeed think Dave's Ranna advertisements were cool. The ads depicted a hero for their beaten and lonely generation. A hero assaulted by a figure of authority that did not understand him. Middle class youth around the globe recognized their champion, and saluted him. The strapline 'Game won' now seemed a prompt for teenage revolution. The ads became a cult classic in less than one day. They were exactly what Eddie Radacker had wanted them to be. They were cool.

The fact that he was able to keep his business was a great consolation to Philippe, but when he called Jessica, he did so with a heavy heart.

'I am a man of my word,' he said. 'I promised to buy your next three pieces of art, and I will. You can keep your success, but we will never speak again.'

Jessica, on the other end of the line, felt the ground move beneath her feet. Philippe knew that she was not 'Anonymous'.

'Philippe?' she said. 'What do you mean?'

'You heard me,' said Philippe. 'You heard what I said.'

'But Philippe,' she said. 'I can explain.'

Philippe spoke slowly, with flat deliberation. As though he was speaking to a child.

'I will not mention the fact that you are not "Anonymous",' he said. 'And you will not mention the fact that this business with the Ranna films was accidental. We cannot let the world know what happened last night.'

Jessica, on the other end of the line, realized that without Philippe's support, she would eventually come unstuck. Once he'd stopped buying her work, harsh questions would start to be asked. It wouldn't take long for the establishment to discover she was not as good as they thought.

'I'm sorry,' she said.

'So am I,' said Philippe, and he put down the phone.

Chapter Thirty-five

The hangover

Dave stepped out into the cold air accompanied by the landlord of the Workman's Rest, who had let him spend a drunken and uncomfortable night in the red velvet armchair. Deciding that it was better to have an unconscious body in his pub than an angry drunk, the landlord had kept pouring Dave drinks until he didn't look capable of causing trouble. Then, feeling somewhat responsible for the young man's condition, he'd covered Dave in a curtain and left him snoring like a donkey.

'Well, it's a new day,' said the landlord, blinking at the white morning light. 'Your problems still look big?'

Dave thought about his problems. He had destroyed an advertising campaign costing millions of pounds. He had supplied Jessica with the wrong tapes, completely ruining his plans for revenge. His problems, if anything, seemed bigger than they had the day before.

'They look insurmountable,' he said to the landlord.

'That's a long word for a man with a hangover,' chuckled the landlord. 'As long as you're coming up with big words, I reckon you'll figure out what to do.' He patted Dave on the shoulder and wandered back into the pub.

As Dave unchained his bike, he thought about what the landlord had said. The man was right. It was time he figured out what to do.

He was tired of looking for revenge. He was tired of trying to compete with Jessica. Ever since he'd known her, his life had been miserable, and ever since he had come to London to work in advertising, it had been more miserable still. He was tired of trying to express himself artistically. He was tired of trying to please people who thought he was 'technically competent'. He didn't want to be jealous of Jessica any more, and he didn't want to be an artistic failure.

Dave made up his mind. He decided that he should not have anything more to do with either advertising or modern art. He was not going back to Laurent Création, and he was not going to stay in London. He had no idea if he could leave the capital without his tormentors giving chase, but he was certainly going to try.

As he made his way home to pack, Dave noticed the beautiful patterns the diesel fumes made above the Thames.